THE JOURNEY PRIZE

STORIES

WINNERS OF THE $10,000 JOURNEY PRIZE

1989
Holley Rubinsky for
"Rapid Transits"

1990
Cynthia Flood for "My Father
Took a Cake to France"

1991
Yann Martel for "The Facts
Behind the Helsinki Roccamatios"

1992
Rozena Maart for "No Rosa,
No District Six"

1993
Gayla Reid for
"Sister Doyle's Men"

1994
Melissa Hardy for
"Long Man the River"

1995
Kathryn Woodward for "Of
Marranos and Gilded Angels"

1996
Elyse Gasco for "Can You Wave
Bye Bye, Baby?"

1997 (shared)
Gabriella Goliger for
"Maladies of the Inner Ear"

Anne Simpson for
"Dreaming Snow"

1998
John Brooke for
"The Finer Points of Apples"

1999
Alissa York for "The Back of the
Bear's Mouth"

2000
Timothy Taylor for
"Doves of Townsend"

2001
Kevin Armstrong for
"The Cane Field"

2002
Jocelyn Brown for
"Miss Canada"

2003
Jessica Grant for
"My Husband's Jump"

2004
Devin Krukoff for
"The Last Spark"

2005
Matt Shaw for "Matchbook for a
Mother's Hair"

2006
Heather Birrell for
"BriannaSusannaAlana"

2007
Craig Boyko for
"OZY"

2008
Saleema Nawaz for
"My Three Girls"

2009
Yasuko Thanh for
"Floating Like the Dead"

2010
Devon Code for
"Uncle Oscar"

2011
Miranda Hill for
"Petitions to Saint Chronic"

THE BEST OF CANADA'S NEW WRITERS

THE JOURNEY PRIZE

STORIES

SELECTED BY
MICHAEL CHRISTIE
KATHRYN KUITENBROUWER
KATHLEEN WINTER

EMBLEM
McClelland & Stewart

Emblem is an imprint of McClelland & Stewart,
a division of Random House of Canada Limited

Emblem and colophon are registered trademarks of McClelland & Stewart,
a division of Random House of Canada Limited

The lyrics quoted on p. 138 are from the song "(I'll be with you) In Apple Blossom Time."

A cataloguing record for this publication is available from Library and Archives Canada.

We acknowledge the financial support of the Government of Canada through the Canada
Book Fund and that of the Government of Ontario through the Ontario Media Development
Corporation's Ontario Book Initiative. We further acknowledge the support of the Canada
Council for the Arts and the Ontario Arts Council for our publishing program.

Published simultaneously in the United States of America by McClelland & Stewart, a
division of Random House of Canada Limited, P.O. Box 1030, Plattsburgh, New York 12901

Library of Congress Control Number: 2012941714

Typeset in Janson by Random House of Canada, Toronto
Printed and bound in Canada

McClelland & Stewart,
a division of Random House of Canada Limited
One Toronto Street
Suite 300
Toronto, Ontario
M5C 2V6
www.mcclelland.com

1 2 3 4 5   16 15 14 13 12

ABOUT THE JOURNEY PRIZE STORIES

The $10,000 Journey Prize is awarded annually to an emerging writer of distinction. This award, now in its twenty-fourth year, and given for the twelfth time in association with the Writers' Trust of Canada as the Writers' Trust of Canada/ McClelland & Stewart Journey Prize, is made possible by James A. Michener's generous donation of his Canadian royalty earnings from his novel *Journey*, published by McClelland & Stewart in 1988. The Journey Prize itself is the most significant monetary award given in Canada to a developing writer for a short story or excerpt from a fiction work in progress. The winner of this year's Journey Prize will be selected from among the thirteen stories in this book.

The Journey Prize Stories has established itself as the most prestigious annual fiction anthology in the country, introducing readers to the finest new literary writers from coast to coast for more than two decades. It has become a who's who of up-and-coming writers, and many of the authors who have appeared in the anthology's pages have gone on to distinguish themselves with collections of short stories, novels, and literary awards. The anthology comprises a selection from submissions made by the editors of literary journals from across the country, who have chosen what, in their view, is the most exciting writing in English that they have published in the previous year. In recognition of the vital role journals play in fostering literary voices, McClelland & Stewart makes its own award of

$2,000 to the journal that originally published and submitted the winning entry.

This year the selection jury comprised three acclaimed writers:

Michael Christie's debut collection, *The Beggar's Garden*, was longlisted for the Scotiabank Giller Prize and the Frank O'Connor International Short Story Prize, shortlisted for the Rogers Writers' Trust Fiction Prize, and won the City of Vancouver Book Award. He received his MFA in Creative Writing at UBC in 2008. A two-time Journey Prize contributor, he now lives in Thunder Bay, where he is at work on a novel. For more information, please visit www.MichaelChristie.net.

Kathryn Kuitenbrouwer is the author of the novels *Perfecting* and *The Nettle Spinner* as well as the short fiction collection *Way Up*. Her short fiction has been published in *The Walrus*, *Granta Magazine*, and *Storyville*. She is the inaugural recipient of The Sidney Prize for Short Fiction. She is an award-winning creative writing instructor through the University of Toronto School of Continuing Studies and Associate Faculty with the University of Guelph Creative Writing MFA. Please visit www.KathrynKuitenbrouwer.com.

Kathleen Winter's first novel, *Annabel*, was longlisted for the International IMPAC Dublin Literary Award, shortlisted for the Orange Prize, the Rogers Writers' Trust Prize, the Amazon.ca First Novel Award, the Governor General's Literary Award, and the Scotiabank Giller Prize, and won the Thomas Head Raddall Atlantic Fiction Award. Her debut collection of stories, *boYs*, won the Winterset Award and the Metcalfe-Rooke Award. She lives in Montreal.

The jury read a total of eighty-two submissions without knowing the names of the authors or those of the journals in which the stories originally appeared. McClelland & Stewart would like to thank the jury for their efforts in selecting this year's anthology and, ultimately, the winner of this year's Journey Prize.

McClelland & Stewart would also like to acknowledge the continuing enthusiastic support of writers, literary journal editors, and the public in the common celebration of new voices in Canadian fiction.

For more information about *The Journey Prize Stories*, please visit www.mcclelland.com and www.facebook.com/TheJourneyPrize.

CONTENTS

INTRODUCTION

Juries are tricky things, and though a blind jury has its advantages, it also comes with complications. Writing is an ethical as well as an aesthetic profession, and as readers and judges we fought at times against ourselves: would the stories in the anthology justly represent Canada and its multiplicity of voices? Should that even be a consideration? The jury for the Journey Prize is meant to come up with both a selection of the best stories and something like a cohesive anthology. Ultimately, though we kept a hope of achieving a balanced representation of voices in this country, our jury made decisions based on overall craft – we cared about stories realizing their full potential through their gorgeous attention to words, and their forceful drive toward their own meaning.

We learned that unlike the proverbial customer, the reader is not always right, especially when charged with the near-impossible task of picking the best stories from a sea of almost uniformly impressive works by new and emerging Canadian writers. A few stories were overlooked on our first reading. But as we chose the long list there were spectacular reversals. Many stories that initially refused to yield their riches bloomed upon subsequent readings, and jurors cozied up to others they had declared insufferable. Other stories that wowed us at first lost their flavour after a second look. Throughout, we cajoled and convinced, we argued and wooed, we decamped and betrayed.

We were three jurors with vastly differing perspectives and taste, and we saw first-hand the beauty of this – the joy of convincing and shifting one another's views while feeling our own preferences evolve. In the end, we are all happy to have a collection that represents craft, brilliance, audacity, subtlety, and force. We couldn't have done it without listening carefully to one another and being willing to question ourselves. More than anything, we were each able to pluck our heels out of the dirt and change our minds. And we believe that after surviving the messy inexactness of this process, the final anthology is stronger for it. But enough of us, the stories are the true reason you're reading this anthology. So here's how they moved us and why we chose them.

In "Why I Read *Beowulf*," Shashi Bhat's exquisitely lucid tone keeps opening out into greater and more perilous surprises. We admired the matter-of-fact way Bhat introduced astonishing statements. Our hearts leapt in fear as we progressed through this wry study of the shifts between predator and prey.

Kevin Hardcastle's "To Have to Wait" uses condensed lines to ignite this story of two brothers on a road trip to bring their father home from a desperate place. We loved Hardcastle's deadly dialogue, his natural precision, and his mastery of relationships. The structure and pacing impressed us, as did the piece's emotional elegance.

Grace O'Connell's breathtaking story of the love between two friends repeatedly conveys the whole from a study of parts. Natural dialogue shows us a friendship that is strong yet ever so fragile. "The Many Faces of Montgomery Clift" manages to show how friends can achieve a kind of immortality despite social constraints that fertilize hypocrisy and lies, and the writing bursts with transparent colour and freshness.

We lauded "Daughter of the Dead Reeds" for its elusive and enigmatic meaning. A strange admixture of dirty realism and fantasy, this story's filthy secret only submerged us deeper within it. We never fully understood this story and we didn't care. Martin West gave us that sinking feeling that belies all art, and we marvelled at it.

Jasmina Odor's "Barcelona" meted out its riches in a way that forced us to embrace the story and be slowly danced toward an accumulating articulation of meaning. We recognized a complex marriage of theme and form in this story, and were moved and impressed by it.

We were delighted to learn we'd selected not one but two stories from Andrew Hood. The first, "Manning," a foray into the absurd underbelly of a collectors' convention, is a joltingly funny reminder that there is indeed such a thing as heartbreaking callousness, especially when it's exhibited by a child, and especially when this child and his mother were left with only twenty-nine boxes of worthless sports cards as their inheritance. (Who would've thought such pathos could be wrung from a near-worthless Rance Davis baseball card?)

We loved Eliza Robertson's "Sea Drift" for its strange regressive narrative, how it worked backward toward sense and built a gossamer matrix of imagery to hold that sense. We enjoyed its light touch, and its insistence on deconstructing myth into the personal. The story sparkles.

Andrew Hood's second story in the anthology, "I'm Sorry and Thank You," is a hilarious encounter between two disparate souls. Restrained and subversive, this piece uses clever shorthand and radical leaps that give it a feeling of liftoff. We loved Hood's natural language, his deft implications, and his exacting use of carefully selected words to large effect.

"Ashes" is a study in the use of telling details. We appreciated its snappy pacing – clipping along and never flagging – and its use of a framing device that works well with the subject matter. Nancy Jo Cullen uses concentrated phrases to say big things, and her respect for accuracy gives this story its sharpness.

Alex Pugsley's "Crisis on Earth-X" sets up countless impossible hoops and then proceeds to jump through them in ways we could not have foreseen. Its sentences and its story surprised and amused us. It even broke our hearts in the way an excellent story can, so that we were glad to have them broken.

In her story "Ice Break," Astrid Blodgett ties, hangs, and tightens a noose of narrative with a masterful touch. Every word in this story is essential, and you can almost hear the text cracking beneath you as you venture out upon it, inching further from the shores of its beginning. In this quiet prelude of tragedy, Blodgett has crafted a tale that lives in your mind long after you've broken through.

Kris Bertin sets up the more traditional narrative of a recovering alcoholic who takes a job as a night janitor, before veering things into a surreal devolution. In the world of "Is Alive and Can Move," dashed middle-aged ambitions exist beside the unreasonable expectations of youth, monastic purity beside boozy excess, and careful celibacy beside sexual abandon. Besides, where else could you find this sort of linguistic gold: "I barely finished my cleaning that night because I was so fucked up over the lizard."

"You Were Loved" by Trevor Corkum is an exquisitely paced and unflinching examination of how pain begets pain, a story about the long echoing aftershocks of parental absence and the dark crypts that exists inside us all. Corkum refuses all pat psychologizing, conjuring a complex, wayward man whose only defense is one of depersonalization and avoidance. With a sexual frankness rarely ventured in Can Lit, the story is nothing short of heart stopping.

Ultimately, as a jury, we were left with the impression that Canadian journals are not only locating and publishing top-notch fiction but also, in doing so, raising the bar, taking risks, and evolving our national voice. It was gratifying to be able to read such a wide range of strong entries. We are proud and heartened to be in the company of so many new and talented writers. We hope the experience of being put forward by these journals acts as a kind of mentorship for all the writers whose stories we read, and not just those who made the anthology. Carry on. Make more art. Be tenacious.

Tell us your stories.

Michael Christie
Kathryn Kuitenbrouwer
Kathleen Winter
June 2012

THE JOURNEY PRIZE

STORIES

SHASHI BHAT

WHY I READ *BEOWULF*

I started reading *Beowulf* about a week ago, not because it was on the syllabus, but because I am in love with my English teacher. I would read anything for him. The cover of my copy of the book has a black background with the title in white block letters, and under those the jacket designer has placed the silhouette of a man, but just his top half, like a passport photo, except that the silhouette is made entirely of silver mesh. I keep turning back to this picture on the cover and wondering how they made it look three-dimensional, and half-expecting the pattern of metal to bulge into discernable features, to turn into a man's face.

Once I finish the book, I will begin to drop casual references to it in class or at English club meetings. "This reminds me of my favorite epic poem," I will say, pretending I don't know that it's also my English teacher's favorite epic poem, and then I will quote brilliantly, lingering on the alliteration. Mr. Sears will pause, turning away from the blackboard to face me, holding a piece of chalk in his hand. Sometimes, in my most reckless moments of imagination, I see him dropping the piece of chalk in amazement.

I am not sure yet exactly which passages I will quote, because I am only on page four. I reached page four this morning, as I sat in the hallway of the school with my best friend, Amy. Every day we have our mothers drop us off exactly forty-five minutes before the bell rings, and we sit on the ground outside the English office. I'm usually reading and Amy is usually peeling the varnish off the floor. The varnish lies in a loose coat over the hardwood and cracks as we step over it. Our school building deteriorates at an exponential rate; it seems like every day another part of it breaks off. One time I bicycled by and looked at the school and thought to myself, with fierce affection, "That is my high school," relishing the still-newness of ninth grade, and just at that moment, a piece of one of the window frames creaked loose and fell from its hinge to the pavement.

Amy regularly peels the floor in patches all over the school. We eat lunch in stairwells, our backs against the concrete walls and legs crossed in front of us, sandwich bags in our laps, cackling at each other over inside jokes we've had since second grade, and she'll take a break from peeling the floor to peel her tangerine, trying to remove each peel in one long strip. She peels the floor in the gymnasium during stretches, and then leaves the waxy scraps in small piles here and there so that later, when we're made to do push-ups, people's hands and shoes accidentally land on these piles and their limbs go sliding sideways.

I keep telling her not to do this, but lately she's sort of been turning on me. I do think it's natural to get irritated with your best friend, with whom you spend so many hours, encountering so many opportunities for disagreement – over which movie to see or whether to eat at Subway or Tim Hortons or whether Americans have the right idea about making the drinking age twenty-one or whether moustaches worn ironically can ever look really handsome – but once you have invested so many years in a friendship, such things should cease to matter. I'm not sure Amy recognizes this. Although our lives have run parallel since age eight, when, in Mrs. Hollifriend's class, we both agreed that dinosaurs were not as fascinating as everybody else seemed to think, lately I've been thinking that Amy might easily drop me, like a jacket with a hole in it, like a hair elastic that's lost its stretch. So today, we're sitting there outside the English office and I go, without really thinking, "Amy, what's wrong with you? Why do you always have to peel the floor and deface our school?" and she turns to me and goes, "At least I haven't memorized every article of clothing owned by my English teacher." It's sort of a joke of hers that I spend so much time gazing at Mr. Sears that I must have his clothes memorized by now, except that it's not really a joke, because I know that he owns six button-downs (three different shades of blue, one white pin-striped, one yellow, and one grey) and white athletic socks that show when he sits down, and four pairs of pants that are all sort of beige-ish brown. Only once did I see him wear a pair of jeans, at the English Club fundraiser, which was a car wash to raise funds and awareness for literature from the Augustan period. We used the money we made to buy used copies of *Gulliver's Travels* on Amazon.com and then we just handed them out to people on the street. Mr. Sears called it "Spreading the Word." He smiled when he said it, his mouth an open oval. It took me the first half of the car wash to adjust myself to that new jeans-wearing version of my

English teacher, but then I found something beautiful in his effortlessness, and decided that his casual style did not take away in the least from his devotion to our cause.

I like to record these lists of clothing, and also all my related thoughts and observations, in a notebook, a Moleskin notebook like the kind Mr. Sears said Hemingway used.

Also, sometimes in class his socks fall around his ankles and I want to duck down on to the half-peeled floor and crawl under his desk and pull them up for him.

Because of all this pent-up sexual frustration, I've cultivated a new hobby, namely, interacting with pedophiles in Internet chatrooms. Or not pedophiles, but one pedophile in particular. His name is Ronald, and we've been talking online for about a month. He has asked me to think of him as my boyfriend, though he's really more of a manfriend, because he is forty-one years old. When I told him I'm fourteen, he typed, "Your age is my age in reverse," as though that means we are meant to be. He says he thinks I'm exotic because of my Indian background, so I didn't tell him I was born in Canada. After I'm done with school and English Club meetings or band practice, I go home and go on "Internet dates" with Ronald the pedophile. We'll Google important political figures and then discuss our findings, or we'll furnish an imaginary home with furniture we imagine buying on eBay, and sometimes we'll go to Freerice.com and spend hours defining words and ending world hunger.

Usually while I'm doing this, my parents are either working late or in the basement praying. They have created a "God Room" in the basement, where all of our Hindu gods and goddesses hang in rows around the blue walls, staring out with peaceful expressions.

"You are as beautiful as a goddess," Ronald said to me once, after describing himself as an agnostic. I'd added him on Facebook, though he's on limited profile so he can't see my address or anything, but I did allow him to see my photos, so he looked through all the ones of me and Amy and told me that I'm infinitely more desirable than she is.

I regularly watch *To Catch a Predator* on *Dateline* and am amazed at how often the child molesters resemble the guys my dad works with. I told Ronald about this and he found a bunch of episodes of the show on YouTube, and so we watched those on another Internet date. We witnessed one predator wearing a large shapeless hat atop his large shapeless head, entering the house, unaware of the NBC cameramen drinking coffee behind the decorative curtain. Then the decoy thirteen-year-old chirps something about going to change into her bathing suit and the guy with the large hat smiles to himself and actually, literally starts rubbing his hands together in anticipation, and I bet he has really dry hands so bits of skin are flaking off them, and also he has this backpack on that's maybe too small for a grown man, and he takes that off and started rifling through it, but before we found out what monstrous equipment he has in this backpack, *Dateline* correspondent Chris Hansen emerges from behind the decorative curtain and introduces himself, and the man with the hat removes his hat and uses it to cover his face.

"Don't worry, my darling," Ronald said to me, "I am ten times the man he is," which makes me wonder if Ronald knows how math works. Ten times a pedophile, I think, as I look through his Facebook pictures. Unlike most people's Facebook photos, Ronald's feature no other people. Mostly they show him leaning against a blank wall, his head rounded in a way that indicates he took the photo himself with one outstretched arm.

In my most recent conversation with Ronald, he asked me for my phone number. I was reading *Beowulf* while talking to him, and thinking maybe I should rent the movie instead, and I was caught up in thinking about Mr. Sears and whether the movie version would be significantly different from the book version and checking Wikipedia to see whether the movie script used quotes from the Seamus Heaney translation. So I'd pushed the Ronald conversation window to the side of my screen, and all of a sudden he typed, "Are your parents home? Can I call you? What's your phone number?" all three questions in a single row. I pictured him on a sofa, his laptop on his lap, sinking back into the cushions as he waited for my reply. And maybe due to all my unreturned love and daydreams for Mr. Sears, I started imagining what would happen if I fell in love with Ronald the pedophile. He lives in the next town over, so it wouldn't be a long-distance relationship. Instead of Internet dates, we could go on actual dates to local hotspots and events like Heritage Village Day. We could climb each of the 144 flights of stairs to the top of the CN Tower in Toronto, something I have always wanted to do, but Amy refuses to go with me. "Would you climb the CN Tower with me?" I typed, and Ronald said, "Yes," with a winking emoticon, and so then I typed my phone number in one swoop of momentum, with no spaces or dashes.

He dialled the numbers just as quickly. I let the telephone ring four times, fanning myself madly with my copy of

Beowulf, the mesh face fluttering forwards and backwards as I wondered whether to answer the phone. But then I realized if I didn't answer, the call would go to voicemail. Ronald would leave a message accessible to anybody in my family, because this was our landline and not my cell phone since my parents for some reason won't get me a cell phone. Also, my parents were not out at work or at the store or at a baseball game or wherever it is parents go when strangers call the house. While a weird man preyed on their child, my parents prayed in the basement, singing light religious tunes in their atonal voices and clanging finger cymbals that clashed with the ringing phone. My parents might put down their photocopied Sanskrit mantras at any time and unfold their piously curled bodies to get up and answer it. I wondered if Ronald would pretend to be a salesman, and then I thought, if my parents pick up the phone, Ronald will probably never speak to me again. So I answered it.

There was no pause at all, and I heard a soft, wheedling voice say, "You didn't think I'd call, did you?" And then the door to my bedroom opened, and I saw a man standing there, peering around the doorframe at me and grinning this slow grin and saying, "What do you want for dinner?" because the man was my father, so then I immediately hung up the phone and told my dad rice was fine as always for dinner, and when he asked what I'd been doing the past hour, I said (very convincingly, I think) that I'd been researching the incarnations of all the various Hindu gods.

In English class, third period, Amy has disengaged herself from me and moved to sit with this new boyfriend of hers. His name isn't even worth mentioning, but he was in my fourth grade class and he used to try to join conversations but everybody hated him and ignored him so then he would just give up and stare at the wall. But then one day, he started talking to the wall, and telling it things and asking it questions, *why won't they talk to me?*, *all I have is you*, and so on, and I wonder if he and Amy have similar conversations now.

Before Amy started dating him, and before I had fully fallen for Mr. Sears, we would spend all of class laughing silently behind our open notebooks. The first book we read in this class was *Washington Square*, and we both hated it, so we left Post-It notes throughout the pages of our copies, to warn future readers. Our notes said things like, "I hate this book," and "Don't read any further," and "Aunt Penniman is a flat character," but now I regret writing those Post-Its and wonder if I should retrieve my copy from the library and remove them. I won't though, because that would be like erasing our history when already I can feel Amy slipping away, and it's different from that time she bleached her hair orange and became cool for a week and sat on the radiator where all the cool kids sit. It's different partly because relationships of weird teens last forever. It might never be me and her sitting and laughing together ever again.

Instead of socializing with Amy, I try to imagine Grendel from *Beowulf* and draw pictures of him across my notebook in red pen. I compile monster parts from passages in the book and from generic TV monsters, heads that nearly aren't there dissolving into the lines of the page, wide white teardrops instead of eyes, teeth protruding through stretching mouths. Their bodies have torsos disproportionate to arms, veins visible through the surface of skin like the bulging, textured veins of leaves, legs narrowing into a pair of skeletal feet that leave bony, blood-filled footprints, footprints that stalk over the page of notes that I'm supposed to be taking. Instead of grammar exercises, I've drawn penciled, mesh-faced men, weaponless, knees curling under them like paperclips.

Mr. Sears goes on with his lesson, and in the background I hear someone call him, "Oh Captain, My Captain," because he is one of those teachers who tears up textbooks and says there shouldn't be a rubric for poetry. Mr. Sears delivers an impassioned speech about some Alexander Pope poem and then he asks me a question, but since I've been drawing monsters instead of paying attention, I only know that the poem may or may not have something to do with haircuts. I curse myself for not listening and wonder if this is karma for the time I invented a Hindu holiday as an excuse for skipping gym.

"Disappointing," Mr. Sears says, and his head tilts sadly sideways under the weight of his disappointment. "You have to do the reading," he tells me, "or there's no point in coming to class."

I want to tell him that I have done the reading, I've done more reading than any of these other fools, but he turns away and makes a joke about how his wife never reads any books either, with the exception of Harlequin romances.

In the romance corner of the room, when Mr. Sears turns to the board, Amy and her boyfriend caress each other's faces. In an online article, I read that if a boy touches your face, it means it's true love. The boyfriend bends his head and lays it onto Amy's shoulder, and he looks almost handsome. It's the only time I've seen him look anything other than stupid. The only person I can remember being that close to me is my mother, and I find it painful to try not to yearn for that strange, solid, intimate warmth of a human head. Amy sighs her chin into the boyfriend's palm. She pulls at his nose and he embeds his fingertips into her cheeks, and I worry that they will accidentally gouge each other's eyes out.

I wait for Amy after school as I always do, but she doesn't show up. I duck into the library. Nobody's using the computers, so I sign into my account and find Ronald online.

"What a terrible day," I type.

"You're early," he replies, and then, "What happened?"

"My friend ditched me for her boyfriend," I type, and then, because it's not like I'm in a committed relationship with this Internet pedophile, I tell him that I have a crush on my middle-aged English teacher and about my moment of embarrassing inattention in class.

There's a pause, and then Ronald types, "Pretend I'm him."

I suppose what Ronald wants me to do is to lean into my screen and enact an elaborate sexual fantasy I have about Mr. Sears via the Internet. It's true that I spend much of class time and much of my own time fantasizing about my English teacher. I imagine us in a warm fireplaced room with burgundy wallpaper and clawfooted furniture, but we've disdained this furniture to sit on the floor. We read to each other from a shared copy of *Beowulf*. Mr. Sears holds the book and I turn its pages. Our heads are pressed together, my hair over his shoulders. For some reason in this fantasy I have flaxen hair, despite being Indian, and I'm wearing an empire-waist gown and a wreath of flowers, and Mr. Sears is dressed similarly in eighteenth-century garb, like maybe a navy waistcoat and white pantaloons. We're sipping from glasses of wine, no, goblets of wine, no, chalices of wine, and we're uttering guttural words to each other in Middle English, as the fireplace flashes at us like an unanswered chat window.

The problem with these fantasies is that I never actually get past the reading part, so I don't know what I'm supposed to describe to Ronald, and so, to diffuse the situation, I type the letters LOL.

"What's so funny?" Ronald asks.

I try to think of something provocative to ask him. I type, "How old were you when you lost your virginity?"

There's a long pause and then Ronald types, "Haven't we had this conversation before?" which doesn't make sense because Ronald and I have certainly never had this conversation before, or even this type of conversation, since our imaginary dates have remained pretty tame and educational, and it occurs to me that I am not the only teenager with whom Ronald regularly speaks on the Internet.

Ronald starts typing long strings of text, full of typos, and I realize that he's describing all the things he's going to do to me, except I don't understand most of the terms so I open up a separate window to look them up on Urban Dictionary.

He begs for a response. I'm thinking of his Facebook pictures and how he could be a guy that works at my dad's office. My dad could be right there in an adjacent cubicle, entering numbers into his computer with the Lord Ganesha desktop wallpaper, working overtime for the money to send his daughter to medical school, because I haven't yet told him that I plan to get an English degree and concentrate in pre-1800 literature.

I humour my parents, because they are pious and kind and easily deluded, and if you try to have a serious discussion with my father, he will always bring God into it.

Ronald's words become more garbled and he's used the F-word at least four times. He waits for me to say something. I consider the keyboard and then type the letter "M" repeatedly so it seems as though I am moaning, and I follow it with exactly seven exclamation points.

"You are so beautiful," Ronald types, though he spells beautiful wrong, and I assume he's looking at my pictures, and then he says, "Are you still having a terrible day? Let me come there and comfort you."

Through the library door, I see Amy and her boyfriend walking through the hallway. They are peeling the floor together, in one unbroken strip. They walk slowly, as not to tear it, focused on the piece of varnish that passes through their collaborating hands and curls and trails behind them.

It's possible that Ronald is talking to four different girls right now, four different fourteen-year-olds typing covertly in their high school libraries before catching the school bus home. One by one they must sign off, until he's left with a single girl who does what? Answers the phone and talks to him? Invites him home?

"Okay," I type to Ronald, "I can be home in fifteen minutes." I give him my address, 53 Pickett Crescent, near the intersection of Elgin Mills and Yonge, and I send him a link to the Google Map. "I can't wait to see you," he types, and I don't let myself wonder what he means by the word *see*.

I leave the library, and see the shapes of Amy and the boyfriend's bodies as they turn the corner at the end of the hall.

I head in the other direction, towards my locker, and on the way I notice the door of the English office is partway open, and spot Mr. Sears.

When I knock on the door, he tells me to come inside. I shut the door behind me and begin speaking without making eye contact. I count the posters of authors that line the top third of the room's walls.

"I just wanted to apologize for class today," I say. He's wearing the lightest of his blue shirts and standing, half resting on the desk. The other English teachers have all left, and I realize I've never been alone in a room with Mr. Sears.

"That's all right," he says in his infinitely understanding way. "You've just got to stop being distracted in class. I know you love this stuff."

I almost drop my backpack at hearing him use the word "love," and I walk up to him tell him, "I do love this stuff. I love books. I'm even trying to get through *Beowulf*, though I admit it's going a little slowly . . ."

Mr. Sears has chalk on the pocket of his shirt and I reach my arm across the arms' length between us and brush the chalk off his shirt with my fingers. He grabs my hand and holds it in place. He frowns in a way I haven't seen on him before, the skin of his eyebrows pulling together and downward.

First he glances at the door, perhaps double-checking that it has no window on it. Then he kisses me. It's unfamiliar because I have never imagined this far. He picks up the straps of my backpack and slides them off my arms. He lifts me up as the backpack drops on the floor with the thumping, cluttering sound of books and pencils, and he places me on the edge of the desk. The lights in the room are white rectangles in lines across

the ceiling, and I look at them because I'm not sure if I'm supposed to look at Mr. Sears, whose head I want to hold in my
hands, but I have this awful feeling that the second I place my
hands on his face, his features will turn to mesh, the metal
cutting the tips of my fingers. He pushes his head next to my
neck and when he breathes, he smells like coffee, like cough
drops, like an old man. On the pocket of his shirt is a tiny
embroidered penguin; a clothing detail I have already memorized and written down in my Moleskin notebook, where I also
keep track of my friends' birthdays and my better homework
grades, and where I record it when a day is particularly beautiful. He moves one hand to grip my spine like it's the spine of a
Norton Anthology, and I think of five things: Thought number
one is of all the times I've seen him pick up a book in class and
slam it face-down, pages spread open on the table. Two, I consider Amy and her boyfriend, and wonder how far around the
school hallways they've gotten, hand-in-hand and laughing.
Three, I think of Ronald searching the houses for number 53,
parking in my empty driveway, pressing the round yellow door-
bell, thinking he's about to rape some stupid little girl. Four, I
hope my parents arrive home from work fairly soon, so when
this is over, I can phone them to pick me up. And five, I remember the time I overheard Mr. Sears speaking to another male
teacher and saying, "What a dog," in reference to a girl, an
expression I didn't know people still used, and it had taken me
a moment to realize what he meant, before I convinced myself
that I must have misheard him, before I pictured the head of a
dog on a female human body, sad-faced and teeth bared.

KEVIN HARDCASTLE

TO HAVE TO WAIT

They came out of the house with the risen sun beating down on the weather-worn porch. The summer had come early this year. The heat burnt the grass brown and took the nearby river down a foot by June, the high watermark lying naked on the granite banks. Paul went down the porch steps with a plastic cooler that had their lunch inside. He stopped on the gravel driveway and had to squint to see. There were waves of heat trembling atop the hot black mastic of the bordering concession road, the air fat with humidity and hard to draw in. It felt as if his nose and throat and very insides ran hotter with every breath he took. He shook his head and stood there, tall and thin, his dark hair flattened down by the dampness of his scalp.

"Shut that door behind you," he called back without turning around. "And make sure it shuts. That mangy farm dog got in there one night and Mum lost her damn mind."

Matthew came out with his shirt half on and he was still wet from the shower. When he pulled the T-shirt down it darkened in patches, sitting ridged and crooked across his heavy chest.

He left it like that and pulled the door shut as he came out. He took a step and then stopped and went back. He gave the door a shove. It came open so he leaned back inside and grabbed the knob and pulled as hard as he could. This time he heard the metal latch click. The door stayed put when he shoved it again.

"That door's a piece of shit," he said, coming down the steps in ragged old skateboard shoes. When he got down to the gravel he trod heavy on the rocks and they shot out as he walked past Paul to the passenger side of the car. Matthew tried to open the door and it wouldn't give. He stared down at the handle and muttered something, his hand still trying it. His fingers kept going even when he knew the door was locked and finally he stopped and put both arms on top of the roof. Inside of a second he yanked them clear and cursed a string of nonsense at the car and the heat and the world altogether.

"It's hot as absolute hell out here," Matthew said. "This car is going to be a billion fucking degrees inside."

Paul nodded and spat on the ground. The phlegm was thin and parts of it started to vanish right away on the stone. He exhaled hard and went over to the car and stood facing his brother, both of them the same height, Matthew much larger in build. They had the same eyes though, the same hairline. They had the same shape of mouth and sometimes made the same expressions on very different faces, Paul's thinner face with its squared jaw and Matthew's rounded face with a rounded jaw and that thick, wide-set neck below it. They looked at each other for a while. Paul's eyes were clear, though they skittered around. Matthew's eyes, bloodshot from the drink, were still as the burnt and breezeless world around them.

"Was Mum outraged last night?" Matthew said.

"She didn't say one way or the other," Paul said, "but I guess you probably could have come back here first to drop your shit off. Instead of straight from the airport to the bottle."

"I know. I should've."

"I talked her down though, before she took off for work. Told her you'd be back to the house this morning to go with me an' that you'd see her tonight. I also told her your future wife was likely at the party. That you might shack up with some townie and quit your fuckin' philandering."

Matthew stood there with his mouth partly open. He blinked hard and his eyelids were out of sync. Paul started laughing at him.

"You're still plastered, you idiot."

Little laughs came out of Matthew's maw for a few seconds, and then he inhaled hard and stood up straight. "You should've come out last night."

"I'd say I'm sort of way past partied out. It's not so bad when you just come back home for a little while and cause some shit. But when you live here you'd rather punch yourself in the dick than go out with those idiots."

"You just didn't go 'cause you couldn't have driven today. You'd be in bed 'til five with your hangover."

"I have to drive 'cause your licence is suspended."

"It's suspended 'cause I was driving your uninsured fuckin' car when you were too hungover."

Paul looked at Matthew for a second and then turned away. He nodded. When he turned back he had a crooked little smile on his face. "Yeah, I know," he said. "We'll sort that out too."

Paul put the key in the lock and turned it, then opened the door. The heat inside swarmed him. He made a funny sound and hit the button to unlock all the doors. Matthew still couldn't get in.

"Stop fuckin' pulling on it," Paul said.

This time when he hit the button Matthew's door unlocked, and he opened it. Matthew leaned back from the car when he felt the air and then he took a deep breath. He looked over at Paul and they shook their heads and got in. Paul put the key in the ignition and turned it, and they wound down their windows before shutting the doors.

"I don't care about losin' the licence," Matthew said. "I don't even have a car."

Paul looked over at him and nodded. Then he turned the radio on.

"Yeah, but you might have one someday," Paul said.

"Fuck it. I ride the bus. I'm gonna get a bike maybe."

Paul smiled. "Man, you'll die riding a bike in that city."

"I don't die doing anything," Matthew said. "And it sure as fuck wouldn't be in that city." He let out a short, loud laugh.

Paul fished a bottle of water out of a cooler in the back seat and drank deep. Matthew waited for him to pass it over, and all the while he stared through the front windshield at the house they'd grown up in. The narrow two-storey farmhouse stood at the head of the driveway, simple and ancient. If it had not been handed down to their family with the outlying fields and firs they would have had little at all. Not ten years ago those boys had set down to eat a mess of bacon and eggs and fried steak in the damp, stone-walled kitchen, their parents gone for the night. The greasy plates had just hit the suds in the sink when a black sedan rolled into the driveway carrying five men, all of them bent on laying Matthew out and stomping him bloody into the gravel. Paul racked rock salt shells into an old double-barrel scattergun and went out to meet them. By the time he came back inside Matthew had soaked a rag through with spirit, jammed it into the bottleneck, and was trying to spark it with a barbeque lighter. Paul wrestled the bottle from his brother and cursed him out until Matthew sat down at the kitchen table and put his head in his hands. He was sixteen years old. Paul was just two years older. Later that night they drank the bottle dry, sitting together in the dark waiting for the men to locate their guts and come back. They never did.

"You miss that house?" Paul said.

"I don't know. It's hard to believe I lived in it."

"What's it like out there where you live?"

"Like Mars."

"You gonna ever come back east?"

"I think so."

"When?"

"As soon as I made enough money to live off the bullshit wages back here. Or as soon as they start throwin' money at people with grade twelve who can dig the hell out of a pipeline ditch."

Paul smiled. Matthew turned to face him.

"You could live with me when I move back," he said. "Get a cheap place somewhere in a town that ain't this one."

"I like it here."

"Nobody likes it here. Not anybody smart as you."

Paul shrugged.

"In a world that wasn't so fuckin' silly," Matthew said, "I'd be able to stomach being here while you took another run at that college. Even with no money and old enemies gettin' fat just down the road."

Paul nodded but he didn't say anything. Matthew shifted in his seat. He spat out of the window and hung his head.

"Truth be told, man, this place makes my fuckin' skin crawl. I don't feel right until I get ten miles past the township line."

Paul backhanded sweat from his brow, wiped his hand on the seat cover.

"This place wasn't ever kind to you," he said.

Pointing west, Matthew said, "Out there I do okay. I ain't shit in this town."

"You are right now. Trust me."

Matthew shook his head.

"Of all the days to be here," Paul said, "this is the one."

He fiddled with some of the levers and knobs on the console. Then he gave the dashboard a whack with his right hand and the air conditioning came on.

"Yes," Matthew said.

"You want to get out and wait until it cools down?" Paul said.

Matthew looked at him and then looked past him out of the driver-side window at the fields of high grass, the hazy outline of pine trees rising from the slope of the mountains to the north.

"No," he said. "Let's get going. He'll be waiting for us to get there. I don't want him to have to wait."

Paul nodded and put his seatbelt on. Matthew sat back in his seat and shifted some more. He pulled at his shirt and seemed to make it more crooked by trying to fix it. Paul studied his brother for a few seconds, then put the car into gear.

"Okay," he said.

—

They drove along the single-lane county roads to avoid the traffic, the tourists, and the travellers. They passed farms with empty fields and others with crops of corn and soy, new metal silos lit up by the sunlight and old wooden barns gone to rot. They saw very little cattle. There were horses grazing close to the road on one property, one head sticking out through the wire of the perimeter fence, the ears flicking. Soon the car followed the rear boundary of another field. This time the fencing was reinforced by wooden slats, and there were some high sheet-metal walls with barbed wire running along the top. Way off in the distance the field went up a hillside and there were strange shapes moving out there, creatures that were too tall or ran on two long legs, and some with horns that no animal from that part of the world should have. Matthew mouthed a profanity and squinted as he tried to figure out what he was watching out of his window. Suddenly he started nodding and turned to his brother. They had gone there as children. Paul had been old enough to walk the grounds with his father, and he'd recognized the place right away. Matthew frowned at him and turned back. They observed a battered wooden sign with something like a tiger's head painted on it. "Elmvale Jungle Zoo," it said. Matthew watched the sign go by and shook his head as it went.

"That place is retarded."

"Remember when that tiger got out and went into the town and the cops came in and shot it before anyone could get to it with the tranquilizer gun?"

"No," Matthew said.

"Man, I do."

Matthew wouldn't stop shaking his head. When they had long since cut through the township he still had a troubled look on his face. Paul knew his brother wasn't fretting that hard about the ramshackle zoo. He waited and soon enough Matthew spoke up.

"How has she been without him there?" he said.

Paul held the wheel in one hand and ran the other through his hair. He wiped a palmful of sweat on his shirt sleeve.

"You know, you take for granted the kind of feelings they got for each other, forget they been through shit that would kill most folks," Paul said. "Then you see one of them without the other . . . Shit."

"Yeah."

Paul bit at his nails, then put his free hand back on the wheel. "She goes to work and she fusses around the house and gets on with it, but there's nothing behind it. All those old routines don't mean shit anymore. They just pass the time."

"What about when he was home?"

"Before, when he was there between the treatments, he wasn't really himself. They put you under and hit you with that juice and it saps the life right outta you. He came home worn out. Couldn't remember a lot of things. It was weird. So this last time he asked just to stay in there until it was done."

Matthew leaned back in his seat and set his arm on the window ledge. His skin stuck to the plastic. Then he too wiped his brow with his T-shirt. He coughed and had to roll down the window to spit. A torrent of warm air came in at them. Matthew shut his eyes and took a deep breath.

"You might as well leave that open," Paul said. "This air conditioner hasn't done shit for us in its life."

Paul also put his window down and they drove for a long time with nothing but the sound of the rushing wind and the low wail of the radio through the car speakers. Paul thought Matthew had gone to sleep until his brother sat up straighter in his seat and wound his window halfway up and sat there scratching his head. Paul rolled his window partway up as well.

"How do those things work? Those treatments?" Matthew said.

"They send a current through your brain to make you seizure."

"Does it hurt him?"

"You're out when they do it. They say you don't feel it. But the anaesthetic does a number on you. And like I said, you forget shit for a while and you wake up without that fucking awful shit on your mind. That's why epileptics don't get depressed. Their brain hits a point and just says no more and they seizure. Nobody knows for sure how it works."

Matthew took a deep breath and let it out slow. He rubbed at his eyes with the palms of his hands, leaned forward and crossed his arms on the dashboard. Then he rested his chin against them. "I don't know, man," he said. "Anything with the brain freaks me out. I might rather be depressed than risk it. But you're closer to it than I am. I don't know."

Paul stared out at the open road. The greying tarmac ran straight for miles and miles and shimmered under the blazing sun, and far off on the horizon a fog of humid heat obscured the country ahead. Not one cloud was above them, and he knew they were still far inland and had a long way to go. "I'd rather have seizures," he said.

Matthew raised his head and stared at Paul for a while, but Paul didn't look back.

—

In the early afternoon they pulled into a gas station at the edge of town. There were only two pumps and one of them only ran diesel for the tractors and trucks that came through. The station sat in the bottom of a valley where a dozen houses had been built maybe a century ago and half were boarded up or left to slow decay whether people lived in them anymore or not. The two-digit sign that stood high above the lot couldn't keep up with the price of gas, and so now it just read double-zero, the going rate guessed at by those passing through. Paul pulled in from the road and came up to the pump and stopped.

"We runnin' low?" Matthew said.

"I missed a turn somewhere a ways back," Paul said. "I'm gonna ask somebody how to go straight from here, and yeah, we could use some gas too."

Matthew sat up straight. He rubbed at his face and exhaled hard. Then he opened his door. "You pump, I'll pay," he said.

"Okay."

Matthew went toward the gas station store, his arms stretched out wide, the back of his shirt dark with sweat. Paul waited a second and then got out of the car. He walked around it and stretched his arms as well, blinking under the open sky where the sun sat lonely and ruthless. He took the nozzle out of the pump and flipped the metal switch so that the gas would flow. Then he pulled the nozzle to the rear of the car, the hose tethered to the pump by a line with a rusted metal coil at the end. The gas tank's cap had been lost for years, so he just opened the flap, shoved the nozzle into the hole, and squeezed. He thought of something and turned in time to see Matthew open the front door of the station before stepping in.

"Hey," Paul yelled.

Matthew stopped short in the doorway and turned around. He stood there waiting.

"Get us some drinks for the ride back if you want."

Matthew nodded and went inside. Paul looked over at the closing door for a few seconds, and turned back to the pump and watched the numbers cranking over, the digits distorted by faulty electronics in the display. He got near enough to the amount he wanted and guessed where to stop, then walked the nozzle back to the pump. He saw what looked like twenty-six dollars and eighty-eight cents worth of gas and let out a little laugh, thinking about Matthew's face when the attendant told him what he owed. Paul went over to the back of the car to shut the gas-tank flap. As he did so he saw three men about his age walking into the lot toward the store. Two of them were wearing ball caps and cargo shorts and the other had short, ragged hair and torn jeans and no shirt on. They all had the rough look of a long night, but they were talking and laughing, so Paul called over to them.

"Hey guys," he said. "How's it going?"

The shirtless man turned as they came by and they slowed up but didn't stop. None of them said anything. They just looked at Paul.

"You guys from around here?" Paul said.

"Yeah," the shirtless one said. "Why's that?"

"I passed by the turnoff I was lookin' for and ended up here. I wonder if there might be another route to where I gotta go without havin' to backtrack."

"Where you goin'?"

Paul studied the three men for a moment. The two men with caps were taller and they seemed uninterested. One took off his cap to wipe his brow and he had a bad haircut with a bald patch at the centre of his head. The shirtless man was shorter and well-built and he had a cross tattooed across his shoulder, the work poorly done.

"We gotta get to Pineridge. You know the place?" Paul said.

The man smiled. "Yeah, I know it."

"Good."

"What you gotta go there for? Who you got in there?" the man said.

Paul looked into the man's eyes and then he turned and stared out past the gas-station lot at the firs that rose up the valley hillside. He cleared his throat and turned back. The man was still waiting for an answer, still grinning. Paul didn't like the man at all. "So, how do we get there from here?"

"Nobody wants to go out there," the man went on. "People go in there for a reason. They don't come back out. You know that old guy that shot that cop in the head in the bar a couple years back. In front of all those people. He's in there. So's the fucker who did all them kids. All kinds of wackos in there. For real."

"I'm not fuckin' goin' to that part. That's the maximum-security part. He's in the other side. Where you get treated and you get out."

"Who is?" the shirtless man said.

Paul kept staring at the three men, but he didn't have anything to say to them. Now they wouldn't move along. They just stood there smiling and mumbling things to each other, and then Paul heard the creak of the shop door and he saw Matthew coming out with a plastic bag in his hand. Matthew was looking down. He spat on the ground and when he looked up he saw Paul. He hesitated and then went on. Paul turned back to the men and went around the car to the driver-side door and opened it. The shirtless man watched him go, said something to his friends over his tattooed shoulder and kept staring Paul down. Paul still wouldn't say anything more.

"Who you goin' to see in there?" the shirtless man said. "Ain't nobody from around here, that's for sure. That loony bin is for fuckin' psychos and diddlers, and if you got family in there you ain't from here neither and should keep your crazy asses outta here. They fuckin' set up shop there and bring all these sickos from everywhere and fuck up our town. Creepy bastards. That place should be burnt to the fuckin' ground with whoever you goin' to get in it."

Paul shut the door and the shirtless man drew himself up big and held his hands out in waiting. But Paul wasn't looking at him. He was looking at Matthew, who had dropped the bag on the ground and had come up behind the three men.

"Hey," Matthew said.

The shirtless man turned. He was still grinning and didn't see it coming. Matthew dug his feet in and threw a short left hook from the hip and caught the man right on the mouth and the man sat down hard on the sand-strewn asphalt and stared up in utter confusion, blood coming out of his nose in a thin steady line. Matthew had his right cocked, but the shirtless man didn't try to get up and his two friends just stood there. One swore, but he didn't move. Matthew looked at each of the two men and back at the downed man. Then he looked over at his brother. Paul had come around the car and stood beside the pump shaking his head.

Matthew raised his eyebrows. "What?" he said.

"Get in the car," Paul said.

Matthew stayed calm as he picked up the plastic bag and side-stepped the three men, the one he'd punched still sitting on the ground with his hand over his nose, blood between his fingers and hate in his eyes. Matthew went over to the car and Paul opened the passenger door and waved him in. As Matthew sat down the door shut behind him. Then he heard the sound of gravel shifting as the man he had hit scrambled up to holler something at them. Matthew turned to Paul, but Paul was already making his way over to the men with his long deliberate strides. Matthew got out of the car but he wasn't quick enough. Paul had already hit the shirtless man three times before Matthew got to him. The man had only been on his feet long enough to say a few words. Now he was lying on the ground again with his hands pawing at the air. If the other men had thought about doing something they gave it up when Matthew came back. He grabbed Paul around the chest with both arms and pulled him away. Once he had been dragged clear he shucked loose and started for the car without looking back and without even looking at Matthew. His face was flushed and his teeth tight together and his knuckles were slathered with blood from the man's ruined nose and mouth. The brothers walked to the car together and Matthew had his right arm over Paul's shoulder. His heavy hand lay flat against Paul's chest and Matthew held him close, patting his palm hard against a fast-beating heart.

The car crested the north ridge of the valley by the late afternoon and started down the other side. For a few minutes Paul and Matthew were high above the town, staring out together at the shoreline with its maze of docks and piers and boats coming into their slips and others drifting out into the bay. The water shone green in the sunlight. There were no waves because there was no wind, but the surface shimmered and shifted just so slightly. Far off in the bay were tiny islands of shield rock and some were topped with dwarf white pines and bowed willow trees. The horizon line lay out in the distant waters and if there was land beyond you couldn't tell it by sight.

"That's a nice place, isn't it," Matthew said.

"It would be."

They could have driven straight through the town, but Paul took them around it, coasting down on a zigzag route through the streets until the car came out onto a long, level road that took them past parks and marshes and a massive retrofitted power station before leading right to the bayside of the town. Here they merged into sparse traffic on a four-lane shoreline roadway and drove a little more than a mile east around the outskirts of the north end before leaving the winding coastal road. A large promontory rose up toward the water's edge, blanketed by pines and larger deciduous trees with their foliage burnt and dried above the tree line. Further up the tree cover thinned and there were great, smooth boulders jutting out of the hill-face as renegade knobs and joints of the earth's very bones. On the plateau sat an enormous modern building made of grey stone and newly forged metal and heavy slabs of glass set together to form a near-seamless westerly roof.

"That's one hell of a fuckin' building," Matthew said. "You really need to make it stick out like that, in case anyone would ever forget it was there in the first place. Jesus."

Paul nodded, but he didn't say anything. He had taken to wringing the steering wheel with his hands as he drove and when he saw the sign he was looking for he turned left and took the car up the hillside road. They climbed up to the place under the ever-shifting shadows of the wooded pass and at the top the road flattened out. Paul slowed the car as they came to the front gates. There an old man with a guard's cap and uniform sat in a glassed-in booth and when they pulled up he pushed a button and asked them what they were there for.

"We're going to the northwest wing. To pick somebody up."

"Okay," the man said and relaxed somewhat.

Paul gave their surname and the man said it was all right. He opened the gates and waved them through. Paul nodded and drove on.

"Doesn't take much to get in or out of here," Matthew said.

"That's 'cause people don't care about this part of the place. It's that one there they're worried about."

Paul cocked his thumb toward the passenger side of the car and Matthew looked out of his window. A fork in the road ran toward another set of gates, solid metal doors sealed fast between barricades that stood twenty feet tall with razor wire fixed between spikes at the top. The building that they had seen from the road sat far away behind the barrier. The car followed the gentle curve of the road until they were driving away from the structure. Now they saw another one ahead. It was older and made of limestone and red brick, with dozens of its windows shut except for a few on the lower level beside the main entryway. There were no gates and no guards. They pulled right up to the front steps and Paul put the car in park, but he left it running.

"Can you park here?" Matthew said.

Paul just sat there for a moment and then he took a deep breath before opening his door.

"Hey," Matthew said.

Paul turned. "You stay here in the car. If somebody tells you to move then move it."

"I'm coming in there with you. We're gonna get him together."

"It's not like that in there. It won't make it any better. I been in before so I'll go get him. The sooner we get him outta there and on the road the easier it'll be."

"What the fuck are you talkin' about?" Matthew said. "I want to go in there and get him with you."

"Why the hell would you want to do that?"

"What?"

"Listen to me. Stay here. I've seen him in there before. You haven't. He'll remember it that way. Just you being here with him in the car, not in there. It won't make it any better for you to go in."

"What the fuck you mean, 'any better?'"

"It won't make it any better for him."

Paul got out of the car and stood there with the door open. He stared up at the building and then looked west toward the seemingly endless waters. He swore then and shut the door and leaned down so he could see in through the open window on the driver's side. Matthew kept looking at him, but he didn't say anything else. Paul nodded. He slapped the edge of the window with his palm and then stood up and walked around the car and started to walk up the stone entryway steps.

"Tell him I'm waiting out in the car," Matthew called out.

"Okay," Paul said, but he didn't look back.

When he came back down the steps a few minutes later Matthew was sitting in the backseat. Paul was carrying a small suitcase with their father right behind him at his shoulder. He had gone nearly all gray, though his hair still grew thick and his dark eyes were the same as Paul's, as were his small ears and slender nose and the shape of his chin as well as the narrow shoulders, the wiry arms and legs. If he weren't so much shorter than Paul the future would have seemed utterly foretold. Matthew got out of the car and looked at Paul as he went by to put the suitcase in the trunk.

"Hey Dad."

"Hello son."

Matthew smiled crookedly and went over to put his arms around him, the man's chin pushing against his shoulder. His father seemed not to know what to do at first, but soon enough those aged, familiar arms rose and held fast and then he was patting his son's back with his worn-out hands.

They drove with the sun sinking into the jack-pine forest to the west. Paul was still behind the wheel. Matthew sat in the back seat and he could see his father's eyes in the passenger-side mirror and he had never seen their reflection in that mirror before. The three of them had never been in a car at once without their father as the driver. The old man stared out of his window at the fading day and must have seen something there because he sat very still for a long time. When they asked him about the hospital or about his health at all he only gave them a few words back and after he replied he would look away again and seemed to be thinking too long about what he'd said.

He appeared eerily calm until he turned to answer another question from Paul and saw the swollen knuckles on his son's right hand.

"What the hell is that?" he said.

Paul shifted in his seat, lifting his hand off the wheel like he might hide it somewhere. There were lies circling about in his head and he glanced up at the rear-view mirror at Matthew for just a second.

"It's nothing."

"Who did you hit? Why did you hit them?"

As he said it he reached out and took Paul's hand in his and examined it close, his own scarred and misshapen fingers going over the damage with great care. Faint red stained into the ridged skin over the knuckle joints. Paul didn't say anything.

"The man needed to be hit," Matthew said from the backseat.

"Matthew," their father said sharply and Matthew went quiet. He didn't even have to turn around. He looked over at his eldest son and his eyes were wide and full of concern and other things that Paul had never seen there before and couldn't identify. He let go of Paul's hand and shifted back into his seat properly, but he kept his eyes on his son.

"I couldn't help it, Dad," Paul said. "I didn't even think about it."

"Did they hit you first?"

"No."

"What did they do to you?"

Paul ran the injured hand through his hair, then scratched at the back of his neck. After a few seconds he lay on the wheel again.

"They said something about you," he said.

Paul tried to keep his eyes on the road, but his father kept studying him. The old man put one of his heavy hands over his mouth and then took it away and bit at his malformed nails. Soon he stopped and looked at his hand and then lay it flat on the window ledge. He stared at it for a very long time before he spoke again.

"You can't do that, Paul," he said. "Unless you are in real trouble you can't do it. And never because of me. Someone shits on my name it doesn't make me happy, but I won't have you risk coming to any harm over me, not you or your brother."

In the rear-view mirror Paul saw Matthew rubbing at his chin with his palm. Saw him snort and let out a heavy breath. Paul watched the road and kept quiet. He nodded.

"Paul," his father said. "You promise me that."

He stared at him until Paul looked back.

"Okay."

Paul turned to the road ahead and his father watched after him. Then he reached up and put his hand on his son's neck and squeezed a little. When he let go he did so with some hesitation. Everybody in that car knew that they had heard a promise that would never be kept.

They were all quiet for a long time until Matthew spoke up.

"Dad," he said. "Do you want to stop? You haven't eaten anything."

"If you want to get something then sure, we can stop wherever."

"We're okay, Dad," he said. "It's up to you."

Their father turned and looked at Matthew for a second and then at Paul.

"If you two are okay I'd rather just keep heading for home."

"Sure," Matthew said. "Let's just keep on going. Paul's been driving a long time."

"That's what I figured."

The car turned onto the county road in the near dark. There were stars in the sky already and just a shred of the moon and in the dusk there were birds flying in tandem and others perched on the power lines in small groups and a few standing alone. From far down the road they could see the old familiar shape of the wooden farmhouse, the shadows of their clothes rising and drifting out from the metal skeleton of the rotary clothesline in the yard. The breeze that moved them had come in from the north and it played in the trees and when the car crept up to a stop sign they could hear crickets singing in the charred thickets of tall grass and off in the fields the distant sound of a dog barking. They went on through the crossing toward two lights burning, one in the front porch, another in the kitchen.

Matthew slumped against the open window. He hadn't seen his mother in over a year. He stared into the half-light blindly. Inside the house she would be watching their arrival through the window, standing over the sink in her nightgown with a cold bottle of beer on the counter beside her. Their dinner would be on plates in the oven, warming there while she worried about them coming in so late and about the drive that was now over. She would be wondering if they had eaten already while she waited, her appetite lost to nervousness. They would come in and she would fuss about them and say something about them being late and then she would hug their father very hard and

Paul and Matthew even harder, as if they had been locked away with him. She might not expect them to eat, but she would lay out their supper and make them sit down at the table, the four of them together. She would take her place last, having waited with the phantoms and the dark corners and the pictures of their long-gone relatives, the part that was missing returned to her and their house made home again.

THE MANY FACES OF
MONTGOMERY CLIFT

Lewin was named after his drunken grandfather and Micah was named for the Old Testament prophet who said, "Do not trust a neighbor; put no confidence in a friend," because Micah's mother had been both converting and going through a bad time while pregnant. Her mother thought it was a girl's name when she saw it in the table of contents; she was new to the whole Bible thing, and it was an innocent mistake. But most people at John Huss Christian High School were named Joy or Stacey or Matthew, and being a Micah meant there was a slight blurring around her, the smallest mark of strangeness that was sometimes enough to leave Micah feeling as though there were a tiny satellite delay between herself and everyone around her, that she was isolated one half-second ahead in time.

So she was intrigued to hear that a Lewin was transferring in. She had never heard the name before, and she pictured someone tall and thin, with a mean-looking mouth and tired eyes. When she saw Lewin for the first time, at his father's funeral, he looked just like the picture in her head, so much so Micah thought she had, to a certain extent, invented him.

At the funeral, her mother told her to go and speak to him, to say she was sorry for his loss and that she looked forward to having him in her class. She did this, and told Lewin about Bible Challenge, the Bible trivia competition that John Huss participated in along with the other Independent Christian schools in the region.

"It's really fun," she said. "We get to go away for tournaments. One of my teammates graduated, so maybe you can be on my team."

If this was an inappropriate conversation for a funeral, Micah didn't know, having never been to <u>on</u> before. She hadn't known Lewin's father, but because Lewin was soon to be a student at John Huss, Principal Garmash had activated the telephone prayer chain, and everyone had been told to go.

Lewin was examining a crustless cucumber-and-cream-cheese sandwich while Micah talked.

"I've already started studying," she said. "We're doing James first. It's short. But there's this one verse about the double-minded man that I know they'll have a ton of questions on."

Lewin didn't respond, but he moved his gaze from the sandwich to Micah, so she went on.

"He looks in the mirror and forgets his own face. That's the verse."

Lewin said, "He has two faces?"

"No, he's double-minded, not double-faced."

But even as she said this, Micah was thinking she had gotten the same wrong impression while reading – that she had pictured the double-minded man as having one face on the front, the regular one that he looked at in the mirror, and another, forgotten one on the back of his head. And the one on the back wasn't a face at all, just blankness.

"Could you come with me for a minute?" Lewin said.

The sentence hung together all wrong, it sounded corporate and suspicious and formal all at once. Micah went with him and they entered a broom closet near the washrooms, Micah going in first while Lewin held the door. There was a bottle of white wine on the shelf. Lewin unscrewed it and offered Micah the first sip. It was warm and slightly oily, almost carbonated in its sweetness. Micah could feel her tongue all the way around her mouth, more than usual. Usually it just sat there. She had never had a drink before.

Lewin said, "I really didn't want to leave my old school," and Micah said, "I'm so sorry for your loss."

Because she was trying to be polite, Micah hadn't told Lewin she was the top-ranked player in Bible Challenge, certainly at John Huss and sometimes in the whole region. When he was assigned to her team, she was conciliatory and patient. She explained that instead of hand-held buzzers, the teams sat on chairs that had sensors on them, and to attempt an answer, they had to spring to their feet to release the sensor. They spent some hours practising this, leaping forward and giving answers, over and over.

"So basically, we have to move our asses?" said Lewin.

All the Joys and Staceys and Matthews in the room stared at him.

"Basically," said Micah.

—

By the time the winter tournament arrived, Lewin and Micah were neck and neck in the region. They both had excellent short-term memories and they would sit together in the drama room before practice, cramming. They leaned up against one another, back to back, and Micah could feel the knobs of Lewin's spine pressing against her.

There was a minister's son from Wiarton who had a photographic memory. His finger would trace along in the air while he read words only he could see. They were determined one of them would beat him at the spring competition. All of the tournaments were held in small towns or sad suburbs, places like Mississauga or Stoney Creek or North Bay, with cinderblock basements where the paint was an inch thick on the walls. There were dusty tins of Orange Crush and Dodge minivans. For the weekends away, Lewin would dress up in a green mechanic's jumpsuit or plaid pants and tuxedo shirts. He bleached his black hair and Micah helped him spray it so it stuck straight up from his head.

Back at home on Sunday nights, they loafed together in his room, and Lewin would carefully make his face up with cosmetics from the drugstore, his hands steady and light. His skin was bad then, and the medication he was on made it flake off, even from his lips. He looked raw all the time. With the makeup it was both less and more noticeable. Lining his lips in warm sienna, he told her, "It's important to line the mouth you have, not the mouth you want. Everyone can tell the difference." Then he went into the bathroom alone to wash up, and Micah waited, the house quiet, and she thought about what might happen if someone broke in with an axe, with long whispery coils of white rope. With a gun. When Lewin came back, the skin on his face was damp and angry-looking, but his expression was serene.

Micah's ex-boyfriend had been on the Bible Challenge team before he graduated. He had a guitar and cracked his knuckles, and his handwriting was scattered with pinpricks because he pushed too hard with the pen. He wrote in capitals. Lewin said only serial killers wrote in capitals. After Micah took top honours at the Alliston tournament in April, Lewin convinced her to burn all the love letters her ex-boyfriend had written her.

They went to the park near Lewin's house and burned the letters at dusk near home plate. Micah pushed the ashes into the gravel with the toe of her sneaker and hated Lewin for making her do it. But they walked home hand-in-hand to his empty house. His mother had been gone for some weeks, with a widower from the church who had introduced himself to Lewin as "Uncle Don." He said Lewin was the man of the house now and he could probably have all sorts of fun on his own for a little while. He said Lewin's mother needed cheering up. The house was big and new and the walk home from the park was pleasant.

While they walked, they pointed out the cars they would buy when they were older and married. Sometimes Lewin would put his hands over Micah's eyes and quiz her on the models of the cars. They memorized the makes and years the way they memorized verses and chapters. There never seemed to be anyone else walking around in Lewin's neighbourhood, just the polished cars sliding silently in and out, like sharks in the cool glow of the street lamps.

At the house, Lewin and Micah went out back to the trampoline, the way they always did whenever it was warm enough. There was a hot tub too, under a fleshy leather cover.

When they were tired of bouncing, they lay down and Lewin realigned Micah's spine by grabbing onto her head and pulling it until something in her neck popped.

"I learned that from a real chiropractor," he said. "But they're not doctors, technically. Neither are therapists. Psychiatrists are. They can prescribe drugs."

"Why would anyone be a therapist then?" said Micah, lacing her fingers together behind her neck, which now felt loose and boneless.

Lewin went to see a psychiatrist two days a week. They had both decided they would be psychiatrists in the future. Lewin's psychiatrist drove a Mercedes S500.

They lay there sipping diluted whisky from an unbreakable Nalgene bottle, feeling warm. The bottle was scuffed and scraped from their repeated attempts to break it.

Another day after school, while the sun was still up, Lewin's mother and Uncle Don came through the sliding door into the backyard.

Uncle Don said, "Hello, Micah," because he recognized her from church and because someone needed to say something.

Micah and Lewin were sitting in the hot tub, and her legs were wavy shapes stretched over his lap. Their skin was slippery under the water and rubbery above. Micah had her hand on Lewin's arm, which was ringed with dried blood and scars. The fresh ones felt like tree bark.

Lewin said, "So you're back," and his mother said, very quiet, "Sorry I was gone so long."

They all had dinner at a restaurant that night, Lewin and Micah and Lewin's mother and Uncle Don, and Uncle Don's daughter, who slipped off her tennis shoe and slid her sock foot up Lewin's pant leg during garlic bread. A week later, before the summer tournament, Lewin dropped out of Bible Challenge. Micah stayed on at first. She even had the brief sharp thought that it would be easier to win without him there, not just because he was competition, but because he distracted her, his bright outfits flashing at the edge of her line of vision, the dark roots of his hair clanging against the white tips. She lasted a week without him. After she dropped out, the minister's son from Wiarton won the whole regional competition, and then the provincial one too.

Micah and Lewin went to football games, where the boy Micah had a crush on played corner. They brought the Nalgene bottle. Lewin told Micah that when they grew up and got married they would have a rose garden the size of a football field. They talked that way all the time, even though they both knew, in some unspoken animal way, that they would never be married to each other, for reasons no one at John Huss spoke about. Still, they sat together, watching the boys in their slithery polyester uniforms, Lewin leaning forward now and then as if in pain. He'd let his hair grow out after he quit Bible Challenge. The natural colour was too dark, and his raw skin seemed thinner than skin ought to be. When the game was over, Micah's crush would sometimes come to the stands and say hello, looking back and forth between her and Lewin, who had his long, flaking face pressed against Micah's shoulder. And on the trampoline in the evening, Lewin ran his fingers through her hair, messing it up, and she ran hers through his, making it neater. Sometimes he put his hands around her neck and squeezed.

"I could break your neck," he said one night, and she nodded. Then he said, "Do you really pray? Like really really?" and she nodded again. His hand was loose on her neck, as if he'd forgotten it was there.

The Grade 12 summer retreat was the last thing they ever did with the John Huss youth group. While the others canoed or waterskied, Lewin and Micah flopped luxuriously on worn armchairs, watching *From Here to Eternity*. They talked about Montgomery Clift and how no one had appreciated him and how he drank himself to death. They would have appreciated him. They couldn't room together, but they met in the dining hall after everyone else was asleep. The first night, Micah had to wait in the dark, sitting on the stage with the huge antlers and dead fireplace behind her head like a dark sun. The next night, Lewin got there first and she saw him from the hallway, one eye painted over in the gloom and one shining wetly, waiting.

They sat beside each other, facing forward. His eyes were always watering, his eyelids inflamed from the pills, along with the rest of his face. If he had dark eyes it wouldn't have looked as bad. He accused her of being late, of not wanting to come. Lewin smacked his palm against the pitted wood of the stage and the sound was like a gunshot. They both jumped. Lewin's mother had moved Uncle Don and his daughter into the house. Lewin put his head down between his knees and Micah stroked the back of his head. The hair was soft, slightly fly-away, charged with static.

On the last day of the retreat the youth minister told them to pray with a friend, to join hands. Micah sat crossed-legged looking at her own hands, limp in her lap. Lewin came across the floor, which had an orange carpet with a red swirl so bright it felt like someone snapping their fingers in Micah's face. Lewin took her hands out of her lap and sat in front of her, his face passive, dark spots on his lips where he'd bitten them.

They'd only been apart overnight, but she'd forgotten how tall he was. She closed her eyes. He breathed out and it was ragged, uneven. He said, "God, let us stay friends." Micah opened her eyes and looked at him. She felt like her throat was made of wood and someone was knocking from the inside. After a minute or two, Lewin dropped her hands and stood up.

She found him later, standing in shallow water down near the dock. The neatly folded cuffs of his shorts were wet.

"What kind of car do you think we'll get when we're married?" she asked. She stood back from him. "There are so many good ones."

He said, "Remember that wine, at the funeral?" In the sun-light, his skin didn't look as bad. "I heard the caterer yelling at a girl about it. About the missing bottle. The one we took."

Micah nodded. She didn't say, "What do you mean 'we'?"

Lewin asked, "Do you think we would have won Bible Challenge if we hadn't quit?" And then, "When you pray, is it inside you or outside or both?"

Lewin turned away again, looking out over the water. Micah slipped off her sandals and walked in beside him, studying the back of his head, the face that wasn't there. She could feel her own head float upward, her neck popping, and she wanted to leap forward with an answer for him.

MARTIN WEST

MY DAUGHTER OF THE DEAD REEDS

His daughter was dead, he told me, drowned in the river. Claimed by the taupe clay and fouled cattle in the cattle wire of the Red Deer River basin, she would never surface. Come Monday morning her classroom desk would be empty and a pair of ballet shoes would hang unclaimed in the cupboard and no one would help. How can you turn down a plea like that? How can you say no to a man crying on your front step with his cuffs turned up as if he never made it past the third grade?

"You'd better come in."

"She was wearing a bright pink sweater and rubber boots." He came in and there were reeds on his feet and they stuck to my floor. "I told her not to go along the river. But she did anyway. She's got a set of brass bells around her wrist that tinkle like Christmas toys so we can't miss her."

"Where is your wife?"

"She's retarded." He threaded the rim of his hat through his hands and tossed it aside. "She's retarded and she doesn't understand. Not tonight, anyway."

"Haven't you told her?"

"She's off her meds."

She was simple, I knew that. I knew a little. She came to a few of my parties. She had problems with the complicated things in life – area codes, traffic circles, and long grocery lists – but I wouldn't have called her retarded. So I let him in. He sat on the couch. He was cold and he had on a scarlet vest and hip waders from the Salvation Army, but I let him in anyway.

He didn't like my place much. I am a bachelor. I live alone. I live with the petrified skeletons of ancient Badland creatures that I put together for a hobby, and that sort of thing is against his religion. Fossils are popular here. They're not a bad hobby. They don't mean you're derelict or anti-social or have disregard for other people's beliefs, but he sat between the calcified bones and his eyes flitted from femur to cranium and tried to pretend they didn't exist.

I handed him a glass of brandy although I felt a little bad for it. He's a religious man who has lost his daughter and all I did was give him liquor. But he rolled down the brandy in one shot and didn't even wince. Maybe there were things I didn't know. The more time goes on, the more I realize I do not know, like the production of pins or the evolution of Mesozoic flowers.

"Have you told the police?" I asked.

"Why?"

"So they can help us look for her."

"They won't."

"What do you mean they won't? That's their job."

"She has to be gone twenty-four hours."

"No. That's not right. How old is she?"

"She's seven." He nodded. He shut his eyes and counted the years. Maybe he was counting something else, too. "No, wait. She's eight."

"Eight? Then they don't wait a whole day to go looking for an eight-year-old who's missing in the river."

"They will with her."

"Why?"

He shrugged. "She's done it before."

"That is ridiculous. Call them now. I know one of the sergeants."

"Do you have a phone?"

I didn't. I do not like things electronic. They are scabbied. They are horsehair. They get in the way of the real things in life. Real things are bones. Real things are beasts. Real things are proving the past and rye, and drinking with women late into the night and then having them naked on top of you, braids up and down, growling. People spend all day long on cellphones, Blackberries, and computers and don't even know what the insides of their kitchens look like, so I don't bother with them.

"Even we have a phone," he said.

"Let's walk down to the station."

"It won't do any good."

"They have all the proper tools for a search. They have ropes. They have maps and infrared. They'll make it easier."

"You have lights and ropes," he said.

That was true enough. Outside, the sun died orange and sent a long shadow across my workbench just to prove his point.

"Besides," he said, "we've been through this before with them. They'll want to look in the house first. They'll want photographs. They'll want to ask my wife questions."

"So let them."

"No. She'll screw things up. There's always an excuse. They'll never look in the right places."

"What are the right places?"

He did not answer. He sat between a spilled glass of wine and a discarded pair of women's nylons from a weekend party and stared into my vacant living room. There are a few other things you should know about my living room. It is large. It is has high ceilings. Only one couch and one chair. No television. Hardwood floors and no carpet. Along with the fossils there are also remnants of gatherings that happened too near in the past to be fossils. Stains. Smudges. Stilettos. A calendar girl with a blue bikini, a singles magazine soaked with merlot, and a leatherbound address book with many names. He stared out across this smear of a house and the stubble on his chin grew dull.

"Why do you do all this?" he said.

"I like to imagine how those creatures used to be. I know, your religion, you don't believe in evolution."

"I'm not talking about the fossils," he said.

And then he put his head in his hands and he howled. He howled so loud his voice went down into my basement and rattled the jars of preserved plums and the tiny skeleton of a bird encased in formaldehyde trembled, too.

"Don't make me go out there by myself," he said. "I know you don't have children so you can't understand, but please help me find the only thing I've ever loved."

"All right," I said and made my way to the workbench where all the tools of the trade were kept. "I'll help you find her."

Was this a bad thing? Was this a pernicious thing? Did I say yes because I just wanted to shut him up? Maybe I deferred because his wife was promiscuous. She went to parties, that much I knew. She didn't connect well at soirees but it was obvious what she wanted. It was obvious what she wasn't getting at home although I never went there. She would stand there in the corner of a kitchen with a wool skirt hiked up to her knees and a single malt clenched against her ribs. I think her nose was pierced.

We went down to the Red Deer River in the dark. Let me tell you something about the Red Deer River at night. The water is slow and sullen and hides things in the filigreed shadows of cottonwood. It hides alabaster larvae and cardamom condoms; stories of pioneers starving on the banks, of soldiers who went away to distant European wars and never came back. Today, there are stories of automated farming accidents and postmodern suicides because it's such a melancholy place, the pastel grey Badlands sunk below the prairie with spent oil rigs and abandoned wheat kings. But sometimes people just kill themselves because economic times are bad or they have nowhere else to go. They could have done it in Calgary or Vancouver, but this is a better place for it.

I had the flashlights attached to the brim of our helmets. The kind spelunkers used. You could fall in the river with them and the bulbs would still work. Still find the clutches of ancient Pteranodons and the tangle of teeth in the late night sediment. I ran my hand across a layer of prehistoric rock that vanished into the water. Lacerated by the glaciers, the ridges coughed up Cretaceous spines and amber wings.

"Forget about those," he said. "Give me one of those lights and turn them on."

"Why are we looking here?"

"This is the way she always comes."

Laid waste in the mud was the axle of a combine, a weasel skull, and what could have been a free-base pipe.

"Isn't it dangerous this way?"

"Yes," he said. "Of course."

"Then why do you let her do it?"

"Children are like that," he said. "You tell them not to do something, but they go ahead and do it anyway."

His face was dirty. He looked like a miner with my head-lamp on. His breath came out in a white cloud then hung around in a bundle.

"Maybe we should retrace her steps," I said. "What school did she come from?"

"School?"

"Yes, what grade school?"

"I'm not sure."

"How can you not be sure?"

"You bring your dates here, don't you?" was all he said.

There was a kite hung up in the willow. An orange kite with red poppies and a crepe tail like a child would have. In the dark sky between the branches there were other things, too. Underwear and plastic bags, lottery tickets and soiled rags. Beer boxes and plastic ashtrays, relics from unhappy cupboards. Anything that wasn't wanted elsewhere wound up here.

Then in the soft mud by some caragana roots he spotted a set of footprints with the chevron pattern still stamped into the silt. The trail came out of the aspen grove and then mean-dered along the water, left by a small person who was not at all in a hurry.

"Those are hers," he said. "Those are her boots. I know them.

I put them on her this morning. There's a chunk of heel missing."

I got down on my knees. The harsh light fell across the track and on the right foot, and sure enough, the back half of the heel was gone, the rubber cracked and ragged. The trail of boot prints wandered through a cluster of reeds and with each step, they changed a little. The toes sharpened, the chevrons became scaly and the heels narrowed into claws. By the irrigation flue, the tracks were clustered in panic like a child hopelessly lost and knowing so and then they entered the river and were gone.

"What do you see?" he said.

"Nothing."

"You're lying."

"A sign that says phosphates must not exceed ten parts per million."

"That's not what I mean. You're an expert on tracks. What do they say?"

"These tracks aren't new. They're ancient."

"Stop that. I'm tired of hearing about your non-existent fossils. She's been taken into the water right here," he said. He waded into the river and ran back and forth like a dog that couldn't decide where to cross.

"She hasn't gone into the water," I said.

By the mouth of an oxbow pond where the silt lay deep, a coil of barbwire ran from an old cattle fence and was fouled at mid-current. Trapped beneath the surface, a knot of hunch-back clothes bobbed up and down, and because the fabric was pink, I pulled on the wire. The weight sank back. Not like a fighting fish. Not like a salmon or even the dead pull of a codfish, but a fiction that belonged on the river bottom forever. I remember once, as a boy, I went fishing in our boat with my father and uncle. We were out on the deep saltwater and the rod bent down in an arc. My father and my uncle spent an hour reeling the cargo in, and then a bloated dark coil welled up to the surface and just as the limb touched the stern of the boat my father said, "Go inside."

Now my father and uncle are gone and this is a river, not the ocean. But out of the back eddy rose the drowned tangle of soaked wool and rubber boots. The body was small and childish, the limbs knotted in reeds, and the blonde hair strewn with petroleum from the very centre of the earth. Mutilated by the cattle wire, the skull had been stretched into a wedge and around the wrist there was still a string of brass bells.

My neighbour threw his arms around the carcass and the head lobbed back. The eyes were baby blue, but the beak was triangular, and the arms scaly, reptilian wings.

"My Angela," he said.

"What are you doing?"

"She's still breathing."

He put his mouth over the beak, exposed the red gums and razor teeth and blew until the meagre chest inflated. I grabbed him by the shoulder and struck him in the face.

"Stop it."

"How can you say that?" There was blood on his lips and on the sand.

"It is not your daughter."

I cut off the barbed coils with a pair of pliers. The wings flopped apart in an arc of crude oil. Rolled out, the span was six feet. The eye sockets were filled with vitreous humour that had soured in death and the claws on its feet had punctured the rubber boots like ivy grown through concrete.

"We have to bury her," he said. He kissed the leather jaw and did up the blue buttons on the dress. "We have to bury her and give her something proper."

"We have to call the museum," I said.

"Museum? How can you say my daughter belongs in a museum?"

"That is not your daughter."

"She's not an animal, she's not something to be shot with formaldehyde and stuffed in a jar. She's a human being."

"All right, we have to call the medical examiner then," I said.

"No," he said. "They'll just take her away. It would be like everything else. They'd just take her away and then I'd never see her again."

This was long past reason. The dead creature's eye gazed into the stark splinters of poplar night to a place where there was no family and no dawn.

"We have to take her home," he said. He had thought this out. "We'll take her home and we'll put her there on the kitchen table until it's time. That's where all children go. That's the way it should be. We'll burn frankincense and pray. Then I'll find a minister and we'll have a service. In the churchyard, the steepled one behind the train tracks. You'll come, won't you? I want you to come. You're the only one who will come, no one else will. You'll have to be with me when I tell my wife. I can't do it alone. She'll die. She'll crumple in grief."

Then he wrapped his hand around the tiny set of claws that extruded from the wing and squeezed them. Balled inside the fingers was a coil of kite string.

—

Russell Fairbanks had slipped on the front deck of a Massey Ferguson combine and fell down into the blades. His leg was severed at the knee and his femoral artery was punctured in not one but two places. He was rushed to the hospital and I cannot recall if he lived or if he died, because his parents were religious and would not allow a blood transfusion. I remember Lilly Carmine died of frostbite and her parents looked for her everywhere, but someone else found her in an old latrine. Perhaps they were secular.

I thought about these things as I walked up the steps to my neigbour's house. He stayed in the back of the pickup truck with his waterlogged corpse. He kept whispering, "My little fallen fruit," and there was no chance I'd be wading back through that. There are two ways to rationalize a criminal act. One is to say that it is not criminal, that it is for the greater good. Like a crusade, or starting a war. Perhaps keeping a handgun at home. The other is to embrace the criminality and eat your young. I knocked on the door and straightened my collar.

His wife was standing in the sparse living room smoking Virginia Slims with her heel hooked on a coiled hot water heater. She watched the ceiling fan turn. She wore silver bangles on her ankles and her legs were tanned. The windowsill smelled of lemon pledge.

"Oh, it's you," she said.

I closed the door. On the table was a gin fizz and a pair of earrings.

"Are you all right?" I said.

"Why wouldn't I be?" She pointed at a silver tray that held crystal decanters; bourbon, scotch, and rye.

"You've no clue what's going on?"

"With him?" she said. "I'm adjusting."

She turned to the fireplace and twisted a portrait of a small child around to reflect the light from the kitchen chandelier.

"Is that her?" I said.

"Who?"

"Your daughter."

She wasn't listening. She stared into the glass for a moment and then glossed her lips with cherry balm. The portrait was a five-by-eight black-and-white photo of a small girl with blonde hair on a swing set.

"I think I took it better than he did," she said. "He's always been the soft one. He's always been the one that in the end couldn't handle loss. For all of the loves we know, death makes us fonder. That might be Shakespeare. Or maybe it's Hunter S. Thompson. Who knows?"

"What are you going to do now?"

"Do? I'm going out," she said.

"You might want to hang around."

"Why?"

"He's outside."

"What's he done this time?" She scooped up the earrings and pushed the portrait back into place so the glass reflected her lobes. "It's ridiculous, isn't it? But I have to use it. He doesn't tolerate mirrors. He says they're vain. It's got something to do with the book of Daniel. Is there anything going on at your place tonight?"

"No."

"Why not?"

"Because I was just out with your husband in the river. We're both soaking wet."

"In the river?" She stopped and examined the gin. She declined. Perhaps there was something better down the road. "Whatever for?"

"Listen, he dragged this thing out of the water. You might want to have a look."

"What kind of thing?"

"I'm not sure. It's grotesque, really."

"Just give me the synopsis, okay?"

She walked over to the picture window and let some ashes drop into a chrome tray. The ashes fluttered down like owls and I thought for a moment she might lick one up.

"Well, you're going to find out," I said. "He's bringing it inside."

"Figures," she said. "Maybe I'll go over to Jamieson's. He's a bourbon drinker. They've got friends in from the Coast. Why don't you come along?"

"Not tonight."

She opened her mouth a little and the smoke crept out. She reached over and adjusted my lapel. She picked off a reed.

"That's too bad. I need to get away. Look, he hasn't told me much," she said. She shrugged. "I'm leaving. He's keeping the house. I don't care. I don't want it. In case you haven't noticed, he's not the greatest with words. Besides, I don't tell him everything, do I?"

There was sick mutton feeling in the room. The floor had gone gritty with the silt my boots had dragged in from the river and between my teeth there was a dirty feeling too. She reached out and rested the end of her cigarette an inch away from my Adam's apple, then teased me by drooping the ember closer.

"Where is your daughter?" I said.

"What?"

"Where is your young daughter right now, I mean, is she at relatives', or out lawn bowling or drinking Jack Daniel's or in her room sleeping or what?"

"I have not a clue what you're talking about."

"Who is this portrait of?"

She picked the framed photo off the mantel. The girl sat on the swing with a trace of sepia melancholy on her lips.

"I have no idea," she said.

"Where is the photo from?"

"He cut it out of a Sears catalogue, I think."

"He said your daughter was drowned in the river."

"Is that what he told you?"

She sucked on her cigarette with her thumb under her chin. She was nodding, gazing off to the ceiling, perhaps at the crepe-paper chickens, perhaps at the jar of cashews. Not at all at the photograph. The young girl was wearing boots and bells around her neck, dressed up and delicate as if her parents were shipping her off to an event that she was too young to understand.

JASMINA ODOR

BARCELONA

O ver the course of a couple of weeks, Amanda has moved some of her things into a spare guestroom down the hall from her and Earl's bedroom. She now spends a lot of time in this room, rather than in the living room, or the bedroom, or the room that was once her study. She's moved only a few books, her laptop, some underwear, and pyjamas. This move, though deliberately slow on her part, has nonetheless put the entire household on edge: her aunt Grace, her mother Millie, who walks around looking perplexed and afraid, and of course Earl, who has so far been quiet about this problem. Earl strokes his beard a lot and occasionally smokes a cigarette somewhere in the yard, out of view.

When Amanda started being down, crying in the evenings in secret, dressing badly, Earl must have decided that optimism was the best attitude to adopt. Better encourage her than dwell on the sadness. He is nearly thirty-eight and has suffered from depression before; Amanda is twenty-four and until recently has seemed to everyone confident and happy.

Now, no one is sure what Amanda does in her room when she is alone there for hours. Sometimes they'll find her with one of those thick women's fashion magazines spread out in front of her; Earl understands the magazine is probably a cover, but a cover for what? Nothing, it seems. She sometimes gets a little angry when they disturb her, and if Earl asks her whether she'll have supper with the others she might impatiently tell him that she'll eat later. But following that, she also might take his hand, smile, apologize, and thus give him temporary relief.

It is the end of July, and two months since the four of them have returned from a vacation in Barcelona. Millie pleaded and persuaded the reluctant Amanda into the vacation, because she wanted, in part at least, to commemorate the togetherness of the four of them, to affirm how pleasantly Grace, Millie, Amanda, and Earl have lived together. Millie's sister Grace is getting remarried in three weeks and they won't be under the same roof, most likely, ever again. Grace has lived here for nearly a year; she moved in when Dan, Millie's husband, left for the States on business. Grace and Larry's ceremony and reception will be right here at the house. The house is large, as is the yard, and the yard slopes onto a ravine; you can stand at the far end of the yard on the edge of the ravine and see the shimmering surface of the river. There is lots of room for a small outdoor wedding of forty or so guests.

One part of Millie hopes Dan will come back for Grace's wedding as he has told her he would. He has also promised he'd be flying back regularly, and has not been back once in more than a year of being away. But another part of her would prefer not to have the interruption of him at the wedding. Let him come when there are no guests, when the house is empty, formidable, silent except for the rustle of the poplar leaves outside, and Millie is ready and waiting with two glasses of Scotch on the coffee table under the sixteen-foot ceiling. Or let him not come at all. Before Dan went away this last time, he had spent nineteen months at Pennybrooke, a minimum-security prison an hour out of town. He was guilty of defrauding shareholders. Either Amanda or she visited him every week and brought him books to read. Sometimes she feels as if he has never lived here, has never slumped his slim frame onto the sofa and put his feet up after work, has never greeted the neighbours with friendly obscenities, as if it was always she and Amanda, or she and Amanda and Earl here in the house. Many times already she has bartered Dan away for the return of Amanda as she once knew her.

Today they are having dinner together, but Amanda has not shown up yet. Everyone worries about Amanda since she has changed the location of her pyjamas, and especially since she has told them that she wants to go back to Barcelona in the fall, for an eight-week course in Spanish language and culture. Millie has acquired the habit of writing her worries in letters to Grace; these letters often contain things she most wants to say, and she slips them to Grace in passing, on her way out to work, or even while they're sitting in the living room. In the last letter she wrote about a dream she had in which Amanda, looking not quite like herself, tells her that there is no heart left in it, and Millie, panicked and heavy with foreboding, tries to understand what it means, what is the *it*. She wants to ask but for some reason can only touch Amanda's hair, which in the dream is inexplicably blond. She gave the letter to Grace while

Grace was having her one nightly cigarette out in the yard; so far, Grace has not brought it up.

"We have to fix up the yard," says Grace as she spoons mashed potatoes onto Millie's plate. She is just the kind of person to fill your plate when you'd like it to be filled, thinks Millie. She watches with admiration her sister's tall figure, with a straight posture, thick around the waist and hips.

"Is Amanda upstairs?" Millie asks Earl.

"I knocked earlier but got no answer," he says.

"I'll go look," says Millie.

"Oh, she'll come on her own, let her be," says Grace. "Though I do need to ask her about the tablecloths."

They've put Amanda in charge of certain things to do with the wedding, the chair and linen rental, because it seemed beneficial and sensible to keep her involved with the wedding and to give her a preoccupation that could not, as far as they could see, have anything painful about it.

"Good luck getting her up in the morning if you don't," says Earl. They are in the habit of talking about Amanda as if she were quite inaccessible, though she goes hardly anywhere and spends most of her time upstairs.

"I'm sure she's not forgotten. Amanda wouldn't forget. Amanda is efficient with these things," says Millie, and everyone knows that in saying it she is only remembering a time gone by.

When they start stacking the dishes, Amanda comes in from outside. Her brown hair is limp and her jacket undone. She's gained weight in this last year and it shows most clearly in a layer of pudge around her jaw. She was once known for her beauty, and that she is indifferent to it now, is killing it with her indifference, makes the change in her seem, to Millie, an even greater loss.

"We'd all thought you were in your room and didn't want to bother you," says Millie. The look on Amanda's face is part of the inaccessibility: a closed face, eyes averted to just below eye level. Because of the look, no one is sure if it's a good idea to ask what she's been up to.

"You out for a stroll, Mandy?" Earl asks. The feebleness of his voice is disagreeable even to him, but that distaste is not new.

Amanda does not raise her eyes, but makes a sorrowful little grimace as if the question hurts her, physically, and says, "What?"

Watching her now, Millie could weep. Her splendid, beautiful daughter, the kindest person one could imagine. Earl tries to take her hand, lightly, when she passes him to get to the stove and fill her plate. "Oh, what," she says, sighing. "Groucho Marx," he says. He's trying to tease. A friend of Millie's, a therapist, told them once that they should try to coax her out of herself, not let her retreat. Still, this is painful to watch. Millie feels actual tears somewhere behind her eyes.

"We have to landscape the yard," repeats Grace.

"Easiest thing," says Earl. He is a professional landscaper. "I'll do it in one or two afternoons."

"We are so lucky with you two," says Millie. Beyond the kitchen the sun is setting and they all have a golden glow.

Earlier, Amanda was walking through the ravine on the other side of the river; it was warm and there were joggers and cyclists and other strollers out. She could not stand to meet anyone's eyes, not even the few side glances of men; she carried a notebook with her and waited for the urge to write to build in her. She quickened her pace and at the next empty bench sat down and poised her pencil over an already half-filled page. Some time later she was startled by voices.

"Does she not hear? Miss, do you mind?"

"She's pretending. Unbelievable. Hello, Miss, hello there?"

They were two joggers, hardly older than she was, and the man had one bloody knee and a scraped chin; they wanted to sit down and Amanda was sitting in the very centre of the bench. Horrified, feeling her face flush, she closed her notebook and walked quickly away. She walked until she was out of sight for them, and then walked farther to an empty bench. Now she sat on its edge, and opened her notebook again, keeping her pen poised while steadying herself. She could write only a sentence, and it said, *That was a nasty tone.*

Still thinking of it, thinking now of the streaks of blood running down the man's shin, she is glad to be at home and walking upstairs, past the room she and Earl share, and to the guest room. This room is the only place she gets some relief. She lies down on the bed. They demand things of her each day, all day; things she can no longer give. She cannot eat dinner with Earl in a restaurant, can't talk about films or about some friends' breakup or drink wine at one of his friends' house parties, or answer sincerely when he asks what she's been thinking about. She cannot make love. She doesn't know why, but she just can't. She hasn't been able to since before Barcelona, since before spring. The winter, when she was let go from her job at the photo shop, was bad. Neither can she sit with Millie on the sofa, watching some travel show and holding hands, like they used to do for hours in the time after Dan was sent to Pennybrooke. She can't spend the afternoon book shopping with Millie, nor work through an elaborate recipe with her, nor listen to a story from her and Dan's past, some blurry and dreamy time. She can hardly bear the familiar old feeling she still sometimes gets around her mother: love that is a pulsating tenderness for her mother's small frame and brown curling hair.

Oh, she knows that they think that she gets all the time she wants to herself. She knows they talk of her as if it is they who bend to her demands. She's accepted that as just one unremarkable injustice that cannot be fixed. She is sorry for all the things she cannot provide. And she wants to express, somehow, that she is sorry: when the pulsating tenderness appears, it shames her. The shame needs either a dark room, or an action, a gesture. This morning she shocked Earl by making him breakfast – of waffles, bacon, poached eggs, croissants with cheese, and sliced nectarines – because she remembered that they used to, when he worked early mornings and she had early classes, cherish a chance to eat together and linger over coffee. Millie, Amanda can see, is also pleased to see them get along, and Amanda likes to provide some small pleasures for her mother, too.

Although she doesn't begrudge Grace her happiness, she regrets that Grace and Larry will not move in here. Being out of the house, Grace cannot be counted on for her calm presence, her company for Millie, her evening drink with Earl, her general lack of demands, whether explicit or implicit. She reaches for her notebook. The time of Dan's trials – the one that was declared a mistrial, then the second, then an appeal – was a line that split her and Millie's life into two. She and Millie found consolation in long talks over coffee and waffles, or wine and sandwiches, in the nook near the kitchen window. Their talk during that time hardly ever stopped – it seemed as if they were engaged in one permanent conversation, and coming home from work or school they could continue it without warm up, as if it were the real stuff of their lives and the other things were only the technical requirements. Arriving to pick up Amanda, Earl could see plainly that no detail or substance of the world Amanda and he had built was unknown or closed to Millie.

She remembers how she told her mom about Earl. Amanda was seventeen, and she and Millie were walking home from a thrift store, the one at which Earl worked occasionally to make extra money when painting work was slow. While paying at Earl's till, Amanda said to Millie, "Mom, this is my friend Earl." Millie shook Earl's proffered hand. It had rained that day; on their way home, very near the house, Amanda stopped and told Millie that Earl was her boyfriend. She remembers her mother's face, the curling wet strands of hair at her temples. Amanda didn't know then that her dad would be arrested for fraud in a few weeks' time. Millie had hardly ever been angry at her, but Amanda feared she would be angry now. Who is Earl, Millie demanded, and indeed Amanda hardly knew how to explain him. He was fourteen years her senior. He painted houses for a living, worked wherever else he could to help his mother pay off the farm he'd grown up on, the one his stepfather nearly gambled away. What else could she say about him? *I know the kinds of men my mother pictured. And she pictured a procession of them, one after another trying to impress her daughter. But I only wanted my stocky cashier.* Amanda was not only beautiful; there was something good and rounded about her that gave the impression she deserved good things – good men, good jobs, good friends.

To think of them all now as they were then pains her. She will walk down the hall, down the stairs, to her mother's room and stroke her hair. She will find Earl and tell him she loves him and that everything, after all, will work out. But she can't. It is enough that she is supposed to call someone about renting chairs. She dreads this. Dreads the sound of her own voice hesitating and uncertain. She used to be able to do things. When Millie and she were left alone, she was good at calling the plumber, cancelling insurance, firing the accountant, talking to men who called even after Millie changed and unlisted the house phone number. She was good at talking with her mother, good at getting her to like Earl.

Her dad served nearly two years, after the whole process that also took nearly that long. After he was released, came home to a house that seemed emptied of his presence, Amanda moved out with Earl. She can remember those days: they lived in a small flat; Earl's friends were always dropping in; there was a wallpaper photo on the living room wall. She liked Earl's friends. She tries to count back the years to when precisely that was. That tires her. She puts the notebook down for a moment. Last spring her dad went to Phoenix on a business venture. He's supposed to come back, but Amanda no longer waits for it. It seems to Amanda that around the time he left, Millie began to shrink. Her posture changed and she lost about an inch of height. She began to speak in a murmur, knock plaintively on doors, eat her meals out of small side dishes. She had survived the investigation and Dan being in prison, she had accepted Amanda's imperfect lover, but there's a limit to what one can take.

Instead of moving to a two-bedroom apartment downtown, Earl and Amanda moved into Millie's house. None of them wanted to sell it. Amanda would again do – she thought she would, everyone did – what she used to be good at: taking care of things and cheering up her mother. She moved into the house so that she might one day find Millie baking a German chocolate torte, with one of those upbeat chirpy waltzes playing in the background, smoothing the icing patiently and almost hypnotically, winking at Amanda when she caught Amanda watching. *I used to endlessly come across one or both of my parents in some unaware moment, always the observer on the edge of the picture, surprising them – happily, it seemed – with my presence.* Every now and then Amanda and Millie do try to bake together, but Amanda has so little to say. The fake cheer exhausts them both and each needs a lie-down afterwards.

Amanda wants to return to Barcelona. It was with apprehension that she broke this news to everyone, at once, and explained taking the course. She should have told Earl first; she would have, if it weren't so hard to talk to him. Sometimes if she looks him straight in the eye she feels that collapse is imminent. What form would the collapse take – that's still vague for her. The only secret is that there is no Spanish language and culture course as she has told them; or rather, there is one, she's looked it up, she knows how much it costs and what it involves, but she won't be attending it. How she will explain it later she can't quite think about; she hopes it will not matter once she gets away.

What Amanda remembers about the city is the smell of men. During mass at the Basilica, she noticed the discreet colognes emanating from the fresh, upright collars of the men

in the row in front of her. There were other smells: the
colognes were beneath the smell of wood and old prayer books.
She also loved the cafés, with the breeze carrying the scent of
coffee, and the pairs and groups of men and women, packaged,
perfumed, sometimes perfect and sometimes too worn; it all
made her heady.

The rooms of the two-bedroom apartment they rented in
Barcelona smelled of new furniture (the furniture was sparse)
and of linden trees. They had to clean up after themselves, but
a woman came and gave them washed and folded linens and
towels, in various colours, every other day. The woman's name
was Lula and she was thin and stunningly pretty and looked
perpetually fatigued. Whenever Amanda saw her, she either
held her young boy at her hip or her posture alone suggested
a great weight; her lids hung low and she gave the impression
of a person continuously exhaling. She wore dresses in bold
colours – fuschias, and blood reds, and aquas. Her dresses
hugged her waist, hung below her knees, showed plump cleav-
age; her hair was thick and dark and curly and pushed back
from her face. The combination of the mane, the bright
colours, and the perpetual weariness affected Amanda as something beautiful and slightly disconcerting.

On the second day they passed by this woman while she
was talking to an old man in the hallway. He was the owner of
the apartment and his name was Arthur. The woman was his
daughter-in-law, the wife of his son Jude. On the stairs Arthur
invited them all for lunch and they obliged. Amanda liked old
people and she liked Arthur; he was just the kind of old man
she liked. Good-humoured and slightly satirical, as if one
could not be otherwise having sampled the ways of the world.

He treated all of them with interest and politeness. He treated her, in particular, as someone who knows less than he knows of how the world breathes, but also like one who will soon figure things out. His courteousness flattered Amanda because it approached flirtation – or did it approach flirtation only in the mind of the generation that did not expect to have chairs pulled out nor coats taken care of? He liked talking to Amanda about the nineteenth-century French novel; rather, that was the foundation that allowed him to like Amanda. It happened to be one of the last courses she had taken in her degree and so the titles and the salons and the unhappiness were still fresh. Based on two or three informed responses he had assumed, probably, a much wider breadth of familiarity than actually existed. But having a common foundation meant they were free to talk of other things.

Jude was not intended to have a part at all; he was merely the son, beleaguered by a beleaguered wife who was waiting for him to become a lawyer so she might hire a sitter or housekeeper and get some sleep. He was not a man who needed diversion or stimulation or complication, but a man who needed a bigger apartment. He was young – as young as Amanda – but with a child, a toddler, and this small, tired, striking wife. His hair was the slippery blond hair of an infant and his face the kind that passed for good looking in television dramas about small towns – an earnest, manly, serious face. He was not supposed to be in the picture but he was in it, the poorly defined figure somewhere near the edge of it. He smelled like cedar, woody cologne with a whiff of something orange; on the two hottest days, she remembers also being able to smell his skin, coppery and yeasty. She remembers Arthur and Lula's scents, too:

Arthur smelled like just-ironed clothes, and sometimes like caramels which he often chewed. Passing Lula in the hallway, Amanda smelled hair oil and lilac, and there was a whiff of orange around her, too.

———

Amanda's first meeting alone with Jude happened by chance. She was supposed to meet Arthur for an afternoon drink, but she was late. Arthur waited for Amanda at a corner table of the café down the street from his house. This was his regular place; he took his coffee here every other morning. He liked putting on his suit pants and a dress shirt to walk over and be served.

The wind blew wisps of his white hair as he thought about the girl: she was a bit of an unexpected pleasure, a breeze when you thought all the windows were closed. He was not sure that she was as young as a girl; the precise age of the young eluded him. Regardless, here was a person he could get used to talking to. She had a lovely manner, a nervousness that showed in the movements of the hands, and a habit of staring at a person for moments after he or she has stopped speaking. But that entourage of hers – why did they all travel together like that? Though the mother was lovely. Attuned to the daughter – when the girl saw a fly in her lemonade, the mother's eyes immediately searched out the waiter. Did the girl see the mother do that? Another time the mother broke the spell of the girl staring at him by asking her a question – to his regret. The mother seemed nervous too. The aunt and the boyfriend were not nervous. When the mother looked for the waiter to inform him of the fly, the boyfriend watched her as if trying to signal something. She then put down her hand and he went inside the café and returned a minute later with a fresh drink.

The aunt and the mother and the girl resembled each other, and he covertly spent much of their lunch trying to pinpoint the similarities and differences. Around them the girl did not talk very much; that's why he had enjoyed showing her his house and then their brief stroll alone, yesterday, more than the time with the entire package. He thought he started to understand about the family and about the girl. And so he came on the idea of making her an offer. He hardly ever rented the apartment off-season and he liked talking to the girl. He realized he liked her a lot more than he cared for his daughter-in-law.

But now the girl was late and he was feeling his allergy act up. He had nearly finished his coffee and was starting to feel nauseous, a symptom, he suspected, of a new blood pressure medication. The day was hot and he was growing uncomfortable. When he saw Jude walk by, on his way home for lunch, he waved him down and asked him to be kind enough to wait for the girl and tell her that Arthur had to return home. He put a bill into Jude's hand and walked away.

Amanda was hurrying along because she had misjudged the time and now realized herself nearly half an hour late. It happened often that half an afternoon passed before she realized that it was no longer morning. When she saw Jude sitting at the café table, she thought that she must have got more badly mixed up, until he explained about his father having to leave. She had mentioned to Millie that she was meeting Arthur for tea and hoped now that no one would see her here and think she had lied. Jude's smell was a thin edge of cologne mixed with clean coppery sweat; there was sweat at his hairline and on his neck.

"Will you have lunch with us? Lula has made some kind of tuna pasta salad, I think." Because she said nothing, he added, hesitatingly, "Do you like tuna?"

"Sure," she said, "thank you."

If Lula was made uncomfortable by Amanda's unexpected presence at lunch, Amanda could not discern it. She smiled at Amanda through her sleepy lids and pointed her to a chair. She wore a turquoise dress, and held the boy in one arm as she set the table with the other. As they ate, the boy turned his eyes to Amanda repeatedly, prompting Lula to say, "He likes you," the first thing she said since the initial hello. Jude was the one keeping up a conversation by asking Amanda what she and the others had visited.

Amanda had no memory for names and dates of art works, or names of streets, and found it impossible to keep talking about places and things she'd seen.

"He seems very bright," she said of the boy. Shortly after, Lula rose from her seat, put her plate in the sink, and said, to the child rather than either Amanda or Jude, "We're going for our little walk, aren't we." She stopped near Amanda's chair and said to the boy, "Wave bye-bye to the lady." With that Jude and Amanda were left at table with their plates still half full. He moved his plate to the side and she felt it meant that the visit was something of a chore for him, one that could now be concluded without loss of politeness.

She walked out of the apartment minutes later, walked to the corner, and turned left. She was walking toward a vendor's stand where she had seen, the day before, a print she liked: of a field, an open road, and an old-looking horse, in repose. It was a generic print, but she liked the horse, which looked pathetic and unfriendly. The stand was there, and there was a small crowd browsing or waiting to pay. Several Spaniards were involved in a conversation with the seller. She found and took hold of the print. On the last occasion she saw Arthur he told her that if she ever wanted to return to Barcelona, he'd be happy to let her stay in the flat. At the end of summer for instance – she could return at the end of summer and stay as long as she liked. As a young man he had found that it bene-fited him greatly to experience new surroundings, he said; he'd spent a transformative three months on Greece's Saronic islands. She pictured herself walking down this street alone, reaching the street of their flat, past the fountain and up the stairs into a quiet apartment, empty, entirely hers.

The seller was still in conversation and she turned toward the street. Walking not far from her on the sidewalk was a pair of young men; one of them was twirling something like a short thick cable. She would have turned away, but the man then suddenly ran up, quickly, and smacked the cable – it was hard to tell what exactly it was – loudly across the bare thighs of a woman standing near Amanda and among the other tourists. Up close Amanda saw that he was not a man but a teenager. He ran away swiftly to where his friend was and then contin-ued walking at a lively pace, turning back to look toward the woman and laughing. The expression on the woman's face was one of white shock and shame, and pain. The man next to the woman, who was with her, stared after the young laughing boys with an expression of mouth and brow that he might have worn while watching news of violence in other parts of the world, a baffled and concerned expression. Amanda looked away from the woman, to overcome the shame she shared with her. She saw that the woman wanted to rub the place she had been hit, but her hand merely hovered near it. No one else seemed to have seen, or comprehended, what had happened. Amanda shook her head, and said, "They are awful," though she did not know what language the woman spoke; nor was the woman looking at her. After a pause, Amanda put the print back, realizing she could not, anyway, bear to draw attention to herself and ask the vendor if he spoke English. *Nasty*, she thought, and stopped on her walk home to take the notebook out of her purse and write it down. At the flat she complained to Earl of a stomachache, and wrapped herself in the quilt on the bed. He brought her tea, a book, and she let him move the strand of hair falling across her eye, and she let him lie next to her, and she did not go out for the rest of the day.

———

Millie sits at her vanity and thinks about Amanda wanting to go to Barcelona to learn Spanish. When Millie first asked why Amanda would not choose to learn, for example, French instead, Amanda said she had just liked Barcelona so much. This was not one of the things Millie remembered about Barcelona, Amanda liking it so much. To Millie, Barcelona was all hot, sticky air, lush foliage, and corrugated metal shop doors that were pulled down at closing time. But what she remembers about Barcelona most clearly, somehow, is the baggy dress and funny little slippers Amanda wore day after day. It was a short, wide dress, with a deep front, and when they sat down in cafés, the waiters – men, almost all – could see much of her bra.

"It's summer," Amanda would say, inexplicably, when Millie said the dress doesn't fit well. It was warm, yes; in fact it was hot and oppressive and full of people. The dress became a joke. Millie remembers the south-facing apartment and that in the morning they took their coffee on the little canopied balcony. She remembers the bus stop just down the block, and that they would watch people waiting for the bus: youngsters and ladies going for groceries. The bus came every twenty minutes, they had figured out; she thinks now that they never saw anyone run for it. There was an urban sleepiness to everything in that neighbourhood, not stillness, but an unhurriedness to the rhythms of life, the closing of doors, the gentle way the cars pulled away from the curbs. Sometimes Amanda slept in and Earl and Millie and Grace had breakfast without her under the canopy. "Let's leave her for the day," Earl would joke with Millie and Grace, to lighten things. Then, as Millie rinsed plates, she would hear a plaintive voice behind not-quite closed doors, Earl's voice, gently coaxing Amanda out.

Through her window Millie can see Earl pruning a bush. He's not protesting Amanda going to Barcelona, as far as Millie can tell. Would she know if he did protest? She doesn't know if she would know. Earl may not be what she had once, long ago, pictured for her daughter: before he appeared, she had imagined Amanda with many types of men – tall and gallant and intellectual, kind and self-effacing and brilliant. What she got was Earl, his friendly-neighbour manner, a provincial familiarity, advanced age, and few credentials. But she now certainly doesn't want to picture anyone else in his place. She has tried to help them where she could. She gave up the house to him and Amanda – she really only needed one room, two at the most – and a few years ago cashed in some bonds to pay for Earl's two-year diploma. But how are things between them now – she would give up many things to know. Amanda doesn't talk to her anymore, and Earl, of course, won't suddenly start. This tells Millie what she dreads, that things are getting worse. Millie remembers the old man they rented the apartment from in Barcelona, and his son and the housekeeper, the son's wife. It was months before the trip that Amanda's oddness began, and when they were in Barcelona, Grace said it was great to see Amanda engaging with people. She was right – the thing Millie had dreaded about the trip was that she would have to implore Amanda to leave her room at all. It had turned out that she didn't have to do that, most days.

One afternoon, standing by a fountain on the corner of their street, she saw Amanda leaving a café with Jude, not Arthur, walking with her hands in the pockets of her funny dress. She didn't tell Earl what she saw. Amanda came home within the hour, and Millie would surely have cut off her own ear to have Amanda lean into her on the terrace and tell her what she and Jude talked about. Why does a depressed girl have enough energy to talk to strangers and not to her own family? She was encouraged by seeing Amanda choose restaurants and discuss literature, but why should it have been strangers who got the pleasure of the real Amanda, the one Millie has been waiting to wake up to one morning? Millie wanted to help Earl, if only she could. In their bedroom are pictures of Amanda and of the two of them together – Amanda with her mouth full of Timbits and her eyes open wide, Amanda dressed like a 1920s flapper posing for the shot with a gloved arm holding a cigarette in a cigarette holder, Amanda and Earl on a bridge in Banff, night-time and the reflection of lamps in the river behind them, embracing tightly.

Millie looks out again and sees Earl still pruning. She drops her hairbrush, walks out of the room, through the kitchen, out the front door, and into the yard towards him. She sees him notice her and smile. She walks right up, holding up her hand as a shield from the sun, and asks him if he needs a drink – nope.

"It's starting to look good," she says.

"Be ready in a few more days."

"It'll be strange without Grace around," she says, "won't it?"

"I'll miss that old broad."

"Oh, Earl. It will be strange without her. A little bit empty."

"She'll be over lots, I'm sure. If Larry goes away on some contract, she might come and stay here, hang out with you and Amanda."

Here Millie brightens a little.

"She's always welcome, of course. What's Mandy doing?" Millie was in the habit of asking Earl about Amanda as if they didn't all live in the same house.

"Oh, chatting on the phone or something."

This can't be true because Amanda never talks on the phone.

"Oh. Do you think she's serious about this Barcelona thing? The language course thing?"

"Seems like it. Might be good for her. You know there's work in languages – translating, interpreting, things like that."

It irritates Millie when Earl says far-fetched things that side-track her from what she is obliquely trying to say. As if Amanda is going to go to Barcelona to begin a career in interpreting for the United Nations.

"Right. I was thinking I'd feel better about the whole thing if you were going with her."

"Yes?"

"It's only that she doesn't know anyone there. She hasn't asked you to go with her?" He pauses, making Millie fear that she's been far too direct. Earl is capable, she knows, of shutting down conversation, her conversation about Amanda specifically, quite politely and unmistakably.

He says, "No, she's not asked me to come along. I probably could have. Work drops off in the fall."

Millie titters with something like fear. "Well, I think she ought to have. You deserve some travelling as much as she."

He squints at her. "I guess she just wants to do something for herself." He keeps his eyes on Millie as he says it. She can hardly believe she is getting all this from him. What passes through her head is, What doesn't Amanda do for herself these days?

She says, "Oh, I don't know. Has she said that?"

"That's what I think, anyway. I don't actually know, she doesn't explain too much."

"She doesn't?" Millie's heart rate quickens.

"You know how she is."

"So secretive. Oh, I can't tell you how it worries me. Just tell her you want to go with her."

Earl smiles. "She's free to do what she wants," he says. Millie thinks of what to say next, but it does not matter – it is too late, the minute has passed, and Earl is readjusting his work gloves and smiling, and she knows of course what that means.

———

Jude invited Amanda to a music performance.

"That Allejo is a kind of magician, isn't he," Arthur, sitting at the table with them, had said. Amanda had her hands on the table and on hearing the invitation interlocked her fingers. But the tone of Jude's statement so faintly resembled the tone of an invitation that she hardly knew how to answer. He had said, "You should come with me to a concert on Friday," and the suggestion sounded hypothetical and indifferent. Only the old man's just perceptible encouragement suggested it may be something else. Amanda was afraid to accept what had not necessarily been offered.

Jude said, "I like to walk over from the park; you can meet me there and we can walk together." He knew that she was here with others and that she shouldn't have been desperate for company.

"Yes," she said, "I will." She thought, I will tell the others Arthur will be going too, and Lula, and other people. But ought I not to invite Earl, if not Millie and Grace? Well, she had already said yes. She would find a way.

He had not mentioned dinner, but after the performance he guided her to a restaurant.

"So you are a graduate of literature," he said.

"No," she corrected, "of media arts."

"Ah," he said. "I don't believe we have an equivalent of that here. Do you have siblings?"

"No, only child."

"Ah. I have six, but they are all half-siblings. So in a way I am an only child too. In a way I grew up alone. Did you grow up alone?"

"I grew up in a huge house and all the friends I had in school always ended up playing at my house. My parents let us go into almost any room. They were what I think people call modern parents. They were very happy, that's what I remember about them and my childhood. I would exist all day in some imagined world, a fortress of couch cushions, and emerge suddenly into their presence, a shock of happiness."

"My parents seemed to me like such public people – you know? I think I was shy of them most of my childhood. If I caught them in an intimacy, my dad in his shorts, I would get embarrassed. You're here with your family." There was a pause that seemed to stress the absence of her family from this table, here, now.

"Yes, they like it." That was not what she had wanted to say. "We live together."

"In the huge house?" He smiled. She smiled and nodded.

"My aunt, my mom's sister, came to live with us – we could not keep up the house, my mom alone couldn't, not without others. She is reluctant to sell it." He nodded vigorously, as if to show he understood all about the weight of houses.

"It's a unique house. Architecturally speaking."

"Lula wants a house – though my father has several flats we can choose from. She'd like to put all we have into a house. I prefer to keep something on the side – for travel, pleasures."

"A house is a lot of work," Amanda said, thinking of Lula's droopy eyelids. "I would not put all I have into a house."

"We are the same age, you and I, are we not? Your boyfriend is older."

"Yes. I was young when we started dating. I mean, compared to him; I was seventeen. He was thirty-one. My mother, at first, ignored the whole thing so that it might go away."

"Of course," he said, "of course. But you didn't care? I mean it didn't stop you."

"Oh, it could have. But I guess the happiness was already

cracked by then and I didn't have a complete terror of spoiling it."

"Right."

"Only ordinary fear."

"Of course. Should we order dessert?"

"I like your father," she said after a pause.

"Your mother seemed very pleasant. There is quite a resemblance with the three of you, you and your mother and your aunt. You return on the Sunday, you've said?"

For the first time in the conversation she didn't know what his words were intended for. The guilt had not yet started pouring in for her. The lights of all the restaurants, the glassware on the tables, shimmered. She was a woman talking earnestly over dinner with a man. It was what a person wanted from travel, memorable connections. A memory of light reflecting off wine glasses and a stranger's life unpeeling in front of you. No pulsating tenderness, no shame, no love or remorse. Only civility, freshness. Possibility.

"Do you remember when the happiness had started to crack, as you said?"

"Oh, I don't know."

"Right."

"Right."

———

It's the early morning of the day of the wedding, Saturday. Amanda and Earl are in her room; the room is shuttered and lines of light coming through the shutters stripe the furniture. Amanda keeps it this way most of the time. She and Earl sit propped up on the bed. Her long hair hangs down the sides of her face and part of it touches his shoulder; that's how close they are. He's ventured to put his hand on top of her hand. She used to put a lot of work into her hair. He touches a strand of it with his free hand. He has not physically changed since they've met. His fingers are the same. His beard is the same, and the skin on his face is still perfect. He observes the room like a visitor. There is a magazine on the table near the window and a plain glass vase, empty. The room reveals nothing. He puts his arm behind her and around her shoulder, though he knows she might squirm away. This time she doesn't. This is not right, he would like to say. One ought to be able to hug one's girlfriend without fear that she'll pull away as if she's been poked with something sharp.

"It doesn't have to be like this," he says. She closes her eyes. He wishes to not feel as if he were torturing her. "I got a contract for October," he says.

"Oh, good," she opens her eyes. She sits there in fear of what he will ask of her that she won't be able to give.

"Spain will be warmer than here this time of year," he says.

"I suppose," she says. "I might even come back tanned."

"What day do you return?"

"The sixteenth, I think. I have to check the ticket. It's in the drawer there, you can look."

But he won't. Something about that feels false, she telling him to look at the ticket. He doesn't want to look at it. He moves his hand from behind her back.

Maybe he can take her out of this room, out of whatever fortress she has built for herself. He smells her hair, covertly. She leans into him; she leans into him. He won't move, won't ask for more, won't say something and spoil it. He can get her out of it. It doesn't matter what will happen later, but he sees now he can get her out of it.

"What is it?" he says. "Because we can change things."

"Don't – don't talk. I don't know. It – when we were in Barcelona, that woman who got hit."

"Which?"

"At the stand. I was going to buy a print – it doesn't matter what – they just walked by and hit her, with – a cord or something. I don't know. It's just that nastiness."

"Who were – did they hurt her?"

"No – you mean, was she bleeding or something? No."

"You're scared that it could happen to you?"

"It doesn't have to happen to me. It's only that it's out there, always."

There is a timid knock at the door. They don't move to answer it; they know it's Millie. Then Amanda sighs and straightens.

Earl grabs her hand, says just what he means: "I can get you out of this." If not now, he will lose her. She is looking at him. He could cry but doesn't. Millie calls apprehensively, "Hello?"

At supper the previous night Amanda mentioned the good deal she got on her flight. The definitiveness of a plane ticket put Millie in a panic. Until Amanda brought it up, the supper was festive: Millie had cooked, Grace had picked out a fine champagne left in the pantry since the days of Dan. It all threatened to destroy Amanda's resolve. Just yesterday morning all she could think was away, away – that while listening to Earl's humming as he brushed his teeth and Millie starting the juicer. Then in the evening, while Grace was setting the table, Millie knocked on her door, opened it, and said simply, "Amanda, my love, darling." That *darling* cut like a polished, well-prepped blade. Later, sitting at the table, Amanda thought, this is all my mom needs, her family about her, light conversation, an occasion to justify putting out the good china. Me, looking content. And who else but Earl would live in this house and grow to love this family of hers? Barcelona was a risk: it was one thing to be alone in a house full of people, and another to be alone in a stranger's apartment beyond which strangers waited for their bus.

So when Earl came to her room this morning, she was already worn down with a sleepless night and the dread of indecision and the struggle to hold on to the certainty that had been wavering consistently. It would have been a superhuman effort to change tracks and reach out, hold on to him so he might help her. And when Millie knocked on the door, the easiest thing was to open it.

By the time Amanda opens the door, Millie is gone. Millie hurries down to Grace, who will not look at what Millie wrote for Earl.

"Earl is devastated," says Millie, refolding the letter, "he doesn't have to say it – I can see it."

"Jesus Christ," Grace says, "it's only a goddamn course." She thinks, enough of you and your letters. "Do you really think Amanda would have anything to do with that bland Englishman? She'll be back before you notice she's gone." The latter platitude is of course impossible, since Millie notices everything to do with Amanda, but Grace is exhausted. Since Dan left it has been too much of this. God bless Larry.

"You're always welcome here, Grace."

"I know," Grace says, "I read your last letter."

Millie again starts to unfold the letter for Earl. Grace turns away from the lined notebook paper. She has an idea of what Amanda wants in Barcelona; it's not Jude. Earl could have seen that, if not Millie. But Grace is not about to tell them. She has her own life to consider, thank God, and she will not get caught again; no, she will not read any more letters. Instead she will visit with baking for an evening or an afternoon, and her presence in the house will be only the breeziest, lightest caress of a kind hand.

———

At the airport in Barcelona it is indeed Jude who picks her up. She is sick – physically nauseous from the turbulent flight and sick with fear. She packed for the stay as if moving through a dreamscape, as if she were a soldier who doubts the mission, gets a bad feeling in the stomach from thinking of it, but must put her hope in the wisdom of those who planned it. In this state she was driven to the airport, Earl driving, Millie in the backseat. In this state she kissed Earl and hugged her mom, letting Millie hold her tightly for a moment at the airport security checkpoint.

Landing in Barcelona, she wishes to take a taxi, give the name of a hotel where no one could know her and, after putting a few drops of sleeping aid into a cup of hot water, escape into sleep. Jude is courteous, opening the passenger door for her, swinging her suitcase into the trunk. During the ride he keeps his eyes on the road and doesn't try to force talk, so that for some time the only sound is the smooth hum of the car's machine and the murmur of a voice on the radio.

After a while, worried her silence might verge on rudeness,

she says, "It was good of your father to let me stay at the apartment." Jude turns only briefly, smiles.

"He likes you. Anyway, he has other apartments." Another smile crosses his face. What she wonders is, what does he think she is doing here?

When they arrive, he carries her suitcase up the stairs and says, "My father hoped you'd call him when you recover from the difference in time zones." On a pad of paper that sits on top of the shoe rack in the hallway, he writes down two phone numbers, Arthur's and his own.

She thought all she wanted was to sleep, but after he leaves, after she takes off her shoes and her watch and splashes her face with water at the kitchen sink, she then opens the balcony door and steps out onto the tiles, which are warm – it is after ten in the evening, a hot night, though it looks to have rained earlier. She sees people walking on the street, entering buildings, parking their cars and exiting them, talking and laughing and jingling their keys. She can hear their voices. She can hear a distant thump of bass from somewhere in the small building, and a thin sound like an amateur oboe. On the balcony below and to the left of her a man with a fleshy back and light brown hair is lifting undershirts from a clothes line, speaking to someone inside; she cannot understand most of the Spanish, but she picks out the words *mujer* and *dulce*. She can smell warm, wet air and hackberry trees. Her heart begins to beat fast. It is not only fear. It is that she has not slept much in twenty-four hours and has not eaten on the plane. It is that she knows she will have to call home now, and either talk about the Spanish language course or say something true. It is also that she feels the difference between being dead and being alive.

The ugliness deadens one, and then also a hollowness that is hard to ascribe to something specific. Arthur and Jude made her alive, briefly, and now the smells and the people. And her heart also beats fast because she sees that whatever she has begun by coming here, and whether it ends with life or death, this is only the beginning of it, and it will get much worse, before it ends, one way or the other.

———

Millie finds Earl in front of his laptop, his head down on the table on his hands, headphones on his head. She knows he dozed off waiting for a call from Amanda's computer. In the nine days since she has left, Amanda's made some vague but troubling statements. The course did not work out, they found out, but Amanda wants to stay, and extend her ticket even, perhaps. Millie still has the letter she never gave Earl, tucked into the cover of some books that sit on her bedside table. She doesn't like to think of the letter now. She touches his shoulder lightly; he wakes with a shudder.

He was not exactly asleep; he may have sunk one layer below wakefulness, while thinking of the same things he's thought about as the other days since she's been gone – of the fact that it's been eight years. That he's not young, and that there is no consolation for him. All he wants, all he's wanted all along, is Amanda. For her he had let himself get absorbed into her family's palace, for her he used to, years ago, leave parties early and drive across the city in blizzards, tipsy, so she might take a last cup of tea before bed with Millie and Dan. He wanted to love what she loved. Or he feared that unless he did, he would not last, like her friends never lasted. For her he'd learned to understand Millie, had accepted the house, the daily precariousness of moods.

"It's nearly six now," Millie says, "and Amanda must be asleep over there." She says it gently. He takes off the headphones, rubbing the ache they have left around his ears.

"I wanted to tell you I talked to Dan. He wants to come home now. What with Amanda and everything."

"I heard there's a heat wave in all of southern California."

"Oh yes, he's hating it. Here it's twenty-two degrees, perfect. Will you come outside and eat? The air is so lovely. I baked rolls earlier."

"I could smell them."

"We still have to eat," she said, "don't we."

ANDREW HOOD

MANNING

"I'm gonna hit the can like it hit me first," my mom says. "Man the booth, Pickle." She squats, ducks under the table, pops back up on the other side, and, jingling her keys, disappears down the aisles of other booths.

"Hit it like it hit me first" is one of my mom's classic phrases. She's been using it since I can remember being embarrassed of her. It's an okay one, as far as go-to phrases go: not quite smart and not quite funny, but just enough of both of those to elicit at least a smirk. Unless you've heard the hell out of it, then your mouth screws up another way. "Night, Pickle. I'm gonna hit the hay like it hit me first. Don't stay up too late." "Buckle up, Pickle, and let's hit the road like it hit us first." "I'm not against you drinking, Pickle, but keep in mind how your dad would hit that bottle like it hit him first." She'll be here all week, folks.

Dad's splitting has inspired a new number in her repertoire. Everything has to be manned all of a sudden. "Man the apartment, Pickle, while I go out for spaghetti sauce." "Man the car,

Pickle, while I run in here for a lotto ticket." "Man the basketball, Pickle, while I go see if those two black kids want to play two-on-two." As if this one guy – who was never around much anyway, even when he was around – had his finger stuck into some crack in some hypothetical dam and now that he's hit the road like it hit him first, someone else has to plug that hole so everything doesn't just gush and break through and drown everything else. It's like, "Here, Pickle, man the world while I'm gone, will you?"

While my mom's hitting the can like it hit her first, this big pile of human being comes up to the booth I've been left to man. He's got this mustache on his face, but it doesn't look like a mustache he grew. More like he couldn't grow a beard. What he's got on his face is how I imagine the mustache on the main character in this book I'm reading for school called *A Confederacy of Dunces*.

"What have you got?" the pile of human being wants to know. He looks sad about the boxes that we've got opened on the table, and a little tired about them. The good burgundy tablecloth that's been in the family since before Christ was a cowboy does not, as my mom insists, help.

"There's some baseball," I tell him. "Some basketball, some hockey. Some of everything."

"But what have you *got*?" His eyes look like they've been thumbed into his head, like the sunken eyes of a snowman.

"We've got what we've got," I tell him.

The pile sighs like air escaping from a chair when it gets sat on. This has to be his first time to this card show, to be coming to our booth, let alone asking us what we've got. Every month it's the same junk collectors and sad sacks and single dads who come, and they all know that we don't have anything, and that even if we did have anything, we wouldn't even know we had it. They come to the booth to flirt with Mom, maybe buy a card on the off chance that it might improve their chances, but that's about it.

The last Sunday of every month my mom and I pay five dollars to set up our pointless booth at The Arena. This place isn't even really called The Arena, that's just the name it's been given. Where the name was supposed to be, there's just a big blank space. For a while someone had spray painted a weird-looking dick in that spot, but now it's blank again. This is the hockey rink that Corbet's OHL team was supposed to kick ass on. I don't know what goes on, whether they melt the ice or just put a flooring over top of it, but there's always a wet chill here and that sweet chemical smell that all indoor rinks have, folded into the pungency of locker-room-sweat stink. The team the rink was built for was going to be called The Corbet Combats. Something with a bat was going to be the logo. There was even a competition to design some lame mascot. I don't know if someone forgot to carry a one or what, but the way the math of it worked out, the town had enough money for an OHL team or for a rink, but not for both. So we got The Arena for a hockey team, but no hockey team. Now The Arena gets rented out for kids' birthdays, school skating parties, the circus – not the good circus – Neil Diamond that one time, Tom Jones that other, and, every last Sunday of the month, this crap collectors' convention.

The human pile's got a shoulder bag, one of those cheap-ass ones they give away at conventions, and when he adjusts the way it hangs I see that his left hand is a little itty claw.

The other one is in okay shape, though something about the little stubby fingers on it makes me think of baby penises. So with his baby penis fingers he goes through every single card in every single box of Dad's worthless collection. I guess he needs to find out for himself that we have nothing. And I've got to stand there like I'm listening to someone tell a joke I've heard a million times because this is my booth to man now, my worthless cards to man. And the pile is mine to man now, too.

I get the feeling that in life you're rarely lucky enough to know just where the shit has come from that gets cut up and thrown by the blades of your fan. But I can tell you that all of this is Ben Rooney's fault. Ben Rooney is this guy Dad worked nights with at the chainsaw factory who just disappeared one day. Like a bubble that popped, he was there and then he wasn't. What happened was Ben Rooney sold his lifelong baseball card collection for a million dollars and then hit the road like it had hit him first. A wife and daughter were left behind. Claire Rooney went to the same school as me for a few years, though not when her pop popped. She was that girl who in kindergarten would come in from recess during the winter and, starting with her snowsuit, just take all of her clothes off, all the way down to her pointless pink body and get laughed at. Her pop was never heard from again, though I heard of him all the time, because fucking Ben Rooney became like this big hero for my pop. And that's the source of this huge load of elephant dook that got chucked at my fan and got sprayed pretty much all over everything.

"I swear to God," Pop would always say. "A million dollars."

Like swearing to God meant anything. Swearing to God for him was just the same as saying "excuse me" after he'd sneak up on me and belch in my ear.

With dollar signs twinkling in his eyes, Pop started buying baseball cards like rations before a disaster. In his mind, whatever that mind was, this was as good as buying money. Seriously: like buying fucking money. Like he was going out and paying one dollar for ten dollars. That's what he figured out from that Ben Rooney story. I would never ask my mom what on earth she was doing with such an impressive dope because I have this tickling suspicion that I'm the answer. The other answer is that it takes someone just a bit stupider to be with someone so stupid. So, either way, I just don't ask.

Instead of playing catch or something with me in the back-yard we didn't have, or taking my mother out to fancy restaurants this town doesn't have, Pop would be sitting there cross-legged in the basement, unwrapping the cards and stuffing them right into the box, the foil packaging glittering around him like fancy garbage. On the off-chance there would be a hard, dusty blade of gum included, he'd give it to me if I asked before he stuffed it into his own breathing mouth. Card gum you've got to incubate and soften in the hot wetness of your mouth before you can even threaten to dream of trying to chew it. But in all that time it takes to get soft, you just realize that you don't want it anyway.

By the time he popped, like his hero Ben Rooney, Pop had amassed twenty-nine boxes of sports cards. Unlike Ben Rooney, he left all his cards behind when he left. He must have realized what they were really worth. The drool on his pillow on the couch hadn't even dried when Mom packed up those boxes and spirited them to the city and to the first comics and sports memorabilia store she found in the phonebook.

Pop must not have even looked at the cards. He didn't care what they were or what they were about. The cards went from package to box untouched, unenjoyed. Just money in the bank. Rudy – the owner of Rudy's, where we took Pop's boxes of currency – had to peel the cards off one another. I pretended to browse the stupid store while Mom watched Rudy like a hawk that has no idea what a hawk eats.

Rudy, who was dressed entirely in denim – and I mean entirely: a snap-up denim shirt under a fraying denim jacket covered in buttons of all the major league ball teams, and jeans, and a denim hat from the '88 Calgary Olympics, and even his beard was that yellow colour that jeans become when they rot – Rudy offered us $300 for all twenty-nine boxes. Mom lost it like the house keys.

She screamed and all the grown men in the store looked up from their comic books. How dare Rudy try to take advantage of a destitute and heartbroken widow who was selling her beloved husband's beloved collection to afford to take care of her ailing, beloved son, who had contracted AIDS – that's right! Goddamned fucking AIDS, Rudy! – from the blood transfusion he needed after the car crash that had killed her beloved husband? "Fuck you, Rudy!" Mom yelled, as if her and Rudy went way, way back, and she stormed out. She sat out in the car and left me, goddamned fucking AIDS and all, to lug the twenty-nine boxes from Rudy's counter back out to the car.

She didn't say it, but I could tell that Mom, in her heart of hearts – yes, the heart that she has inside of her heart – I could tell that in there she actually believed that after one look at all those boxes, Rudy would open his register and count out one million dollars for her, bill by bill. Like Rudy would take the top off the first box, and this golden glow would bathe him. The heart inside of your heart is always the dumbest. Ask around.

As he stacked the last few boxes into my arms, Rudy, a bit jittery from having been screamed at, gave me a message to give to my mom. The economy of baseball cards, he said, is just like any other economy: it depends on lack. Not many people collected cards in the '50s, say, or their moms threw all the cards in the trash. The harder a card from the '50s is to come by, the more some guy who's stiff for that stuff is willing to cough up for it. When everyone realized how much some people were willing to pay for these useless things, they started holding on to their cards, dreaming of their own million-dollar payoff. But because everyone is collecting now, nothing is rare, and so a collection like Pop's is barely worth the cardboard it was printed on.

I said thanks to Randy and assured him that I really didn't have AIDS. "Yet," I added, and winked, and the look that he gave me said that being nice time was over and now it was time to get the fuck out of his store and leave him to surf online undisturbed for that rare pair denim underwear he needed to complete his look.

I imparted Rudy's wisdom to my mom on the drive home, but telling my mom anything she doesn't want to hear is like trying to give a cat a vitamin. Her fuckbag husband's cards were worth a million dollars and that's all. The next weekend we had a booth at the weird-looking dick-rink. And that was what? A year or so ago?

This book I'm reading right now was written by this guy
who killed himself after no one wanted to read his book. His
mom found the manuscript in a drawer after this guy hooked
a hose to the ass of his car and she started insisting that it was
the best thing anyone had ever written. Luck had it that the
book was awesome, but I wonder if this guy's crazy old mom
ever actually read the thing, like whether or not she just took
the thing out of his drawer and hung it up on the fridge with
an A+ on it. Whatever it was that was his, it was the best thing
ever because her dead son had written it. You can never tell
with crazy women what the value of anything they're trying to
sell you is. But I kind of get the feeling that it's the crazy
women that always get left to man the things that men leave
behind, whatever the things are worth.

From out of twenty-nine boxes and from out of who knows
how many cards, the human pile, with his baby penis fingers,
plucks out just this one card.

"I'll take this," the pile says, and holds up the card like he's
a magician who's just found my card in the deck.

"Okay," I say, and I fix my stare on his deep snowman eyes,
but only because I'm trying to ignore the way that his claw has
something like a slimy sheen to it.

"So how much?" the pile says. He makes for his fanny pack,
which is a NASA fanny pack.

"I don't know." But I'm not thinking about the card, I'm
thinking about an astronaut, done up in all his expensive
hubbub, wearing one of those crappy fanny packs.

"I'll tell you what: I'll give you five dollars for it. It's not even
worth a buck, frankly, but I don't like breaking bills."

"Let's see it," I say, and take the card from him. It's some guy named Rance Davis, a player for Seattle. His baseball card action shot has him in mid-swing. "Who is this guy?"

"He's nobody."

"Nobody's nobody," I say into the pile's eyes, but even against all my best trying, I steal a glance at this sheeny, shiny claw.

"Davis played, like, two games in the majors before f'ing his knee for good trying to steal home. He might have been somebody before, but now he's nobody."

The pile's good hand is out, his baby penis fingers are squirming, eager to take the card back. He's getting nervous, you can tell. The pile's starting to quiver like there's something alive inside of him that's moving around in there, trying to fit in him better.

"If this kid's nobody then why do you want the card?"

"I couldn't give a crap about Davis. He's just the last card I need to finish the '03 Upper Deck season." The pile actually makes a little lunge to reclaim the card but I rear back because I'm not done with it.

As much as I think professional athletes are overpaid and just plain old unnecessary, I can still appreciate that what they do's not easy. A guy doesn't just fall into playing major league baseball. The majors are no chainsaw factory. From before you can make decisions about what you like or don't, you've got to be irrevocably committed to this stupid, silly lifestyle. I know these majors-bound kids in school, and they're just as weird and destroyed as the military-bound ones. You live your life with blinders on, and you work so foolishly hard against the foolish odds that all that foolish work will just lead up to nothing because hardly any-fucking-body makes it to the major leagues, and even most of the guys who do make it all the way there end up being these anonymous henchman types like this Rance Davis guy the pile is so hard over.

Maybe the picture on the card is of Rance's first game ever, of his first time at bat. Maybe this is the picture of the first pitch that was ever thrown to Rance, and he's swinging at it. You give all your dumb life to do this one thing, who are you not to swing? And here in the picture, there's no telling what will happen. He might swing and miss, or he might knock the scalp right off that first pitch. But, whatever happens, something will happen. That's what Rance has decided.

T-ball was as far as I played baseball. Hitting a ball in T-ball is just about as easy as punching the air, but there are those kids I remember who just wouldn't or couldn't swing the bat. The ball was elevated and still and unmistakably orange for them to do whatever with, in a choice position for them to be marvellous champions, but so many of those kids would just stand there stock still, their bat on their shoulder, not quite ready to swing. Not quite ready for anything to happen because of something they did.

To know that not long after this first swing Rance will screw up his leg and bring to a halt everything he has been building is just a bit too much. And it's amazing. All of that is here in this card. So I tell the pile it's not for sale.

"Fuck you it's not for sale," the pile screams a little. There's just a glimmer of cry in his snowman eyes. "Fuck you it's not for sale!"

A smile comes up like a burp, and I try to allay the thing by wrapping it up, by curling my bottom lip over my top, but the look you make trying to keep yourself from smiling is a million dollars worse than an actual smile. Red flowers bloom all over the pile's pear face until it's just one big field of crimson. Little toots of angry breath fart out of his dilated nostrils and he's wobbling and vibrating.

The men that crowd The Arena are basically boys, guarding the crap they have and conniving to steal the crap they want. The crap that they're here after is all that matters in the world. They bicker and they bitch. It's all squirrelly greed and mean loneliness. Sometimes I'll watch them milling and waddling around the rink and imagine their bellies as hatches that open up to reveal some petty, pouting child at the controls of a man. The world that these goons live in is so damned fragile, patched together mostly with opinion, so they're extra careful and possessive of it. I haven't heard the phrase "See with your eyes and not with your hands" so often since I can't even remember when.

The pile tries to collect his huffiness, arrange it into something big and threatening. His little claw looks as if it's trying to grip air while his baby-penis-laden other hand keeps adjusting the hang of his shoulder bag. Some sort of panicked dew has settled onto his moustache and makes it glisten.

"I don't know what the hell your deal is, kid. I don't know what kind of crap you're trying to pull, but trust me, I'm not the guy you want to be pulling it with." The pile sputters this out and all I can think of is shit being pulled on one of those taffy-pulling machines.

"I'm not pulling any crap. There's no deal. The card's just not for sale."

"Well, why the hell isn't it?"

I take another look at the card, at the mid-swing of Rance Davis.

"Because I want it," I tell the pile without looking at him. I don't know how much more I can stand to look at him. "I like this one."

The pile opens his mouth a few times, like he's imitating someone talking. He stops gulping and puts his good hand into one of the boxes and takes out a wad of cards. "Well, what about these ones, smartass? Huh? You like these ones? Are these ones for sale? Huh?"

"I don't know. I haven't had a look at those ones. Maybe they are."

"Well, here: have a look," the pile says, and he winds up and chucks the wad of cards at me.

For an impossible instant, this wad of maybe a hundred or so cards about the thickness of a junior hamburger holds its shape, coming at me like one complete block ready to hit my face like I hit it first. But right in front of me each card catches its own influence of air and they pull apart and go their separate ways. All the cards fall, and flutter, and spin, and swoop down, each of them with some heavy moment on it.

We stare at each other, the pile and me, like we can't believe that what just happened just happened. As if two other people were doing this, and we were just two guys that watched it. My eyes flit back to the pile's claw, and whatever pause button got pushed gets pushed again to make things play. "You're cleaning that up," I say, which I guess presses the pile's own play button, because his mouth opens to say something and his baby penis hand goes to readjust his bag, but before he can say anything, my mom does.

"Pickle!" she yells, and my mom drops to her hands and knees to gather up the scattered cards. They may as well be hundred-dollar bills all over the ground. "Fuck, fuck, fuck, fuck," she's mumbling.

What can anybody do but watch something like that? The pile and me set our differences aside like soldiers on Christmas and watch my mom scramble around on the ground. But then I get a glimpse down her shirt and that's enough of that.

"Mom," I say. "Get up. Jesus."

She wobbles onto one knee and reaches to the pile for help up. Her hand grabs at the empty air where a person without a deformed hand's hand would be. She looks up and she sees the claw, in all its shine and sheen, so she gets up just fine on her own. Once she's standing, she has that dizzy, frazzled look of someone just spun ceaselessly in a chair.

"So who wants to tell me what the fuck this is?" she says. I can smell on her the cigarettes she doesn't smoke anymore. "Pickle?"

"This is your kid?" the pile wants to know. "These are your cards? This is your table?"

Mom looks at the pile, and then at the mess of cards that she didn't even begin to clean up, and then at the pile's sweaty claw, and then at me, and she seems unsure of whether anything here is actually hers. "And you are?" she asks the pile, maybe to bide some time while she figures out who all this stuff belongs to exactly.

"I'm the guy your kid is trying to screw."

"Pickle?"

"I didn't lay a hand on him, Mom, I swear," I say, and though she doesn't, I can tell that my mom wants to smile at that one.

"Listen. Are these cards for sale or aren't they?"

"What? Of course they're for sale."

"Then why won't this kid of yours sell me this card?"

"What card?"

"That one." The pile makes a motion in my direction with his claw, to Rance Davis. "He says it's not for sale because he likes it."

I shoot the pile one hell of a look, as if he's betrayed some confidence.

Mom takes the card and I let her take it. She takes a pointless look at it, stares seriously at it, like someone staring at the engine of a broken-down car they have no idea about, as if seriousness will fix the car.

"I don't get it," she says. She turns to me. "What is there to like about it?"

Not knowing what to say it, I shrug my shoulders. With my face, I do my best to explain about the card, but trying to say anything on purpose with your face is like trying to perform the song you hear in your head on an instrument you just barely know how to play. So who knows what I actually communicate.

It goes to show that you never know what anybody is ever thinking. But you can guess, if you know the person. For all I know, my mom isn't thinking about the card right now at all, but is thinking about whether or not this pile of human being uses his damp claw to cuff his duke or not. But I don't think she's thinking that. It is probably only me who's thinking that. What I think she's thinking about, seeing the way her face gets full and soft from looking at however my face is looking, has to do with Pop. I bet dimes to dollars that she's suspecting that I don't want to sell the pile this card, or any of these cards, because they're Pop's. Like this is all I've got left of that bag of dicks, and so to let go of his cards would be to let go of him. I think that's the way the mind of someone who watches too much TV tends to work. So she nods at me, having gleaned all she's gleaned from whatever my face had to say.

My mom turns dramatically to the pile. "I'm sorry," she says, with this weird, fluffy confidence. "The card," she pauses, "is not for sale."

"I'll give you one hundred dollars for the card," the pile says.

She can't even afford me a piteous "I'm sorry" look. "Deal," my mom says. "One hundred dollars for the card."

"Okay: one hundred dollars."

Now, anyone that's spent any time being nine years old knows that you have to see the money before letting someone you're doing a deal with put their meat hooks on what you're selling. Because even if they do take off without paying you, you at least know that they've got the money to make it worth chasing them down and beating it out of them. Without seeing a nickel, my mom hands over the card. As soon as the pile has it clutched in his baby penises he brings the card up to his claw, as if to feed an animal he's got in a headlock, and tears Rance Davis in half and lets the halves flutter stupidly onto the ground with the rest of the mess he's made.

"Fuck you," he says to my mom, pointing an erect baby penis at her.

"Fuck you," he says to me, pegging me with the same baby boner.

"So fuck us both, then?" I ask.

The pile smiles at me, his mustache like an eyebrow over a hideous yellow eye. "That's right." We finally understand each other.

Giving his shoulder bag one final, absolute adjustment, the pile galumphs away.

All the other men in all their other fanny packs are staring at us. I'm looking at my mom, trying to decide whether or not I can hate her for the rest of my life because of this, if this one time is enough of a reason. Every last Sunday I come here with her, for her – not that I have anything better to do – and entertain this insane delusion of hers. All this for her, and she's ready to sell me out in an instant. People have hated people for less.

I guess because someone has to say something, my mom turns to me and, instead of "I'm sorry," she makes a gross face and says, "Did you get a load of that asshole's little hand?"

"Yeah," I say. "It was disgusting."

Like we'd rehearsed it before, we both, at the exact same time, screw up our faces and distort our left hands and make this guttural noise – like, "Grarrrrrrrrrr" – and this is going to go on to be a shared thing that we do whenever something's disgusting or unreasonable. We make the hand, do the noise, and know exactly where all that came from.

ELIZA ROBERTSON

WHERE HAVE YOU FALLEN, HAVE YOU FALLEN?
(ORIGINALLY PUBLISHED AS "SEA DRIFT")

EIGHT

In the long ago, the rivers bore monsters. One dwelt beneath the foam where the Mahatta ran quick from O'Connell Lake, where the river flowed in faces, geometric and flat and reflecting sun like a prism. Every ripple wore a mirror, and for every mirror, the monster wore an eye. Its tongue lolled beneath rock and sand on the shore, and when villagers knelt on the bank to collect water, the muscle would flex, tremble the pebbles, and snatch the villagers into the monster's jaw. When only a young girl and her grandmother remained, Hilatusala the Transformer visited to inquire what had happened. The grandmother spoke of their missing neighbours, of the monster with many eyes and its tongue beneath the sand. Hilatusala listened, then urged the girl to collect water, urged her to *not be afraid*. So she fetched her pail and kissed her grandmother's cheek and strode the path to river's edge. Before the girl could notice the shifting gravel, she was launched into the air with a speed that knocked her to her back. She opened her eyes to see real birds and clouds and jagged trees instead of their rippling reflections. Then the monster snapped its teeth shut, and the fleshy plates that lined its throat shrugged and expanded and slid the girl deeper into black, which is when she heard Hilatusala's song. The notes screamed all at once, like a raven's shriek and surging water and the whine of a jade knife against cedar. The monster's throat plates shrugged and the girl was hurtled over its tongue, between the teeth, and into sunlight. She landed in the river. Above her, the monster's jowls shook, its lips parted, and the wet bones of the girl's neighbours spewed onto the shore. Spines and sickle ribs and collarbones spilled from the corners of its mouth until the monster had vomited out all of the villagers and coiled back beneath the surface. And so the girl and her grandmother set to work. They matched anklebones to kneecaps, hips to ribs, spine to skull until they reassembled an entire skeleton. Then the Transformer sprinkled the bones with Life Water, and tendons bloomed between ligaments like elastic bands, then muscles and skin and smooth black hair, until a villager was reborn. The more friends they reconstructed, the more friends helped them reconstruct. And so it was that notch-to-groove, vertebrae-by-vertebrae, the girl rebuilt her village.

SEVEN

The canoe poked from the pine tree like a wooden wing, and they crouched ten feet beneath it on either side of a stump. Milton set the plates side by side and sprinkled them with fuel from a plastic lighter. "My grandmother lived up North," he said. "They burned food for their ancestors. For the spirits."

Natalie zipped the collar of her track jacket, withdrew her fists into its nylon sleeves as he dug for something in his pocket.

"I found this in the *Vancouver Sun*." He pressed a folded newspaper clipping into her palm.

She opened it to find a photo of her mom and brother at a swim meet. Her brother wore goggles strapped to his forehead and her mom's good blouse was wet from his arm around her shoulder. They used the same photo in all the papers.

He tossed her the matchbook. She struck two matches at the same time like she'd seen someone do in the movies then dropped them onto the plates.

"Normally you offer clothes," he said, as the fire ballooned, then shrunk into smoke. "But I think it makes more sense to burn something that can help the food find the right spirits."

He nodded to the clipping and Natalie dangled it above the embers, then let go, watching their faces glow as the paper floated and whirled into a half shell of sea urchin, which cupped a meek flame like palms around a tea candle.

"Do you still have her cedar spinning top?" he asked, and pointed his chin at the pine tree, at the canoe.

She tugged the top from the pocket of her cut-offs, the same ones she'd worn yesterday, and tossed it onto the fire. The salmon skin shrivelled and curled on the plates, spitting fat in hot pops. Milton drew the spool of thread from his pocket and nestled that in the embers, too.

"Make the fire bigger," she said.

"Bigger?" His cheeks were long and flat, unaccented by bones, and his black eyebrows stretched low over his eyes.

"More lighter fluid."

He fumbled with the metal valve and dumped a stream of butane into the embers, snapping the flames vertical. The smoke burned thick from the plates, swelled into Natalie's nostrils with the fishy tang of burning oolichan grease. She watched the flames twist around lumps of camas root, watched the shadows cast on Milton's cheeks, how they flapped across the bridge of his nose like crow feathers.

"Let me tell you about the girl who rebuilt her village from bones," he said.

SIX

All the guests were outside, the big house tables papered with greasy napkins and plates. Salmon skins clung from forget-me-not rims, hiding the fishbone tepees that had been quietly erected on the tablecloth. Natalie poured herself pink lemonade as Milton strolled to the food warmers and salad bowls at the far end.

"Normally they dance in here, too," he said. "But outside holds more people." He uncurled the salmon foil and lifted a flank with his fingers onto a fresh plate. "Come on."

"I'm full."

"It's not for you."

Lemon pulp stung her tongue; she swished her mouth with a swig of someone else's cola and joined him at the table. She'd seen the halved porcupines at dinner, the orange meat that hung from their husks in tongues. She never tried one because she had no one to ask what it was.

"A sea egg," said Milton.

She looked up and realized he was watching her. "A what?"

"An urchin."

She took the half-sphere and set it on an empty plate. The salmon remained on the cedar plank it was cooked on. Gummy white fat oozed between flesh and silver in irregular spumes, and it slicked the insides of her fingernails when she separated a hunk from the skin.

"Did your brother like camas root?"

"Camas root?"

Milton laid a wedge of what looked like sweet potato next to his salmon. "How about bannock?"

"I think we baked that on field trips."

"Where?" He tore a corner from the bread in the cookie tin.

"Squamish." She shovelled wild rice onto her plate with her hand. "A cultural centre." She liked the feel of food in her palms, the grains of rice squashed beneath her nails with the salmon fat.

"Genuine Authentic Aboriginal Village?"

"Right," she said. "Somewhere between ski lifts."

"And how authentic were the Aboriginals?"

She fiddled with the tablecloth, fingered her initials in grease on the plastic. "They snowshoed."

"Damn," he said. "How to top that."

"Ever tried? To snowshoe."

"Once. With duct tape and my brother's Ping-Pong paddles."

She maintained eye contact as he grinned at her, made a point to not look away first. He plunged his thumb into a jar of yellow wax and stepped toward her, presenting it like a birthday candle, like she should blow it out. After a whiff she leaned away. "What is that?"

"Oolichan grease." He jerked his hand as though to smear it on her wrist.

She shrunk toward the table and stabbed her own thumb in the jar. Then she faced him, bent her knees, and shadowed his hand, left and right.

He wiped his fingers on a napkin. "One-two-three-four, I declare a thumb war?"

"Bow, shake, corners, begin."

He looked toward the front doorway and stepped from the table. "We should go. Soon they'll come back to clean."

She smeared her thumb in a brassy arc on her plate as he slid out the doorless back exit, then turned to jog after him. He was headed down the path she'd followed yesterday – toward the cove, the canoe in the pine, and her new friend who slept in its hull.

FIVE

At the potlatch Natalie sat next to an Orchid of the Western Sky. The clans had gathered in a tree-webbed clearing of the woods, and the single flower sprouted behind her corner of the sitting log. The pouch bobbed under a white hood between two pea-yellow wings so that the orchid looked like a cheek-less milkmaid, all neck and tongue and cotton frill cap, blonde pigtails out the sides. It must have been planted – her uncle says Western Skies are hybrids.

Sage burned on all sides of the clearing – narrow bundles tied with twine and secured in the dirt with rocks. The smoke smelled stiffly sweet and reminded Natalie of the kids at her old school, who shared joints in the snowberry bushes behind the smoke pit.

A man in a sealskin vest stood outside the spectator ring. He hacked at a cedar log with his knife, and two young girls with chin-length hair distributed strips of bark to guests. Natalie tied hers around her head as she watched the others do. Her uncle stood on the other side of the fire, lilac golf shirt tucked loosely into khaki shorts. He was chatting with the local band chief and a white woman she figured to be a town council member. His eyes shone pale blue in the torchlight and met her own. When he waved for her to join them, she looked down and pretended not to see.

Someone sat beside her, knocked his knees against hers, so she glanced up, saw it was Milton, and turned away.

"I said I was sorry," he said.

She eyed the orchid, her faceless milkmaid, its roseate and waxy tongue.

"Christ, you people think *we* hold grudges." He poked her hip. "Well, did you see Bakwas?"

"No." No wild man of the words for her.

"You look disappointed."

"I'd have eaten his cockles in a heartbeat."

"Don't be silly," he said. "You'd be dead."

The sound of shaking stones rattled from the corner of the clearing, followed by a shrill whistle and drumbeats. A man sat on the far edge of the ring. He wore a mask with a black beak as long as the girl's tree canoe, harnessed to his chest for support. Its lips were painted rust red, its eyes skyward ovoids, and cedar bark hung in shreds over the man's back. He cocked the mask left-right-left-right, and yanked a string that snapped the beak closed. Natalie jumped.

"That's the Man-Eating Raven," said Milton.

The raven capered to his feet, then squatted, then capered again toward the fire, black button blanket flapping at his ankles like heavy wings. Another dancer entered the circle. The beak on his mask was painted pitch and curled like a tidal wave.

"Crooked-Beak of Heaven," said Milton. "Both serve the Cannibal at the North end of the world."

The birds leapt at each other, snapped their beaks with wooden cracks that made Natalie flinch each time. The fire threw their oblong, man-eating shadows onto the faces of the spectators.

"Follow me." Milton nodded to the big house and she felt his rough, moist fingers on her elbow.

FOUR

The canoe in the trees must have been carved for a child because Natalie couldn't lie lengthwise without her calves slung over the edge. She sat cross-legged instead. Next to the bones, which were folded loosely inside a wool blanket. The bundle was wound taut at the feet, but it had unravelled at the hips, maybe picked apart by gulls. A spiny branch of the pine tree poked between two ribs and from it hung a pinecone like a caged canary. Plates of a copper necklace fanned over the skeleton's clavicle, the smallest one dangling in the gap above its breastbone.

The dead grey sides of the dugout were chiselled, grooved, and tree needles filled the bottom. The sky was dark now, and in the moonlight the Chinese beads glittered from the hull like discarded fish eyes. They dribbled from a small, capsized cedar basket and piled in the slanted side of the canoe with the toys – cedar bark tops, buck antler gambling sticks that she recognized from the museum, and whalebone dice, dotted with black grease. A woven doll lay under the Popsicle-stick ligaments of the body's hand. Natalie lifted the girl's finger bone to compare the doll's eyes to the one she found that morning, but at the same moment she heard twigs on the forest floor snap. Leaves rustled; maybe the wind.

She wasn't afraid. She wanted to meet the man who fed you cockleshells, who paddled you to the Other Side, and now she had a companion for the sail. Natalie could return to the girl her second doll, the one with abalone eyes, and they could trade necklaces, her own a silver cross, and the girl could teach her how to spin a top. She'd never heard of Milton's man of the woods, though she had read up on myths before she came. She read about the Thunderbird, who flashes lightning with the whites of his eyes, who eats whales for breakfast. She read about the Tlingit boys who reached the Other Side by a chain of wood-carved arrows. She read about the Hamatsa, the secret cannibal society whose tribe members whirl the dances of man-eating birds – the raven of many mouths, the crane whose beak cracks skulls. She wanted to meet all of them. To find that patch of sky where the stars seep light like milky cobwebs, where the indigo between suns is gauzed.

"Natalie," shouted a voice from a few metres down the path. A beam of light tore between the branches of her pine tree.

Her left thigh felt as if it were filled with sand, so she shifted to release it from her weight. The canoe squeaked against the pine bough and a bead rolled off the dugout lip, but she couldn't hear it land.

"Natalie," the voice said again, from directly under her. "I know you're there. I see the canoe." The flashlight beam quavered along the canoe's lip, then spilled back into the branches. "I'm sorry. It was a silly trick."

She hugged her wrist around her knees and watched the beam shiver back and forth on the tree trunk.

"I let her go. It was supposed to be funny." Milton's voice paused, silent for her response. "Fine. Stay up there all night."

She gathered the spilled Chinese beads one by one and dropped them into their woven cedar basket.

"See you tomorrow at the potlatch?"

She could hear his sigh, and the swish of wet leaves between his shoes as he shifted.

"It doesn't really hurt them."

THREE

The flowers were shaped like paper crowns, as fluorescent as the sockeye that hung in strips outside the smokehouse. Milton stalked the bush with a ball of twine. He looped knots around the wax heads of neighbouring black-eyed Susans and through the lichen-crusted fingers of an overhanging plum tree.

Natalie watched him work from the grass, which reached her waist when she stood and tented over her as she sat. She could feel the air get wetter as the sun drooped copper and low behind the trees. "Milton," she said, and fingered the porcelain beads in her pocket. "What's across the ocean?"

His eyebrows lifted and wrinkled his forehead as he stepped away from the tree.

"Is it China?

"Maybe. Maybe Russia."

"Oh." She clenched a bead inside her fist. "Do things wash up? From the other side?"

"Like what?"

"Beads. Chinese beads."

"You found Chinese beads?" He peeled a slug from his bucket and wrung it between his fists. Slime farted from its tail in wet ribbons, and she stared, lips-parted, as he massaged it into the twine. "Some objects drifted here from old merchant ships," he said. "Maybe beads." He plucked another slug from his bucket. "Sometimes our people traded with the immigrants. The rail workers."

"What about canoes?"

He stared at her. "The canoes are our thing, moron."

"No, I know." She bent low to tie her shoes so that he couldn't see her cheeks. "But what if you found a canoe in the forest? In branches."

"Where were you?"

"Nowhere. What if."

He worked his slugs fist-by-fist along the twine and didn't respond.

She eyed him through the stalks. "What's this for, anyhow?"

He smiled and stepped back to review his strings, then leaned against the tree. "You'll see."

She rested her forehead against the back of her hands and shut her eyes.

"In the long ago, we buried our dead in trees."

Her eyes opened and she flicked her chin to face him.

"Or on scaffolds. But sometimes trees were easier to come by." He swayed his back against the trunk and spoke with the slow luxury of a Scout at a campfire. "We buried our dead in trees so their souls could be nearer to the wild man of the woods."

"Who?"

"Bakwas. He lives with the spirits of the drowned, in an invisible hut in the forest." Milton paused, eyes on the beebalm. A hummingbird had whizzed through the strings, and it hovered above the plant, bill needling into the scarlet throat of a flower. "He feeds lost wanderers the meat from cockle shells. Ghost food. Eat it and you become like him. That's how he takes the dead to the Other Side."

Natalie chewed the ridge that lined the inside of her cheek – had she been so close to a corpse, to the wild man of the woods? "You buried people in canoes instead of coffins."

"Sometimes," he said, and removed a spool of white thread from his pocket. "Sometimes cedar boxes."

She shifted her gaze to the hummingbird – most back home were brown, but this one was silver winged, its tail dusted green, and a high-necked collar of iridescent fireweed. The bird dipped under the balm and cornered right for an exit, but its wing caught the yarn, feather tips welded to slug slime.

Natalie stumbled up, feet tangled, and cried, "It's stuck!" even though its entrapment was plain and Milton didn't seem bothered, and a twine cage wound around beebalm should have tipped her off in the first place. He cupped the humming-bird in his palms, then clutched it in only one. His other hand guided a threaded needle into a hole at the base of the bill, then with a thrust to the other side. He folded the thread so that his fist clutched the needle and knotted end, then spread the fingers of his other hand and released the bird with a gentle bounce into the air. It zipped the length of the thread, then rebounded back, and forward again, whisking the air in hard ovals like the propeller of a beanie, so fast that the shape of a bird blurred into an exhale of white wind that blushed pink in sporadic bursts. Milton held the thread as a kite.

"Do you like it?" he said. Natalie speed-walked past him between the beebalm and the plum tree and sprinted down an overgrown path into the woods.

TWO

"You're the preacher's girl," the older boy said. He wore jeans and a black beater, and he tied his bandana like a pirate.

"He's my uncle." Natalie lay stomach-down on a picnic table. She flicked the cedar bark top she'd found that morning, and it spun out from her fingers until the nose dipped into a crack between table planks.

"So you're going to the potlatch tomorrow? They always invite your uncle."

"It'll be my first."

The older boy carried an empty margarine bucket. He squatted between the peonies in the centre of the church flowerbed and sifted woodchips through his palms.

"What are you looking for?" She studied the line on his bicep where the flesh turned brown-orange. That was their goal back home – sunburnt summers of FM radio, diet colas, and plastic squeeze bottles filled with olive oil.

"Slugs."

She laughed. He didn't. She flicked the top again, but it wouldn't go, and the boy leaned forward onto his knees and snatched something from the paddle-shaped shadows of leaves on dirt. A slug – fat and Dijon-coloured. He held it out for her, the slimed crest of its back contracting between his fingers.

"What do you do with slugs?" Natalie said and pulled herself up. She tugged the squished fiddleheads from her back pocket and laid them on her lap.

"That's secret." He grinned and dropped the slug. It landed in the margarine container with a thwack. "Why'd you move here?"

"Secret."

The boy pinched another slug from the chips. This one was black, and a pearly string of slime linked it to the ground. "Show you mine if you tell me yours."

She waved a fiddlehead in figure-eights through the air and watched him scour the flowerbed. He paused and straightened his spine and watched her watch him. "My mom and brother died," she said. "On that fishing boat." The boy didn't respond. "I stayed with my neighbours in Vancouver to finish the school year."

The silence stretched as the boy bent low to peer again under the peony leaves.

Natalie made a fist and poked the plant in the space between her middle and index fingers. The pea-coloured spiral at the end bobbed forward like her uncle's dashboard Jesus.

"Why do you collect fiddleheads," the boy asked, face shrouded in the bush. Then he pulled himself up and squatted in her direction, the knees of his jeans patched with mud.

"Dunno. I like how they look."

"How's that?"

"How's what?"

"How they look."

She stuffed another fiddlehead into her knuckle. Its infant leaves wrinkly and balled into a bent finger. "Like a baby's fist," she said. She added a third between her pinkie and ring fingers. "Or the end of an octopus arm." She pawed her fist toward him.

"What else?"

She examined the spirals, looped them through the air. "The goose head on Mary Poppins' umbrella."

The boy heaved himself onto the tabletop and plucked a coil from her fist, balancing it in the groove of his collarbone.

Then he knotted his other hand around an imagined bow and arced it against his fiddle's strings.

"You look like a grasshopper," she said. "What's your name?"

"Milton. What's yours?"

"Natalie." She laid her three remaining fiddleheads in a palm-sized fan over the table. "Now what's your secret?"

He beamed at her, laughed with his eyes like a wink. "Meet me tonight at seven?"

"Where?"

"Lane's meadow. By the beebalm."

"The what?"

"The red ones."

ONE

Natalie found the first beads beside the tree trunk. Chinese porcelain – stick letters shaped like tents and Shanghai suns, inked below glaze; she had been scouring the forest floor for fiddleheads. The two beads sat on a bed of wet clovers and pine needles, and she collected them in her palm. Then she saw another a few feet away, and another, so she stuffed the baby ferns into the back pocket of her cut-offs and followed the beads off-trail. The fifth was egg-shaped and painted with a blue lily and the sixth wore a fish tail. The seventh bead, a crane, perched beside a pinecone on the edge of the crag. She pocketed it and searched the rock for more, wiped her fingers through crevices, lifted loose stones – and then she saw the cradle. It had washed up below, on a reef that tongued from the side of the cliff. Woven cedar, a broad hood, empty; the tide rocked it to and fro against the barnacles. A nut-brown bundle bobbed in the surf beside the reef. Natalie sunk to her butt and shimmied down the crag, feet dangling, her fingers curled around lips of limestone until she could jump to the shore. She tiptoed the reef to the bundle and stretched her hand toward water, eyes squeezed shut. Her fingers grazed a stiff stream of hair, then the blanket, which felt like wet suede, buckskin maybe, and she tugged it, bent into the surf to gather the bundle in both arms. She opened her eyes because it felt too light. Tucked inside was a cedar doll – lips painted with salmon eggs, a horsetail braid, and abalone eyes that shifted like oil puddles. She hugged the doll to her chest, felt her heart pound into wood and pretended it was the other way around. Her canvas shoes were grey with seawater, and she felt something under her heel – an eighth bead. She spotted the spinning top after the next wave. A stringy bark cone pierced with a stick, which swirled in a puddle of yellow foam and sea ribbons. She rescued it and stepped into the water. Her eyes combed the waves, her fingers plucked through seaweed, the cold gnawed her ankles. Between crushed clamshells and pebbles she found another bead, and something shaped like a thumb-sized boomerang, carved from bone and etched with black dots. She clenched them both in her fist and gazed at shore, at the trees that feathered from cliff – and that's when she saw the canoe. It jutted from a pine bough, and might have passed as a dead branch if it weren't tilted to show it was a dugout. Natalie waded to shore and up the rocks until she stood directly under the tree, but the canoe wasn't angled right for her to see its contents. Suspended in pine, the wood silvered, it looked like a vessel errant from Nod, swan-nosed and lined with eiderdown, ferrying heavy-lidded children between dreams.

ANDREW HOOD

I'M SORRY AND THANK YOU

He came out onto his porch and there was some hippy mother changing her baby on his lawn. On a Hudson's Bay blanket, the mother was wiping and dabbing at the muddy rolls and creases of her little girl. A gust of wind whipped up leaves around the two, and it was like last night on TV. Some pear-shaped Spanish grandma had been crammed into this glass booth with money being blown all around her. The grandma grabbed at the bills, stuffed her clothes with money, and wore a twisted look of desperation on her face. She looked so stupid. He couldn't tell if the point was to degrade the grandma, but he could tell that this particular grandma didn't care. When the wind in the booth was turned off all the money dropped and lay in a pile at her feet. All that money just right there, but not for her. She had gotten some, but not enough. Never enough. The brittle and wet leaves stuck to the hippy mother's dreadlocks and onto the swamp of the little girl.

"I'll just be a sec," the hippy mom said when she saw him there on the porch. He took a sip from his mug and nodded, slid a hand into the pocket of his housecoat as a sign of being A-okay with things.

The hippy mother stood up with a bundle in her hand and walked to him. The baby writhed on the blanket as if it were trying to crawl along the air.

"Hi," the hippy mother said. She had one of those cute faces that would have been ugly if she had tried to pretty it up with make-up, he thought.

"Morning," he said.

The mother winced at the sun high above them and looked back at him, squinting still.

"Listen," she said, "I'm sorry to do this, but I've got nowhere to toss this." She held up the bundle. "I was wondering if you wouldn't mind taking it for me."

"That's shit in there?" he asked, gesturing at the bundle with his mug.

"Pretty much."

"I don't know why," he said, "but I always think that babies have those things that birds have. Now, what are those things called?"

The hippy mother didn't know.

"You know. It's that thing that birds have where they do a combination of pooing and peeing so you can't tell what the hell it is that's coming out. It's called something, what they have. It's like 'The Cloister,' only it's not. It's right there." He shut his eyes tight and gritted his teeth, trying to force the word to the surface.

"Fuck," he said, popping open his eyes. "It's frustrating,

huh? When you can't think of a word you know. It's like having one of those sneezes where you can't sneeze. Do you ever get those?"

The hippy mother did get those. She was smiling still, but it was a smile that didn't mean anything, like when a car in front of him would leave a turn signal on.

"Do you mind if I just leave this here?" she asked, and anyway bent down and set the soiled bundle on the bottom step of his porch.

"Just so long as you don't set it on fire," he said, and laughed.

"Right. I promise not to," she said. "But thank you. And, again, I'm sorry. She already . . . And I was just going to . . . Anyway, I'm sorry and thank you."

She turned and walked back across the lawn, picking leaves out of her hair.

"Don't forget your baby," he called from the porch. He took another sip from his mug and made a surprised, sour baby face, expecting it to actually be coffee, forgetting about the Canadian Club. The only club he'd ever belonged to, his wife used to say. She had thought she was just a riot, that woman. Now, there was someone he'd like to cram into a booth. But not a booth with money. Maybe a booth full of razor blades or something. How easily could those become airborne?

"Got her, thanks," the mother said, gathering up her squirming girl.

He watched her put the kid into one of those hippy slings that he was starting to see regular people use now, too, and he watched her go, watched her bum as she went.

"Cloaca," he said.

"Cloaca!" he yelled. "It was the cloaca!" he yelled at her. Down the sidewalk, the hippy mother turned to look at him, then turned away and moved off a bit more swiftly.

"Cloaca," he said, feeling good, feeling like he had sneezed that sneeze out, or like he had suffered water in his ear all day from a swim or something and finally it was trickling out now, all hot and amazing.

"Cloaca," he said.

He had come out for the paper when he saw the shitty baby on his lawn. Now he squatted and sorted through the rolls that had built up by his door and found the one with the most recent date. All these people had died somewhere because of something, he read.

He picked out the business section, shook it out as he stepped down the steps of his porch, fluffed the paper, and then spread it next to the bundle the hippy mother had left him. With his bare toe, he nudged the wad of cloth onto the paper and wrapped it up.

He breathed in. There was the sweet and pungent smell, the complicated scent of baby shit. Any smell you miss, even if it's a bad one, is a good one.

Wadding the newspaper and the cloth full of shit into a ball the size of a softball, he walked to the end of the driveway, and then he threw it. The wad landed with a light heaviness onto his neighbour across the street's roof.

Opening his nostrils and opening his lungs, he hoped for that autumn smell, but still it was baby stench. He smelt his hands, but it was not his hands. It was all over the air now, that baby smell.

Another whirl of wind came and tossed the salad of dead

leaves on his lawn. The leaves flirted around him, and he began to grab at them. He snatched all he could out of the air, stuffing them into the pockets of his bathrobe, and then into his robe so they scratched his bare chest.

The wind died and he stood there with the heap at his feet, his pockets full and his chest bulky. A leaf had landed in his mug. He could drink around that.

"Cloaca," he said, feeling pretty okay about himself.

NANCY JO CULLEN

ASHES

n 1976, when I was twelve years old, and my father was still desperate to please my mom, we moved into a new house on Wallace Road. Our part of town was called The Mission, named by Father Pandosy, an Oblate priest who established the first white settlement in the Okanagan Valley in 1859. Wallace Road was lined with identical three-bedroom, bi-level homes. Each house had a dining room which led to an elevated sundeck that served dual purpose as a carport, under which my father parked his 1972 Chevy Nomad station wagon. Our car was beige and embarrassing.

We didn't live on the kind of street where people are fond of their neighbours and share summer cookouts and winter hockey tournaments. For instance, we didn't talk to the German family who ate the rabbits they kept in the backyard, and we barely smiled at – although we weren't openly hostile toward – the RCMP constable who lived next door.

"What a racket," my mother said at breakfast shortly after

we moved in. "I heard them going half the night. I'm telling you, Eddie, he hit her. More than once."

"Do you want me to go talk to him?" Dad asked.

"For God's sake, no!" Mom pressed her forehead into her fingers. "The man has a gun!"

Dad gave Mom a long-suffering look. "Elaine, I don't know why you told me this story."

"Because, Ed, I have a goddamn headache. And you could sleep through the second coming of Christ."

After we had been in the house for three years, my older brother escaped my parents' distaste for one another by finding work on an oilrig near Slave Lake. Six months later, he returned as the protégé of a fanatical Pentecostal minister who had chosen him a sixteen-year-old bride. He was eighteen years old. David didn't even meet his bride until two weeks before the nuptials, to which none of us were invited. One year later, in the spring of 1980, David and his pregnant wife, Charity, moved to a Christian commune near Lumby.

"I give up on the men in this family," my mother said. She lit a smoke and poured a shot of Kaluha into her coffee. "What on earth is he thinking?"

I shrugged. My brother had never been strong on thinking. David failed grade two, and shortly after our move to Wallace Road he was tagging along with Clinton Pelletier, a deranged product of the foster-care system who was a year older than David and brimming with venom.

Clint liked to grab me and stick his tongue in my mouth or push me down on to the floor and grind his crotch into mine, saying, "How do you like that, baby? You want some more?"

David would turn into a mute idiot and just stand there watching. The guy had no will. I knew that, but my mother had her own way of seeing things.

My mother was frantically trying to come up with some alternative names for Grandma, like we'd actually venture out to the sticks to see David and Charity, who wouldn't eat at the same table with us because they believed we were going to hell. "How about Ellie?" she asked during the six o'clock news. We were watching the channel from Spokane, waiting to hear, along with the rest of the Pacific Northwest, what was going on with Mount St. Helen's.

"Crazy old bastard," my father said. Ever since the governor of Washington declared a state of emergency, my dad obsessed over the growing activity around the volcano. And he was fixated on Harry Truman, the old man who refused to leave the mountain.

"Ed! Are you even listening to me?"

"What's that?" he asked.

Mom shook her head. "I might just as well be talking to a wall."

"Make your folks a couple of bourbon-and-cokes, would you, Jeannie?" My dad had recently purchased a twenty-sixer of bourbon in honour of old Mr. Truman, who wasn't just famous for refusing to leave the volcano, but also for his love of bourbon and cats.

"Not for me." My mother's lips were a thin line. "Lisa and I are going to ceramics." There was one neighbour we liked, a nurse named Lisa. On Monday nights, she and Mom went to a basement on Raymer Road and painted mother-of-pearl

Madonnas and speckled frogs with open mouths to hold pot scrubbers. On Mondays, Lisa's son slept at his dad's apartment, so after their ceramics class Mom and Lisa would sit in Lisa's living room, smoking cigarettes and drinking five-dollar bottles of wine. On Tuesday mornings, my dad and I tiptoed around the kitchen and made our way quickly out of the house.

"Well, then," Dad winked at Mom, "make mine a double." He was a well-liked guy, my dad. He made a point of sounding happy, which is probably what made him a successful salesman. For the past two years, he'd been selling time on the local radio station, and he'd found his niche among flamboyant radio personalities, with their laissez-faire approach to boozing and extra-marital sex. Not that my dad was a philanderer, but it was easy enough for him to ignore the sexual revolution with all the good drinking that could be done among those fellows.

My mother snorted and left the room. Dad, who was prone on the couch, turned back toward the television. "Now that's what I call love." He raised himself up on his elbows. "He says he'd die if he weren't on that mountain. His wife is buried there. Now who wouldn't want to feel like that about someone?"

Sometimes my dad went on about the weirdest things. "Do you really want a double?" I asked.

"May as well. Your mother's not home anyway."

When I brought him the drink, he said, "How about we go for a lesson after the news?" A few weeks earlier, on April 16, I qualified for my learners and my dad was teaching me how to drive.

Dad relaxed into the passenger seat and popped the cap off his beer bottle with a Bic lighter. "Do up your seatbelt," he said, although he made no move to fasten his own. I drove carefully out toward the east side of town through the winding hills populated by apple orchards and vineyards. "'Atta girl." My dad had a habit of offering commentary when none was necessary.

The sun was close to setting; tall spruce trees cast long shadows across the windshield. The world was lit in a pink glow, making the trees, grass, and gravel shoulders seem antique. "It wouldn't be a bad idea to turn on the headlights," he said, "just so they know you're coming, not going. I don't think your mother would appreciate a car accident on her ceramics night."

It didn't seem like a statement that required a response, and I was focused on the Bronco heading toward us on the narrow road. "What d'ya say, Jean? Is ceramics class worth all the planning?"

"I don't know."

I had been to one ceramics class with my mom and Lisa, but it was embarrassing. The ladies sat around painting planters and talking about how their kids each seemed to have a marvel-lous talent. Finally, my mother piped up, sounding so chipper you would have thought she was doing a laundry detergent commercial, "Well, I'm perfectly happy with my thoroughly average daughter. Aren't I, Jeannie?"

"I guess so," I had said. Mom couldn't believe it when I said I didn't want to go back the next week.

"Well, your mother remains a mystery to me. Hang a right here." He tapped on his window. "Of course, mystery is what keeps a marriage fresh." He stifled a small burp. "Let's get in some parking practise before we lose the light."

We were on a street of front driveways that safely stored cars for the night; only one turquoise sedan remained on the road in front of a faded yellow-and-white, ranch-style house. "Just pull up beside it and park."

When I stopped the car, he took the last swig of his beer and stepped out of the car. "Hang on." He took several giant steps away from the car and then set his beer bottle down on the shoulder. He placed a big rock beside the bottle and ran back to the car. For a second I saw what kind of kid my dad had been.

When he climbed back into the car he was old again. He grabbed another beer from under the seat and popped the cap. "Now, I'm going to get you to do like you're parallel parking, only instead of another car, it's a beer bottle."

"It's kind of hard to see in this light."

"Welcome to my world, sweetheart." He swallowed the beer in large gulps. "What you really want to do is to get a feel for backing into a spot. And you have to move slowly. Don't let other cars get you all excited. Parallel parking is an art. It demands assurance and attention, like most things worth doing.

"Now, when you pull up beside the car you're parking behind, you want to give it a little space. If you get too close, there's bound to be a collision; if you're too far away, you're just going to lose the whole damn thing. You know what I mean?"

I nodded.

"So you line up your steering wheel with the car beside you – just pull up a little. And you want to be about three feet away."

I aligned the car.

"Good. Now back up. Slowly. And crank it."

I started to turn the wheel.

"But not too soon. Wait until you can see her bumper through the passenger window. And then you want to get about a forty-five-degree angle to work your way in. She's all about how you approach her. Nice and easy does it."

I worked my way into the imaginary space cut off by the empty bottle of Pilsner. I straightened the wheels and backed into the curb, which was also imaginary – the properties on the east side were separated from the road by gravel and shallow ditches. I heard glass crackling under tires and stopped the car. Dad scratched his ear. "Well, that can't be good."

He stepped out to assess the damage. "Pull forward," he called. I inched the car ahead. Through the rearview mirror I saw him bend over and then stand up again and kick at the gravel, sending the pieces of brown glass into the ditch. Then he turned the bottle he was drinking from upside down, letting the last few sips dribble onto the road. He dropped the empty bottle into the ditch, opened the door, and slid back into his seat. "It doesn't look like there's any damage to the tire, but let's get a move on; I don't suppose the folks around here are going to appreciate us littering on their turf."

I drove back down toward the centre of town while Dad nursed his third beer. He didn't like to bring mixed drinks into the car; they spilled too easily. I cranked up the radio but he didn't complain. I guess he had nothing to say. The sun had set and the sky was darkening; I saw my father's face reflected in the glass. I was trying to picture him as a teenager, combing Brylcreem through his hair and chasing after my mom. It was kind of creepy, actually, to think of my parents as young teeny-boppers, before she was cranky and he was a salesman.

"He's got twelve cats," Dad said.

"What?"

"Old Harry Truman. He's got twelve cats. How do you get twelve cats off a mountain like that?"

"You could probably use cages."

"Well, sure. But cats are funny. They don't like change."

"It's better than dying."

"No one knows for sure what's going to happen on that mountain. Harry's guess is as good as anybody's. Turn left at Lakeshore." He emptied the beer bottle and let it drop to the floor. "He's quite the guy."

"Do you remember our old cat?" he asked.

"Funny you should ask," I said.

"How so?"

"I just did a sketch of her in art class." I didn't really remember much about her, except her name and that she was black with a white belly. I drew Sugar as I imagined she'd be now, old and sleeping on the end of my bed. A cat's a nice thing to have around; they're quiet and warm and never pretend to be anything but what they are.

"Well, I'll be damned," he said.

I drove us home, past the elementary school, past the grazing cows, hung a right, and pulled into the carport. The German's squeaky white dog threw himself against their front window, yapping away. "Somebody should put that dog out of its misery," Dad muttered as we made our way to the front door.

"I'm going to bed," I told him.

"Isn't it early?"

"I'm tired. And I have to finish reading *Macbeth* for tomorrow."

"Now Macbeth is a guy who could've learned a thing or two about loyalty." We both made our way into the kitchen, Dad to make another bourbon and coke, me to grab a stack of crackers and a glass of milk to take to my room. "Well, I'll be on the deck," he said. I watched him walk onto the deck in his shirtsleeves with a cigarette burning in one hand and a drink in the other. He pushed a lawn chair against the outside wall of the house and sat down. He didn't turn on a light; he just sat in the dark, knocking the ice around in his glass. When I grabbed a glass of water a few hours later, he was still on the deck in the dark with a drink in his hand, watching Lisa's house.

The next morning, Dad barely spoke a word as we made our way out of the house. I chalked it up to a hangover, but in the evening he continued to be silent; he ate dinner, he watched the news for the reports about Mount St. Helens, he drank another bourbon and coke, or three, but the only time he spoke was to thank my mother for the tuna casserole. Mom, on the other hand, chatted endlessly about nothing. His silence perked her right up. At dinner she asked me about my day at school. She clucked her tongue over the news and said, "Can you imagine? An active volcano this far north?" She didn't wait for either of us to answer before she launched into a commentary about that crazy old man with a death wish and how it was going to end up costing good money to get him out, just you wait and see. Dad stood up and left the room, so she suggested we go to Orchard Park Mall to get new summer clothes on the weekend.

My father stayed quiet for the rest of the week. Mom responded with uncharacteristic chattiness – like they had switched bodies in some kind of supernatural mishap. I stuck to my room, which neither of them seemed to notice. And each night, after the evening news and the reports about the mountain, Dad would knock on my door with a box of beer under his arm and we would head out for a driving lesson. He would crack the first beer as we began and make his way through half the case during a lesson, carrying on conversation like there was nothing unusual going on except the geological surprise of Mount St. Helen's waking up.

When we returned home, Mom would be sitting on the front steps with Lisa, smoking and laughing. My dad would snort and head right to the basement, and my mom and Lisa would be all over me, commenting so loudly that I was forced to hurry inside.

They liked to exclaim, "Oooh, there's a sexy young driver!" Or, "There's no controlling her once she's driving, Eddie!" As if he ever tried to control me. I can't even begin to guess why they thought they were funny.

On Saturday, my dad and I made a long drive through the valley. Mount St. Helen's had stopped spewing steam and smoke and Dad was pretty dejected about the whole thing. "Well, it's good for Harry, but I was hoping for more of a show. How about we go to Vernon for lunch? I could stand a drink." He pulled a cigarette out of his pocket. "Maybe she decided to settle down."

"Who?"

"The volcano. Maybe she's calming down for the old man."

"Oh," I said. Not that he was making any sense.

"I love this time of year." He unrolled the window to release the smoke. "Before everything heats up."

"Whatever happened to Sugar?" I asked.

"Who?"

"Our cat."

"Your mother was allergic."

"She was?"

"Well, she had no time for cats. She said she had her hands full with you and your brother."

"I thought Sugar ran away. Or died."

"Probably." He took a long drag on his cigarette and then let the smoke out in a sigh. "I loved that little bugger."

"What happened to her?"

"Oh, I don't know, honey." He shifted in his seat, uncomfortable I guess. "Your mother took her for a drive."

"What do you mean?"

"Well, you know, desperate times take desperate measures."

"We were desperate?"

"Your mother was."

"Jesus, Dad."

"No one's happy if Mommy's not happy."

"Well, that explains a lot."

He looked at me, surprised, and then began to sing, "I'll be with you in apple blossom time. I'll be with you to change your name to mine. One day in May I'll come to say happy surprise that the sun shines on today."

So Mom got rid of our cat. I wanted to ask how, but Dad was tripping out to old music and generally weirder than usual, and the drive to Vernon is scary and twisty, so I turned my attention to the road and left him to his song and the blooming fruit trees.

When we got home, Mom was gone. She'd left a package of wieners and a can of beans on the counter. "Jesus. Bloody wieners and beans?"

"It's okay," I said. "I'm going out to meet up with Tina and Shelley anyway." We had plans to drop in on a party of grade twelvers that Tina's brother had told her about.

"I want you in by 11:30." He seemed mad.

"Okay."

"I'm going out for a drink."

When I left at seven, neither of my parents was home. I poured a third of my dad's bourbon and a third of his vodka into a jar, topped it off with coke, and headed out to meet the girls. When I got home at 12:15, the house was still empty. Not that I cared; I was drunk enough to want to get right into bed. This gorgeous guy named Paolo had flirted with me all night. I know he wanted me because he gave me one of his Colt cigars. I'd never heard of a guy named Paolo before; he was from the west side but came with his cousin Rick, who went to my school and who was nothing to shake a stick at, either. Anyway, my parents didn't know I broke curfew and I fell asleep with a smile on my face.

I woke a few hours later to my mother yelling, "Don't be a fucking idiot, Ed!" I rolled onto my back and tried to see my ceiling through the dark. I could hear my dad crying.

I wished I'd gotten drunker at the party.

There was some more muffled talking and crying and then I heard my mom again, "There's nothing you can do. I love her."

I hated it when they fought over me.

"And I was happy for you," my dad's voice rose sharply, "because you finally found a friend."

It took a few minutes for that to sink in. My mom was in love with Lisa? And then my dad was crying like a baby again.

"Are you ready?" Lisa must have come in through the back.

"Go to hell!" he cried. "The both of you." Then I heard the back door close and my dad pacing the kitchen, clapping his hands, I think. I wasn't going to touch that with a ten-foot pole, so I turned my face toward the wall and willed sleep to come through my dad's blubbering and the totally embarrassing idea of my mom making out with Lisa. Knowing my mom, she was going to make a spectacle of it, turn it into some kind of show for the cop and the Germans, and the next thing you know, it would be all over the school.

I guess I fell asleep around the time the sun was coming up, because when I opened my eyes it was 12:30 in the afternoon. My dad way lying on the couch, watching the television. "Old Harry's dead," he told me.

"What?"

"The mountain blew to smithereens. There's no way he made it out. Not him, not the cats."

"Oh."

"And your mother moved out."

"I heard."

"Well, I guess that saves me trying to explain it."

"I guess so."

"Not that I understand it." He squeezed his nose between his thumb and forefinger. "Not that I understand it at all."

"Can you drive me to Tina's?"

I probably should have stayed home with my dad, but I felt sick to my stomach from the liquor, or the cigar, or my mom, and if I stayed in that house I think I would have screamed my head off. That night I figured it would be best if I slept at Tina's, I don't know, in case they wanted to fight it out a little more. It was too weird to sleep at our place.

Monday morning I woke to a thin dusting of ash over cars and a hazy sky. Our biology teacher, Miss Franklin, was breathless with excitement over the size of the blast as we mapped the progress of destruction. How everyone could see the explosion coming but how no one really guessed it would be so huge.

After school, I slowly made my way home, not sure what I'd find, but there was my dad, sitting in Mom's favourite chair with a grey tabby kitten in his lap. "I've named her Truman," he said as he passed the kitten to me.

"She's cute."

"Well," he stood up, "I need a drink. There's some sweet and sour chicken balls in the oven, if you're hungry."

"Thanks." I stuck my face into the cat's baby sweetness.

"I'm sorry." He put his hand on the top of my head.

I kept my face buried in Truman's back like I didn't hear him.

ALEX PUGSLEY

CRISIS ON EARTH-X

I was four years old when Uncle Lorne came to live with us. He was my mother's younger brother by twenty-two winters, a mistake of uncertain paternity according to my sisters, and he joined our household when his own was in freefall. "Nanny and Dompa are drunk all the time is why," explained my sister Bonnie. "That's why he's like that." Nanny and Dompa, living in Montreal, were moving into some marital hurly-burly during this time, so it was decided, mostly by my father, that twelve-year-old Uncle Lorne would benefit from the relatively steadier environment of our house in Halifax. I was eager to have such company for in my house I was surrounded by women – my significant mother as well as two sisters above and two below. Uncle Lorne was a singular, decidedly non-feminine addition to our house. He arrived with hobbies fully formed, with habits and rules and secret disciplines. He made models of Iroquois helicopters, completed abstract jigsaw puzzles, and, in an amazing display of home-made engineering, constructed a lunar docking station for our

Major Matt Mason action figures from the parts of a rotary phone, a discarded bicycle tube, and a Fram oil filter. He showed me how to draw propellers and Gatling guns and Batman's cowl – an image I am still known to improvise on unopened letters from Revenue Canada. Uncle Lorne owned more than a thousand comic books, which he kept in boxes under his bed. Each purchase was thoughtfully registered by title and number and condition on blue graph paper inside a mauve Duo-Tang folder. Though he followed many comics, he was closing in on complete runs of *The Justice League of America* and *The Brave and the Bold*, back issues of which he acquired from a mail-order concern in Passaic, New Jersey. This endeavour, among others, was funded by delivering *The Mail-Star*, the city's afternoon broadsheet. Uncle Lorne had a route of 163 newspapers, an ambitious amalgam of three existing smaller routes, and on Wednesdays, when the paper swelled with advertising flyers from Sobeys and the IGA ("Try new Beef Noodle Hamburger Helper!" "Two-for-one 1-2-3 Jell-O!") I was pressed into service as sidekick and all-purpose lackey. The dropped-off newspapers came in bales held together by blue twine. In winter they were fearsome cuboid chunks of frozen newsprint. But the day I'm remembering was not winter. The day I'm remembering was one day away from true summer, a Wednesday in late June, one of the longest of the year. I was now ten, Uncle Lorne was eighteen, and the city was strangely warm, daylight endless, dragonflies soft-lifted on an incoming ocean wind. We were far afield. From the Wellington Street drop-off we had ranged to The Nova Scotian Hotel, back through the Dalhousie University campus, and were now tramping westerly on Jubilee Road. We were covering another boy's paper route – Chris Cody, one of Uncle Lorne's intimates – and this added fifty-two papers to our travels. But even four hours into our overland explorations, I didn't mind. This afternoon alone I had been shown a live seal in the Life Sciences aquatic tank at the university. I had been taught a new climbing technique called "chimneying." And here at the bottom of Jubilee Road I saw that the street literally sank beneath the sea, the Northwest Arm flooding up the slope of a concrete boat ramp, the setting sun a thousand times refracted in its waves. Though I could hear my uncle calling for me above, I took a moment to imagine Aquaman under water beyond this boat ramp, spinning away from the shallows to some murky substratum of the North Atlantic, perhaps rising buoyant through sun-filtered depths, bursting to the surface to rendezvous with the Batboat, the two superheroes racing toward a far horizon. A few weeks before I had read a *Justice League* two-parter about a zombie called Solomon Grundy, a story that featured in a heroic role the grown-up Robin of Earth-Two, and in my mind I decided to place this fully formed Robin in the Batboat. I admired his blended costume, his motorcycle, and how he had assumed the mantle of crime-fighting when the Batman of his world had begun to dodder – because, to be honest, recently I'd been wondering if events might force me in a similar direction. Solomon Grundy had required a team-up between the Justice League of Earth-One and the Justice Society of Earth-Two, and the series had become my favourite team-up story ever. I keenly anticipated the next interworld issues, numbers 107 and 108, copies of which had been ordered from New Jersey for both Uncle Lorne and me. My copies would be considered paid in full if I did eight more Wednesdays on the paper route.

Uncle Lorne called for me again and this time I straggled up Jubilee Road where he was smoking a cigarette. He allowed himself one cigarette after the papers had been delivered. He put out the cigarette on an old and furrowed telephone pole, leaving the filter inside a vertical crevice, and exhaled, his chin bobbing in time to some percussion heard in his head. Uncle Lorne had many internal rhythms whose patterns would remain somewhat mysterious to me, just as he seemed someone whose personality might remain fundamentally unknowable. "Kink-man," he said, using a family nickname. "Ready to race?"

A note of personal history: seventeen months before I had been cut out of hip-to-toe casts, discharged from the Children's Hospital, and told that I could walk again. So I had spent a few years of my childhood either in a wheelchair or on crutches and was only now, at the age of ten, recovering full motion and strength in my left hip, a joint distorted by something called Legg-Perthes disease. Naturally this conflicted with my desires to be the World's Best Athlete because my limp and shortened left leg gave to my walk a crooked, hop-along quality – an extraneous feature, I liked to imagine, that disappeared in the madness of an open sprint. Although I found it tiring to sustain longer efforts, Uncle Lorne had devised a system whereby the distance we ran was increased each Wednesday by twenty sidewalk squares. We had started close – South Street and Tower Road in February – and were now advanced almost to Robie and Jubilee. I was given a head start of sixty resting heartbeats – Uncle Lorne holding two fingers to his throat to count the pulses – then he would spring after me.

Taking off my shirt and tying the sleeves around my waist, as I had seen some older boys do on the Dalhousie campus, I said I was ready. Uncle Lorne inspected the winter pallor of my stomach. "Whew," he said. "*Fish belly!* Fish belly on the old grub." He spoke as if this were a joke already established between us. "Fish Belly Grub. Grub-a-dub-dub. Race with the Grub." It was one of his recreations to explore the associations of words – which he sometimes pronounced in confusing and menacing variations. But I took his meaning as only teasing, tightened my laces, and crashed off, propelling myself down the sidewalk beside the Camp Hill cemetery. I took the corner on South Street at top speed, losing my balance and dispersing my wild centripetal motion by straying into the street itself. As I sped past the Children's Hospital, I heard a commotion somewhere behind me – a rush of sound that was my uncle closing the gap between us. Slinging myself around a stop sign for extra momentum, I met Tower Road with out-of-control, berserker ferocity. I knew, like the grown-up Robin of Earth-Two, that there were do-or-die moments when you simply had to prove yourself. Seeing our house, and sensing a win for the first time, I flashed a giddy look behind me – only to allow Uncle Lorne, on the other side, to dash up the steps of the front porch and, as he always did, touch the door latch, signalling the end of our contest and his victory. I protested if only I *hadn't* looked over my shoulder, losing precious split-seconds, this time I could have won, would've won, *should've* won. Uncle Lorne bobbed his head again, noncommittal, and mentioned that he thought I had run my best race so far. He pushed opened our front door and paused in the evening air. I was just noticing a viral spread of pimples on his chin when he said quietly, "Run your own race, Grub. Run your own race." With that semicryptic koan, he vanished inside to his basement bunker, and I wandered happily into the kitchen. This was a time before microwaves, when the warm-up of a dinner was achieved through the sorcery of a double boiler – which meant leaving a plate of dinner (in this case, a pork chop, mashed potatoes, and carrots sliced with a serrated cutter) on a pot of simmering water. There were two plates tonight, and I saw it as a sign of my rapidly advancing maturity that I had been so singled out. As I touched the dinner plate with the tip of a quilted oven mitt, a song began on the kitchen clock radio that Mom used to check her approaching rehearsal times. I didn't really know what radio songs were, or that playlists turned over, that the song you heard one summer might be gone the next. But "Band on the Run" was around that year, in the way a new neighbourhood kid might be, or in the way you might notice a surplus of ladybugs on a bathroom window one afternoon. I had heard the song before but it perplexed me because the opening was filled with so many different progressions, each sounding like a different song, that I often confused it with other offerings on the radio. But as I identified it for the first time, my continued contact with the warmed plate touched off a number of attendant details in and out of the kitchen. The windows were beginning to lose their evening light. The floaty purple fragrance of lilac blossoms was unmistakable in the backyard. The kitchen cupboards, painted turquoise, showed signs of blue where the turquoise paint had been chipped – and so my response to the song seemed turquoise-blue with an after-sense of lilac, and when a crescendo of horns faded to allow for the strumming of an acoustic guitar, alternating between the chords of C and F-major 7, the song seemed finally to become itself. In a moment of autistic dreaminess, I stood unmoving at the stove, fixed between these two chords, and it was only when the singer sang about rain exploding with a mighty crash was I released from my abstraction – and a multitude of synesthesial meaning exploded for me, moments at once emotional, sensory, and intuitive, and as they shimmered and gathered and burst again I realized it was the happiest I've been without knowing particularly why I was happy, and this song seemed to be a part of it, and not just accompanying it, but activating it, coordinating the mood and circumstance and manifold instant. "Band on the Run" on June 20 was a strangely overwhelming solace for me and it has been ever after linked with the events of that summer, and the possibilities of that year, and though many of the proceedings turned out horribly, I am still grateful to the song for what it engendered in my imagination – for it conveyed a sense of precarious possibilities gorgeously arranged and met and fulfilled.

Uncle Lorne's door was closed when I went into the basement – an obsolete coal room had been done over as his bedroom – so I continued into the rec room, a recently drywalled creation beside the furnace room and home to rainbow-coloured wall-to-wall carpet, a folded-up Ping-Pong table, Nanny and Dompa's deteriorating wicker cottage furniture, and a Sony Trinitron television on a rickety stand. I turned on the TV and stood spinning the channel selector, alert to the probable appearance of *The Six Million Dollar Man*. As I noticed a familiar and quite above-average episode of *Bewitched* – the story where Cousin Serena forces a song on Tommy Boyce and

Bobby Hart – I became aware of some indications I was not the first to set foot in the room. On the carpet, beside a wicker armchair, was an unopened can of Fresca, a bag of Lik-m-aid Fun Dip, and an SX-70 Polaroid camera, a recent Christmas present to my oldest sister, Carolyn. Not that it would be Carolyn who would leave such a gift unattended in the basement – it was, of course, Bonnie, my older, contiguous sister and long-standing nemesis within the family. With the arrival in the house of this gizmo, Bonnie had taken to photographing assorted personalities off the television screen at extremely inopportune moments. Where these photographs were idiotically hoarded I wasn't sure – but lately a number of blurry, underexposed Polaroids of Björn Borg, The Partridge Family, and Tony DeFranco had been found behind the radiator in the upstairs bathroom. I have successfully kept my sisters' specifics out of these narratives but a few words might be appropriate here. Bonnie, two years' my senior, was principally in a lifelong, unwinnable competition with Carolyn, the first-born, who was and has been the perfect child – perfect manners, perfect marks, perfect hair – and thoughtful, serious, responsible, overachieving. Bonnie, when she was alive, was domineering, tactical, and ultraimpulsive – a girl never slowed by an unexpressed thought. She stood now in the doorway of the basement rec room, holding a CorningWare bowl full of homemade popcorn, her head tilted to one side, looking at me with the smile that Tolerance gives to the Misguided. "Uh, what do you think you're doing?"

"Watching *The Six Million Dollar Man*."

"Uh, no, you're not. Because did you say 'reserve?' Were you sitting down and did you say 'reserve?'" Bonnie quickly touched her tailbone to the wall, repeated this code word, and straightened up again. "Because if you weren't and you didn't then we're watching what we want to watch. Plus I was here first and you're out-voted, so tough titty."

My two younger sisters now materialized in the area behind Bonnie. They were clad in worn and matching flannelette nighties and each held in her hands a cereal bowl of popcorn – the effect was rather like two novice members of the junior choir advancing with opened hymnaries.

"What're you guys watching?" I asked, stalling, not prepared to walk away from the television.

Bonnie explained they had been planning all week to watch a movie called *The Parent Trap*. I had not heard of this plan. I was offended by this plan. And I refused to believe I'd been consulted about this plan. What was this movie even about?

Uncle Lorne came out of his room to investigate the crowd in the newly boisterous rec room. "What is *what* movie about?" he asked.

"*The Parent Trap*."

Uncle Lorne looked to the ceiling, as if to properly assemble his thoughts. "It's about these kids." He glanced at Bonnie for verification. "Twin sisters, right? And one night they're waiting for their parents to come home and then – Grub, do you know what gelignite bullets are?"

I said I didn't.

"Plastic explosives used primarily in automatic weapons where –"

"That's *not* the movie, Uncle Lorne," said Bonnie with maximum indifference. She was now pointing at her stash of junk food, ready to launch into a further defense of her viewing rights, when from upstairs we heard Mom and Dad come in the front door, their shoe-steps resounding over our heads. All of us, through acquired habit, wordlessly decoded the noises above for signals of disposition, humour, inclination.

"Mom's drunk, you guys," concluded Katie, my youngest sister, with casual nonchalance, nibbling a single piece of popcorn. "Bet you any money."

Our mother, as it would turn out, was not yet drunk. She and our father had been at a party celebrating the opening night of a play, *A Midsummer Night's Dream*, the gathering held across the street in the rented rooms of some new friends, Mr. and Mrs. Abbot – although my sister Bonnie maintained these two were not formally married. When first informed on this point, I wondered if Mr. and Mrs. Abbot were perhaps a gypsy duo who assumed diverse identities and travelled the country-side, defrauding townspeople out of their children. But the Abbots, it turned out, were not gypsies or con-men. They were something else altogether as exotic: they were draft-dodgers, expatriate Americans from Wheeling, West Virginia, who had driven to Nova Scotia on a Honda 450 motorcycle in the summer of 1968. They lived first in an unheated commune in the Annapolis Valley, on the other side of West Paradise, but came to Halifax two years later when their two daughters reached school age. These two daughters, September Dawn and Jessamine, were fourteen months apart in age and inexplicably identical to me. Both wore tie-dyed shirts and homemade pants with no pockets. Both had blonde hair down to their waists. Their hair was sometimes held back in pinched thickets by glass-baubled elastics, but September Dawn, and especially Jessamine, did not care for these elastics and often the

girls ran around with hair loose and unfastened – so encountering them in a neighbourhood game of hide-and-go-seek was
like coming face-to-face with a feral child who had been lost
some months in the black mountain hills of Dakota. The
Abbot household had a somewhat lax philosophy toward personal upkeep, and one or the other girl was always scratching
a sty out of an eyelash or separating a scab from a kneecap.
Since arriving in Halifax, Mr. Abbot had secured a situation
as the stage carpenter for Neptune Theatre. Mrs. Abbot had
some undefined connection with a new organization called
the Ecology Action Centre. She was also a folk artist of some
commitment. She worked mostly in macramé, collage, and
silkscreen. Because my father had done some pro bono legal
work for the Abbots regarding their immigration, our family
had been the recipient of two silk-screened prints – and, as we
kids trooped up the stairs from the basement, I saw my father
was now in possession of a third, a sort of lacquered beige silhouette of three ponies in a salt marsh.

"Jesus, Mackie," he said to my mother, shaking his head.
"Where are we going to *put* this goddamn thing?"

My mother, who this evening was wearing a lime-and-
purple-print dress – what my sister Carolyn called the Jo Anne
Worley dress – pulled open the refrigerator and reached for a
bottle of Blue Nun wine before saying, "Your father made us
leave the party early. Like anything's new."

My father put the silk-screen print down on the kitchen
table and made a slight tip of his head, his eyebrows contracting in bemused concentration. It was a familiar gesture which
meant he was wondering whether or not he should imply his
real reaction – which was, in this case, that he considered the

party overrun with dubious people and dubious practices – or simply forgo any response at all.

"Because," continued my mother. "This one couple was passing around a marijuana cigarette. As soon as your father saw that, we were out of there."

"Well," said my father. "How's that going to look? It happens to be against the law."

"Loosen up. Their friends were very nice. When in Rome –"

"Okay, Titania. That's plenty, thank you. Time to get these kiddles to bed." He pointed at my youngest sister. "You? Bed. Now. And I mean it, Ditsy."

My mother grabbed a plastic juice glass from the dishwasher and poured herself four fingers of white wine. "They're anti-war, you know, these people. Flower children. They think anything's possible. The wife's a women's libber. Vivien. But very sweet. Him? I'm not so sure. Wes is the saintly type. Wants to do good. Like build a barn for mentally retarded kids in New Brunswick." She tossed back half the wine. "Sure, why not? But what are they going to do with a *barn* – shear sheep? Honest to God. Be careful of these so-called saints, children. Believe me, people who act like saints – a lot of so-called saints are trouble. They're living in a dream world. Telling people what they don't want to hear in the first place. And the more Wes is doing good for some retarded kid, the more he's neglecting his own family, you watch."

My parents' conversation continued over the next few hours, sometimes softly in almost inaudible murmurs, other times erupting into strident tones of outright drunken hostility. By this time I was lying in my bed, sleepless, restless with every wrongful twist of my bed sheets, staring at my ceiling.

The lights in the street created a familiar overglow in my room and I stared as tiny dots of winking dimness generated patterns on my paint-cracked ceiling, patterns I often collected into recognizable images – the man with the nose, the happy cow, the mud-splattered ogre – the last of which I was having trouble looking at more than once. As I heard my parents make their way up the front stairs, I closed my eyes and prayed to God they wouldn't get divorced again.

"Stewart, would you mind not being such a –"

"Mumsy? I don't want to hear another word of this."

"– prig. They're just trying to do good in the world. Their life isn't only about making money."

"Sure, sure, Mumsy. Relax. Relax, kid."

"I hate it when you get like this."

"Here we go. Here it is. It's all coming now. I'll take the rest of that wine, thank you very much."

"You want to lose your hand? Just tell me something. Why don't you try something new for once in your life – like in the last forty years? That's the problem between me and you. You don't care two shits about the environment. And I do."

"The environment? How in the *hell* are we talking about the environment?"

There were a few thudding and bumping noises – which I guessed to be my mother's foot slipping off a step and her subsequent stumble into the creaking banister. "Well," she said. "I hope *I* never ridicule what is wise and good. That's a quote. You can look it up."

"Yes, Mackie. Beautiful performance. Exit stage left with a bear."

"It's exit pursued by a bear. Get it right, for Christ's sake. For once in your crumb-bum life, would you get something *right*?"

This exchange was followed by the closing of their bedroom door, a brief lull, a night shriek, and the smashing of a bottle. My parents began as actors – they met in college in a play – so we kids were used to these kinds of theatrics. But tonight seemed a return to the drear uncertainty of five years ago and as I tried again to fall asleep I began to wonder if what I wanted for myself was really relevant at all.

Uncle Lorne was an archivist, a tinkerer, a published poet. The year he came to live with us, when he was twelve, he was seized upon by the middle school English teacher, Mr. Jones, who chose three of Uncle Lorne's poems for the literary section of *The Grammarian*, the school yearbook. Two were about Third Empire Rome ("Roma Aeterna") and a third, and for me most vivid, was titled "Wild Dogs." It moved with the pace of a Blake lyric and started with the line, "Perturbed eyes and carious teeth. . ." What was this word – *perturbed*? or *carious*? or *gelignite*? In what furnace burned these words? Where had he gleaned such lore and stuff? The poems were signed "Lorne Anthony Wheeler," one of the few times I saw my uncle's full name in print. When he was in Montreal, living in Notre-Dame-de-Grâce, Dompa had given him a rubber stamp with his full name and address on it (a very Dompa gift), and this blue, inky imprimatur appeared on the cover of many of my uncle's earliest collected comics – before he realized making such a mark might devalue the artifact. Uncle Lorne left Montreal just before Expo 67 and, though he seldom talked about it, I could feel, from how he once pinned to our cork-board postcards of the geodesic dome and the Habitat 67 housing complex (communiqués from Benoit Charbonneau and Thompson Oldring – precious friends I'd never meet), that Nova Scotia must have seemed for him a far and distant outpost of the empire, and Halifax, vis-à-vis Montreal, a city much reduced in circumstance. I decided it was to cosmopolitan Montreal that he owed his strange intelligence. My uncle and his abilities I regarded mostly with reverent awe, though I knew he was somewhat eccentric – as if his clockwork required further assembly. Because while Uncle Lorne was made up of a lot of quick parts, not all of them worked, and some were changing colours, and still others awaited their final function. His vocabularies, his silences, his keen intrigues and esoteric associations were all clues, as I sensed them, to the inverted kingdom of his imagination. "My brother's mind certainly works weird," my mother would say. "No, Lorne's brilliant, he is, but he's not always exactly *here*, you know. In the real world." I sometimes wondered if I would ever understand him. And I wanted to – I wanted the fellowship and solidarity and stability such an understanding would supply. My sisters had no idea how Uncle Lorne thought and had mostly stopped trying. "You know," said Carolyn when the gelignite comment reached her desk. "That's just Uncle Lorne humour." Bonnie agreed. She tended to speak about Uncle Lorne in a respectful but detectably marginalizing manner – and sneaking into her tone lately was the implication that Uncle Lorne was increasingly out-of-touch and peculiar – as if, for her, he was already beyond the point of no return. At the end of June she said to me, "You know the Abbots are atheists, right?"

"So?"

"So Faith asked Uncle Lorne what atheists were and you know what he said? That atheists were families that drown their own pets. Is that supposed to be funny? Like a Chris Cody joke?"

"Faith knows what atheists are."

"But what if Uncle Lorne tells Katie that? She's young and she'll believe him." There was no attempt at a tolerant smile here – Bonnie was offended by Uncle Lorne's deliberate sub-version of a religious matter and she would attribute this wayward attitude to the growing influence of the other paper boy, Chris Cody. Christopher Cody was a giggly, bushy-haired teenager who would arrive at our backdoor door ostensibly to watch *Kung Fu* with Uncle Lorne. Later, he might be found shambling around our furnace room in tinted aviator glasses, eating Munchos Chips, and listening on headphones to Grand Funk Railroad or Badfinger or Santana – albums whose psy-chedelic cover art used to frighten and confuse me as a small child. To my uncle, Chris was Commander Cody, a name always spoken in a hoarse, back-of-the-throat style, as if Uncle Lorne's voice were suddenly parched with fatigue or thirst. This voice was used in all manner of Chris Cody settings, often with purposefully sinister implication, and recently even in non–Chris Cody situations, when a bored Uncle Lorne might seek to surprise you by creeping into the TV room to whisper into your ear, "Boris the Spider!" which was the name by which this diversion came to be known – as Uncle Lorne's Boris the Spider trick.

I was wary of Commander Cody. On a winter Wednesday at the newspaper drop-off, he once chased me into a snow bank and put snow down my back. In May I was kicked out of the

TV room so he and Uncle Lorne could watch a Clint Eastwood movie. And lately, now that both had grown greebly moustaches, Chris Cody had taken to commandeering my uncle on missions into the musty Halifax nightlife, to places with names like The Hollis Street Tavern, The Ladies Beverage Room, The Green Dory, and some bar called Angie's. On Dominion Day Sunday, stepping out our back door to walk to St. Matthew's United Church, my younger sisters and I happened upon Chris Cody's recent vomit, some of which had fallen through the porch slats, but most of which was still intact, congealed in a kind of fractal dispersion pattern, swirls and streaks emanating from a wet epicentre not far from an unfortunately situated Malibu Skipper doll. Chris Cody was found in his clothes in our basement bathtub, Uncle Lorne in the wicker armchair, and our family's station wagon on a sidewalk on Barrington Street, the passenger's side of the vehicle wrapped around a utility pole. My father, not known for his severity, grounded Uncle Lorne for the rest of the summer and grimly recommended to him that he seek out a better class of companion than Christopher Cody, who had been driving the car.

"Commander Cody has crash-landed," my uncle said afterwards in his Boris the Spider voice. "He will be flying with his Lost Planet Airmen no more. He has been marooned on the Red Planet. Commander Cody, over and out."

My sister Bonnie was blunt in her relief. "Thank God – that guy was such a gook."

"A *gook*?" Uncle Lorne said. "Bitsy, do you even know what a *gook* is?"

Bonnie used the term as she and Carolyn always did – to

mean an awkward or unseemly person. "Chris Cody's a gook," said Bonnie, flatly.

"No, Bitsy," said my uncle, with some impatience. "A *gook*'s a Viet Cong. As in Victor Charlie. As in they *were* blown up with gelignite. Why don't you get that straight?"

That Wednesday there was no race home after the paper route. Uncle Lorne's mood precluded it. He chain-smoked all the way back to Tower Road, preoccupied and changed. In the last few years, I had noticed divagations. For most of my youth, Uncle Lorne was the lilting fall of the Byrds' high harmony line in "Mr. Tambourine Man." He was the kid staring with steady excitement at the movie poster for *Endless Summer*. He was that brief half-second when he bent his face forward before clearing his bangs from his eyes with a flick of the head. But now – now he was no longer the sort of candid, open-air kid you might approach on your first day in the Scout Troop or at the soccer skills camp. He was no longer a kid. In one moment he was my colleague and pal, ironing the creases out of a comic book, constructing a lunar-docking station, and the next he was bringing home a fluorescent black light to place above a felt poster, or watching Bruce Lee movie marathons in cut-off jeans, his dark bangs so swoopy and shaggy they barely allowed for a sight line. By June of that year Uncle Lorne had become a long-haired freaky person, a hippie in an untucked T-shirt, a fringed leather jacket, and bell-bottoms fraying beneath the soft heels of his red suede Adidas sneakers. He was reedy, stretched, finishing a growth spurt that would top him out over six feet, taller by far than Dompa or my father. He was still proudly himself, equal to any context, unsurprised by developments

great and small, but he was losing interest. Just as I was beginning to really read and appreciate and care for *The Justice
League of America*, Uncle Lorne couldn't care less. For a while
his curiosity was stayed by the Marvell Comics universe,
specifically the metaphysics and Kirby dots of *The Silver Surfer*,
a loner adrift in the cosmos, as well as the Kirby titles started
at DC, *The New Gods* and *Mister Miracle*, but his previous fas-
cination was no longer evident. It was an effort for him to
dream the superheroes when before they had dreamed him.
His thoughts entered their mythology only when my presence
reminded him. "This place, Grub," he said to me on that walk
home, dropping a last cigarette on the sidewalk and scuffing
it out with his suede sneaker. "This burg . . ." He sighed as if
unable to delay a judgment that had become screamingly
obvious. "It's like living in the Bottle City of Kandor. It's so cut
off, it's bogus. It's beyond bogus. It's so bogus, it's *rogus*. It's an
embarrassment of rogusness. And everywhere fossified. Fwa!"

———

Arriving at our house, we saw my mother had left a note taped
to the door, "Dinner at the Abbots! love Mom." There had
been considerable interplay between the two households since
the solstice. My sisters Faith and Katie were turning seven and
five that summer, and September Dawn and Jessamine were
turning six and four – and so best-friendships were made fast
and fixed. It worked for my mother not only because she was
in *Midsummer* every evening but because she was rehearsing a
new play during the afternoon – something called *Godspell* – so
she was at the theatre day by day by day, from eleven in the
morning to eleven at night. When he wasn't in New Brunswick

volunteering at a summer camp, Mr. Abbot was building sets for *Godspell*, so Mrs. Abbot became the de facto guardian for both families – a responsibility she met with deliberate composure. Of the two, it was Mrs. Abbot who seemed to me saintly. Vivien Abbot was the calm of a Peter, Paul and Mary song. She was slimness and silence and ovals. She wore her hair long and unstyled and parted in the middle, shaping her face in the oval of a cameo brooch. Soft on her nose were the side-lying ovals of her granny glasses. From her neck, a pendant swayed in elliptical arcs as she stirred a vegan stew made from backyard zucchinis. Beside her, leaning against the kitchen wall, were two twin-arched gothic windows rescued from a falling-apart farmhouse, and, as she looked at us kids with calm, impassive eyes, supplying us with a very patient, open-ended expectancy, it was as if, in all her self-effacing ovals, *she* were somehow transparent – as if she were merely a frame through which to view the world. She was, on the contrary, at least to us kids, highly palpable, for she conveyed in an instant her respect for the aims underlying a child's inarticulacy, mystification, and helplessness. Vivien Abbot was one of those vigilant, soft-talking mothers who never had to raise her voice because children, sensing her intrinsic decency, never wanted to disappoint her. She went about braless in paint-flecked peasant smocks and overalls, sometimes the side-swell of a breast plumping into open sunlight. But Mrs. Abbot, and the Abbot family in general, acted as if nakedness wasn't anything to particularly panic about – a principle rather new to our street. For some reason she had a reputation as a free-thinker and radical – censures I tried not to hold in mind as I was worried they would lead to restrictions on our visits. Earlier in the summer she let September-and-Jessamine and Faith-and-Katie paint the kitchen furniture any way they wanted – I was sitting on a chair splashed with many colours – and I decided these kinds of experiments explained her reputation for licentiousness.

The Abbots' house, if not actually under construction, was primitively open concept. An interior wall had been partially demolished, plaster-and-planking waiting by for the insertion of those gothic windows, and the place had the air generally of a workshop or folk art *atelier*. There was no real distinction, say, between Kitchen and Bedroom, where September Dawn had forgotten three dinner bowls on a bedside table, or Painting Studio and Bathroom, where a collection of unframed canvases were furled and stored in the plunger stand beside the toilet. When we delivered the evening meal to Mr. Abbot in his garage workroom, it was not a shocker for Uncle Lorne and I to pass a salamander's terrarium given pride-of-place in the middle of the dining room table, or to find the back porch steps littered with yarn-and-stick God's Eyes and covered in sundry books, where, for example, *Harry the Dirty Dog*, a long-overdue library book, competed for stair space with two hardcover copies of *Zen and the Art of Motorcycle Maintenance* – an apt combination, as the day would have it. For Mr. Abbot, wispy in a plaid shirt, wide-wale brown corduroy trousers, and Wallabee shoes, was working on cleaning and reassembling the Honda Black Bomber he and Mrs. Abbot had ridden to Canada six years before. But, even to me, it looked like a never-ending side project, with all those parts and pieces lying on the floor and work table, sacred relics of their fourteen-hundred-mile pilgrimage across the Allegheny and Appalachian mountains.

But, as a single moth sputtered against the swaying light bulb that hung from the garage ceiling, shadows forming and re-forming under Mr. Abbot's eyebrows, I remember shivering with an augur of different days to come as Uncle Lorne, placing the bowl of zucchini stew on the plywood work table, asked in an unusually clear and respectful voice if Mr. Abbot might like some help repairing the motorcycle.

———

Godspell in our town was an event, a portent, an advent of the Sixties a few years after the decade had passed. Stages in Halifax were mostly determined by Noel Coward and George Bernard Shaw and, as my mother called them, "these jeezly Agatha Christie adaptations." My mother's loathing was a by-product of her rising animosity for Dawson Redstone, the artistic director of Neptune Theatre, a cunning Yorkshireman from whom she got, or sometimes didn't get, parts in plays. But these pommy, cobwebby dramatic choices faded into the shadows beside the bright lights of *Hair* and *Jesus Christ Superstar* and *Godspell*. My mother was forbidden to audition for *Hair*. Regardless of the purity of the work's vision, my father thought it professionally questionable to pursue a situation whereby a client might hire a lawyer in the morning only to see that same lawyer's wife "flouncing naked downstage" later that night. A deepening feud with Dawson Redstone precluded involvement in *Superstar*. But *Godspell*, the Broadway soundtrack for which was rarely off our living room turntable, set off my mother's sense of possibility and vocation. Now in the newsreels of my mind, my father often appears in black and white. There he is in skinny suit and tie, holding a swaddled

Carolyn for her christening photo. Or there he is in a formal, grey-toned studio portrait to mark his appointment to Queen's Counsel. Or there he is in a white-bordered snapshot where he seems to be giving the toast to the bride in the bigger dining room at the Waegwoltic Club. But the images of the 1970s were suddenly free of borders and crowded instead with bright instamatic colours – just as the designs of the day were crowded with starbursts and poppies and flowers. My father's concession to this freedom was to grow for a few months frizzly sideburns, and to acquire, while on a vacation in Antigua, an absurdly speckled batik sports jacket that he was permitted to wear in continental North America exactly once. But my mother's response was manifold. My mother came of age in the 1950s – when Doris Day was the very model of the modern wife-and-mother. When a social situation required my mother to be on her best behaviour, she went first to a Doris Day routine. She twinkled with good humour, good will, and good grace – with what a young woman thought was pleasantly expected of her in Polite Society. There was a pressure of unsaid opinion, yes, most often released in the steam of an awkward pause or an abrupt turn in topic. This implied what was thought but was never directly stated, so, moving on, no one need feel embarrassed. My sister, Faith, thinking later on this distillation process, would say, "You could never say anything bad with those ladies but the truth would always come out in a kind of backhanded compliment – making everyone feel weird and uncomfortable anyway." Now my mother, after managing five pregnancies and six children, more than once blew a gasket. "Motherhood sucks," was her post-partum remark when bringing home a final baby from the Grace Maternity. But her policy in public – in her mind – was always on the safe side of convention. She was a 1950s mom stranded in the 1970s. But meeting Vivien Abbot (and to a lesser extent another woman, Madge Wicker, who lies outside the purview of this current history), changed my mother, adjusted her understanding, and moved her to consider new strategies altogether. Why should she have dinner prepared every night at six o'clock – hurrying home to float olives and sliced radishes in a cut-glass water dish? Why should she be the one to ferry the kids to gymnastics and piano and basketball? There was an informal Sunday drop-in session at the Abbots. With *Godspell* up and running, Mom began attending what Gregor Burr, a colleague of my father, would describe as "some leftist, radical women's lib bullshit." How much value my mother saw in Vivien Abbot's persevering logic and fair-mindedness I don't know – but these meetings appealed to something not yet fully formed in her character and my mother, who for various reasons was always looking for the other half of her personality anyway, began not only to question the assumptions and conditions of her life – but to cast around for a means to transform them.

All of this belonged, of course, to the doings of the adult world – a parallel universe a ten-year-old boy did his best to disregard. I kept to my crafts and sullen arts – stayed on the watch for super-villains, mutant zombies, alien invaders – mostly on the lookout for radioactive spiders and the remains of the intergalactic space pod that had brought me here from some distant, red-sunned planet. Charging recklessly down the basement stairs, I touched only the steps that didn't squeak. This

meant leaping the bottom three stairs and immediately som-
ersaulting – purely as a means to dissipate the tremendous
shock of impact. This feat accomplished, I swung my hand into
the darkness of the rec room – not wanting to be surprised by
enemy operatives – and found the wall switch and flicked on
the overhead light. Satisfied I was alone, I turned the television
on and, in a show of private athleticism, jumped backward into
the wicker armchair. There settled, I began to consider my
future with the cast of the PBS series *Zoom*. They were not the
Justice League, true, but there was a costume of a sort (a hor-
izontally striped crewneck sweater and bare feet) and one did
have to bring to the side one's own signature power, witness
Bernadette's arm-swinging thaumaturgy. My musings were
interrupted by my sister Bonnie. She stood between me and
the glowing television, portentously flicking the pull tab on an
unopened can of Fresca.

"What are you doing?" I asked. "I said 'reserve.' And I'm
sitting down."

"You can't watch TV right now. You have to water the ficus."

"What ficus?"

"If you don't water the ficus, it will die. And you're supposed
to fill the humidifiers. Mom said."

"She's not home."

"She will be. She's coming home for the family meeting."

I said I didn't know about any family meeting, but even if I
did, there was no knowing for certain if I would be there.

"Oh, you'll be there," said Bonnie. "Everyone has to be
there."

Continuing my own line of reasoning, I made a comment
about people being surprised by what I might do. If, for

example, I decided I wished to become a professional decath-lete and compete in the Montreal Olympics, then how did anyone know for sure I wouldn't win the Montreal Olympics? Obviously they didn't. I was unpredictable.

"Yeah, like you'll go to the Olympics," said Bonnie. "You can hardly run. You'll probably never be able to run like a normal person. And you're supposed to get a hip replacement when you're thirty-five. That's what the doctor told Mom. The orthopedic surgeon. So you probably won't win anything."

This interpretation did not exactly square with my own plans for myself and, in a gesture of correction, I slapped at the can of Fresca in Bonnie's hand, sending it flying towards the wall where it collided with a metal bracket on the exposed underside of the folded-up Ping-Pong table. The can was now spinning on the carpet, a thin mist of Fresca spraying from a dented perforation in its centre.

Bonnie watched it for a moment, unmoved, then addressed me with matter-of-fact sangfroid. "You're paying for that."

I said I was not.

"You're getting me a new one. You're replacing it."

I said that if I wanted, I could *run* to the store and replace it. I just didn't happen to want to run to the store at the moment.

"You couldn't run to the store."

I said that of *course* I could run to the store – and back – and faster than she could ever dream of running to any store any-where in all the worlds of the universe.

Bonnie considered her own thumbnail. "You want to make a bet?"

―――――

The proposed race is to The Little General – an ice cream dispensary and grocery store whose storefront is decorated with a bootleg Cap'n Crunch figure. It is on Spring Garden Road, not an insurmountable distance for me, though it does almost double my recent Wednesday runs. Bonnie takes off like a shot. I choose a steadier pace, knowing that these "rabbits," as Uncle Lorne calls them, tend to peter out after the adrenalin subsides. But Bonnie does not peter out. She vanishes up Tower Road until her shirt is a speck of blue wavering into invisibility. By the time I arrive at the store counter, Bonnie has come and gone, a localized ache is persistent in my every other step, and I am unable to keep from limping. Trying to stay focused on the race, I draw on my reserves of berserker ferocity. It lasts two blocks before a searing pain escapes from my hip, as if my femur is beginning to crack. On College Street, I stop running and swear at the sky, repulsed by my inadequacy, crazed to be living on a planet where such injustice is allowed to occur. In a sulk, I do not finish the race, and a half hour later, I am walking up the back steps with a pint of chocolate milk and a *Haunted Tank* comic. The back door, strangely, is a quarter open, the hallway empty. On the kitchen table, double strangely, a mug of coffee is still steaming and so is the meatloaf-and-rice on the seven served plates. I call out for my mother, my sisters, my uncle, my voice wending its way from righteous confusion to plaintive unease as I traipse upstairs to a vacant second floor. In the bathroom I turn off a hot water tap. There is not a soul in the house and only now do I recall previous evenings when we have been directed to the Abbots' for dinner. But ten minutes banging on both front and back doors rouse no light or movement. I am in the third stage of panic, my worried brain flashing with paramedic scenarios, when our station wagon coasts up the street, everyone in it but me: the family meeting. Uncle Lorne, untangling himself from the back seat, is wildly overtaken by my youngest sister, Katie, in such a rush her yellow flip-flop is left on the grass behind her. "Oh, Aubrey!" she says, ecstatic with information. She hugs me around my waist, her head sideways at my elbow. "We're moving. We're getting a new house! It's *so* big. And everyone gets their own room – even me!"

———

We would be leaving the only home I had known. The new house, on Dunvegan Drive, was not far from the Jubilee Road boat launch where Uncle Lorne and I strayed that June afternoon. It was a split-level modern place with brown wall-to-wall carpeting, white-painted rail banisters, up-to-date plastic windows. And it was big – the finished basement had five rooms of its own. There us kids were given a rec room big enough for the TV, the now fully extended Ping-Pong table, and the old living room stereo, an all-in-one Clairtone console. Carolyn had come home with the *Band on the Run* album and one evening I was staring mesmerized at the spinning green apple of the record label, the headphones fully on my ears, when the ceiling lights flashed on and off – a phenomenon I connected with Bonnie's presence in the doorway behind me. "What are you *doing*?" I asked, talking over the music in my ears and indicating by my tone that I was moments away from all-out rage.

With tired officiousness, Bonnie mentioned that I had to come upstairs for another family meeting.

"Another family meeting?" I took off the headphones. "What's it for?"

Bonnie exited the rec room. "Didn't you hear? Mom's leaving Dad again."

"Who said that?"

Bonnie started up the stairs. "Because she wants to start her life over. She's leaving. You really didn't know, did you?"

I sat beside Faith and Katie in the spare living room, all of us on chairs pulled from the dining room. My youngest sisters' legs were not long enough to reach the floor, and their flip-flops swung hysterically back and forth as they tried to keep from crying, though their faces were already wet with tears. The meeting was notable for their efforts to choke away their sobs, my parents chain-smoking menthol cigarettes, and the serious monologue that issued from my father as he informed the family that he and our mother would be separating in the next few days, explaining that she would be moving to Toronto for an unspecified period of time. I stared at the systems of cigarette smoke as they rose and dissolved into the corners of the ceiling. Apart from numb surges of sympathy for my father, I wasn't sure what to feel, but I remember thinking it was repulsively inappropriate that Uncle Lorne was not present. He had lived with us for eight years, as long as Faith had been alive, and, yes, he had misbehaved, but he had been grounded for it, and to decide not to include him in such a family meeting seemed irresponsible and insensitive and just *wrong*. At that moment, as if only a little behind cue, Uncle Lorne pulled open the side door. All of us in the living room went silent and for a few moments we listened to Uncle Lorne move about the new house. There was the sound of two brief nasal sniffs and the noise of him sorting through the most recently re-routed mail, before he went still, having heard Faith and Katie's sniveling.

My father called to him. "Lorne, would you come in here a minute?"

Uncle Lorne stepped into our proceedings, shared a glance with my mother, and then, as if acknowledging a pre-existing understanding, simply shook his head and turned around and glided back out the side door.

I ran to him and found him on Jubilee Road smoking a cigarette in front of a telephone pole, his chin bobbing in time to his imaginary music. In his left hand he held a packaged envelope from Passaic, New Jersey. "Whose race you running now, Grub?" he asked, smiling, contemplating me with amused affection. He carefully slid the comic books out of the package, showing me the newest team-up issue of the Justice League and the Justice Society. "*Crisis on Earth-X*, Grub," he said, reading the issue's title and presenting me with my copy. The story was about a mix of superheroes sent through a dimensional transporter to an alternate world where the Nazis, having won that earth's Second World War, control everybody with a mind control ray. It was a bit much for me to absorb all at once and I asked to look at Uncle Lorne's comics. Spying the distinctive checker-top of Silver Age DC comics, I realized with an excited jump that his new acquisitions finished a run of *Justice League* and that my uncle, Lorne Anthony Wheeler, was now in possession of a perfect, unbroken consecutive sequence of the *Justice League of America* from November 1960 to the present moment. There were rumours of two cousins in Dartmouth who had amassed a whole run, and a brother-and-sister team in Cape Breton who had all but the first three issues, but those were achievements shared between two people. Uncle Lorne had done it on his own, as he moved from city to city to city, as he'd moved from his own family to ours. A collection started when he was seven years old, with a purchase at a Lawtons Drug Store in Truro, was now inviolably complete as of August 26, 1974. I asked about his plans – to complete another title? To put his *Justice Leagues* in a vault? "Negatory, Grubster," said Uncle Lorne, pushing his still-lit cigarette into a wrinkle in the telephone pole. He moved his gaze to look across the North West Arm, contemplating the far horizon, before speaking to me in a tired voice, suggestive of the Boris the Spider diversion, but more as if he really *were* tired. "I don't think so. Time to exit the Batcave. Time to leave before the planet explodes. Time to get the hell out of Dodge."

———

"What happened that summer?" my sister Faith would ask me many years later. "We were like the perfect frigging family. Mom and Dad's friends were shocked. Weren't you? I remember Mom saying she felt Dad was just checking things off. 'Get a law degree? Check. Get a job? Check. Get married and have kids? Check.' But without stopping to think what it would mean to her. I'm not sure that justifies running off with what's-his-nuts who played Jesus in *Godspell*. That lunatic in the Winnebago. But do you know I have not seen Uncle Lorne since the day of the family meeting? Since that summer? He didn't come to Carolyn's wedding, did he? My God, do you blame him? Why would he? What a sin, the poor thing. It falls apart with Nanny and Dompa and he gets fobbed off on us. It falls apart with Mom and Dad and what's he going to do? Live with Aunt *Kate*? The poor bastard." Faith's choice of words was not consciously literal, and however treasonous it might have been to suggest in childhood, later evidence would point to such an assessment – that someone else beside Dompa was Uncle Lorne's father. What were Uncle Lorne's secret origins? I never knew. Even my father, keeper of a hundred of the city's secrets, may not have known. Uncle Lorne makes a cameo appearance in a Super 8 movie of Katie's fifth birthday. In that footage, he runs beside the birthday cake to smile absurdly into the camera, squinting from the incandescent camera light, but holding his smile in close-up, setting both sets of teeth together before prankishly kissing Katie and withdrawing offscreen. He must have been eighteen at the time and you could tell how, in his adolescent years, his features had elongated – eyes slanting, eyebrows darkening on the crest above his nose – charismatically vampiric. He always had for me the dash and darkness of a nocturnal superhero like Deadman or Nightwing or Dr. Fate. It was only when this birthday film was transferred to video twenty years later that I saw with adult eyes, when he withdrew into the shadows, just how shy, how recessive, how Asperger's-y, how *nervous* eighteen-year-old Uncle Lorne really was.

———

What happened to my parents' marriage was happening everywhere. Divorce, a social state prohibited the generation before, rushed toward its 1970s statistical zenith. Many families were dissolving – there were crises on infinite earths – but this did not exactly reassure me. After reporting to a bearded pediatric psychiatrist who asked rather over-placidly which parent I wanted to live with – and me not being able to answer – I lapsed into a surly, uncomprehending funk. Everything seemed in disarray and, as we began the exercise of unpacking in the new house on Dunvegan, I was noticing omissions. There was a yellow water pistol that had not made the move, a number of *Laugh-in* stickers, and, most ridiculously, Uncle Lorne's entire comic book collection. "We moved everything," Bonnie informed me. "Carolyn said the old house is finished. There's nothing left but garbage."

"It's *not* garbage –"

"If it was in a box, Aubrey, it got moved. Did you check the basement? Why do you even care? They're just Mom's brother's old comics."

I began to explain the reasons why this collection was significant but, for whatever reason, my ideas came out all at once – emotional, jumbled, and, in anticipation of Bonnie's disapproval, abruptly defensive.

She regarded me with a mix of puzzlement and disdain. "I feel sorry for you," she said, gradually, shaking her head. "You're just like him – weird. You're going to be just like him – weird and alone with no friends and pathetic, loser."

Quite immediately I formed an interior resolution that Bonnie would have to be considered absolutely irrelevant if I wanted to preserve any of my own ideas about my life – and, in response to her last statement, I simply made for the side-door and pushed it open.

"Where do you think you're going?" she asked. "You can't be like this if you live with us!"

I did not answer and, stepping outside, I swung the door shut so it cracked the door's peek-through window. From inside the house Bonnie asked again where I was going and, already sprinting away, I screamed that I was going to the store to get her a Fresca – to get everyone in the world a fucking Fresca – *that's* where I was going. But I ran without knowing where I was going. I was passing by the Camp Hill cemetery before I realized – as some maple seeds helicoptered into my eyes – that the late summer evening had darkened into night. For some minutes my mind had been empty of self-awareness and turning the corner on Summer Street I eased into a single-pointed, euphoric state where I was, finally and simply and transcendently, running my own race. I arrived at our Tower Road house as the last hints of colour vanished from the sky. I went to the back door, where Chris Cody often banged to be let in, and turned my key in the old Otis lock. I stood a few moments in the back porch, my clothes damp with sweat, listening for cues to other occupants. Curiously, recalling the Marie Celeste moment of a month before, a plate of dinner had been left on a double boiler but, as I could quickly see, the water had boiled dry and the meal was crusted and cracked and sticking to the plate. I turned off the burner and opened the unplugged refrigerator – four tins of Coca-Cola, a shrivelled carrot, a mouldy jar of Dijon mustard.

I took a Coke, closed the fridge, and walked to the front hall. There was a trace of Mr. Clean in the air – a faint and bitter smell that made the few straggly details all the more hopeless, remote. The rooms were bare but here and there were a few abandoned expressions of our family. A plastic container of Kaopectate, a chalky medicine Carolyn used to swig during exams, stood like a forgotten sentry on the front stairs. The fallen leaves of the departed ficus plant, whitened, dried, dead, trampled into the shag carpeting of the living room. At the end of the hallway, a mimeograph from Katie's kindergarten forgotten on the floor. I picked up the page and saw it was a spelling test that once had been folded into a paper fortune teller. Katie had made some effort to decorate it using a blue Flair marker. But all the verve of the home, all the dreams and desires, all the hopes and fears of all the years, of course all of that was gone. The Tower Road house was now some anonymous structure – hardwood floors, stained carpets, mottled walls where late Mrs. Abbot's silkscreens had hung. Turning from the living room, I opened the basement door and descended the stairs two steps at a time, calling out for Uncle Lorne. In the centre of his room, a fluorescent black light tube was stuffed in a metal garbage can along with a pillow, a broken model of a gunboat, and his mauve Duo-Tang folder. I took a moment to open and drink my Coke, feeling the taste from the tin, the sense of disturbed dust in the air of the basement. Then I dropped the can into the garbage and retrieved the Duo-Tang. Across from each entry, in Uncle Lorne's expert and miniature handwriting, was a dollar value for each comic book. At the bottom of each page was a tally and, flipping to the end, a grand total for the entire collection, the circled figure of thirty-four hundred dollars. He would not use any of this money for the motorcycle – the Abbots, free-minded Americans, would give him that as a gift – and he spent very little as he motorcycled along the Trans-Canada, sleeping in campsites, staying with the Oldrings in Vermont, and a cousin in Calgary. The purple of the Duo-Tang and the blue marker on Katie's fortune teller paper I found very calming, in the way that the colour combination of lilac and blue can calm you when your family is falling apart and you have no control over your future, and the colours recalled to me my experience of "Band on the Run" and so the song returned unbidden inside me, complete, continuous, the soundtrack to a few more moments of my summer, and in the upstairs hallway I found a blue mattress, diagonal on an empty floor, and fell on it, face down, my hands under my hips, and lay there, exhausted, sweat evaporating from my forehead, soon falling asleep, knowing I was absolutely alone for the first time in my life.

ASTRID BLODGETT

ICE BREAK

We're a long way out on the lake when the ice breaks. It's late, after three, probably. The sun is low in the sky. We've driven past a dozen men squatting on their three-legged stools over small round holes and staring into the blackness. We haven't found our spot yet. We haven't even seen Uncle Rick.

Everywhere I look outside there's the lake and the sky, both the same grey-white, blurred together so you can't see, way out there, what is lake and what is sky; and here and there in the middle distance men hunched on stools, dark silhouettes; and up close the dashboard, dark blue, covered in a thin layer of dust except for the handprints I left when Dad turned too quickly off the gravel road onto the lake, and I grabbed on, handprints like claws.

———

Earlier, Dad had asked Mom to come.

Mom said no. She always said no. She was doing some work, some financial stuff she needed to catch up on. She'd already told him it was late in the season, the ice might not be good; what did Uncle Rick say. Dad told her they knew what they were doing, they'd been doing it for years, they always assessed the risks before they went out. So she didn't talk about the ice anymore.

Now she said, "I know how much you love it."

It was after noon. We'd slept in, my sisters and I, and we'd been reading the coloured comics and doing Saturday morning chores. Mom looked over at us – Marla, Dawn, Janie – all in a row on the kitchen bench, eating brunch. Tallest to shortest. Oldest to youngest. Each in our own spot.

"Sam," Mom said, "You could take Dawn."

Sometimes they did that, one parent, one child. Every six months, it seemed, we had a family meeting about it, and it worked okay for a week, one or maybe two of us doing something alone with Mom or Dad, and then they forgot about it till the next family meeting. Or two of us wanted to do whatever it was Mom or Dad wanted to do with just one of us. So it never really worked.

Dad looked at me. "You'll have to get ready quick. Uncle Rick and the cousins are probably already there. They won't put up with any dawdling."

Marla finished chewing and took a swig of milk. "No going to Jack's without me." Sometimes we stopped at Jack's Drive-In for ice cream, if we were good. Marla couldn't come today. She had a babysitting job down the street.

"No one said anything about Jack's," Dad said. "Hurry up, Dawn." Dad got up and went outside. He looked grumpy.

Probably we wouldn't stop at Jack's today because he was in a bad mood.

Mom said she'd pack a thermos of hot chocolate and some cookies.

———

In the truck, Dad hits my left shoulder hard. It doesn't feel hard, not now anyway. He hits me again and I turn to look at him, slowly. It takes ages to move my head.

———

Janie and I cleared the table. Marla went to the bathroom to get ready for her babysitting job.

"Janie," I said. I've piled the dishes into the sink and run water into it. I plunged my hands into the sudsy water. "Want to come?"

"Naw, I don't want to," Janie said.

"Dad'll probably stop at Jack's." I didn't know if he would or not, but it was worth a try.

"Dawn!" Mom poured hot water into a thermos. "Don't push. She can go if she wants to, but she doesn't have to."

"But you're making me go."

"Not making you." Mom looked out the window. Dad backed the truck out of the garage. "It's a good chance for you two. You don't do much together." She twisted the cap on the thermos and went downstairs to the laundry room.

"I don't want to go anyway," Janie said again.

"I'll give you a dollar," I said.

———

His face is red and his mouth is moving like he's shouting, but I can't hear anything. I've gone deaf. His eyes are close to my face and bulging.

———

"I know something you don't know," Marla sang when she emerged from the hallway. Her eyes were dark with eyeliner and mascara, and her hair was done up in a pony.

"What?" Janie and I said. We were still doing the dishes.

Marla smiled in her teasing way and said, "Tell you later."

"No, tell us now!" I said.

We heard Mom come up the stairs.

"Remember Mr. and Mrs. Pichowsky down the street?" Marla said in a loud whisper. She went to the back door and put on her boots and coat. "See ya!" she called out. "Bye, Mom."

The screen door slammed behind her.

———

His lips are fat and his cheeks are rough and stubbly. He didn't shave that morning. He doesn't shave to go ice fishing.

———

"What?" Janie asked me. But Mom was in the kitchen now and I didn't want to say. Mr. and Mrs. Pichowsky got a divorce last year and moved. We never saw the kids anymore. They stayed with the mom, who moved to Deepest Darkest Mill Woods. Nobody ever went there because it was miles away, and if you did go there you'd just get lost. That was what Dad said. Marla must mean that Mom and Dad were going to be like Mr. and Mrs. Pichowsky. Marla was just being cruel. She always did that, said a little bit of something, and then left. I wasn't going to tell Janie what Marla meant. It was too mean.

Mom went down the hall to the big bedroom.

"Mr. Pichowsky went away, didn't he?" Janie said. "And Mrs. Pichowsky went somewhere else."

"Mmm-hmm." Now I had another reason for Janie to come. If Marla was right and Dad was leaving, then for sure Janie should come today. To have one last visit with Dad.

"I'll give you a dollar if you come," I said again.

"A dollar?" Janie made a face. "That all?"

———

Dad yanks at my seatbelt, and I pull at it. I'm not just deaf, I'm slow and stupid. I can't unclip the buckle. My body is weighing it down. The front wheels have gone through the ice, the truck is tipped forward, and I'm leaning into the seatbelt. My fingers are stiff and fat and useless. They could not take a five-dollar bill and fold it in half and half again if they had to. They could not do anything so delicate and so careful.

———

If I'd stopped to think about it just for a minute, I probably wouldn't have said it. But it just came out: "Okay, five dollars." Five dollars was a lot. But I really wanted her to come. I didn't want to be alone with Dad. He was always grouchier when it was just him and me. He was scary when he got mad. And he never knew what to talk about with me so it was uncomfortable and we both ended up saying all the wrong things. I'd heard them talking once, him and Mom. He said he'd tried to talk to me and I just wasn't receptive; and Mom said he had to get over it, he had to get over the idea that someone will be how you imagine them to be, and just accept them. "You can't change people, Sam," Mom said.

"Really?" Janie said. "Five dollars?"

"You can have my five-dollar bill." I said. It wasn't any five-dollar bill. I got it when I started babysitting last summer. It had come straight from the bank: it was crisp and smooth and flat, like a page from a brand new book. There was not a single crease in it.

Janie's eyes lit up. "You mean it?"

I nodded. Mom came into the kitchen. I thought she would make Janie change her mind, but she didn't.

"Show me."

———

All of a sudden, the sound is turned back on. Dad shouts and swears. He looks angry. The wheels and now the hood are under water.

———

I went to our bedroom and pulled it out from under my mattress. "Here," I said, walking back down the hall.

Janie took the five-dollar bill and looked at it closely, both sides. I counted. She didn't say anything for at least thirty seconds. "Okay. I'll come."

She laid it on the table, lined it up lengthwise and folded it in half once, and then again. She slipped it into her jeans pocket and bounced around the kitchen, patting her pocket and making little dance steps with her feet and squealing. Then she tilted her chin up a little and smiled so her teeth showed.

Dad opened the screen door and called, "You ready, Dawn?"

Mom looked at him. "Last chance this season, like you said. Have fun!"

"Janie's coming!" I said.

Dad looked from me to Mom.

Mom nodded. "She wants to. Just take them both. I'll get my work done this way."

———

Dad unclips his seatbelt, flings his body onto mine, and rams his shoulder against the door. He's sitting on top of me now, all of him, pinning my legs to the seat. He pushes against the door again and it opens a crack. Ice cold water seeps in. He undoes my seatbelt and flings it to the side. The buckle whacks my cheek. He smashes my hip against the door, over and over, pushing me hard against it. The door opens a little more and water gushes in. He stops and takes a huge breath and looks into the back seat and makes a long, loud howl.

———

We piled into the pickup truck, me in the front and Janie in the little seat in the back. Dad backed out of the driveway.

"Looking forward to seeing your cousins?" Dad asked.

"It'll be boring," Janie said.

"Is that what your mother says?" He pulled onto the Yellowhead Highway.

"No, Dad," I said.

"Are we stopping at Jack's on the way back?" Janie asked.

Dad didn't seem to hear. "Man, I hope Rick's still out there. We were pretty slow getting going." He tapped the steering wheel with one hand. He was already annoyed. "Hey, Dawn," he said, turning to look at me. I hated it when he did that, when he turned to look at me and not at the road. I wanted him to watch where he was going. He wiped his forehead, pushed back his hair. "Mom said to ask you about your reading. How's it going?"

For just a moment, I wished Janie wasn't there. I hoped Janie wouldn't pipe up that it had been weeks and I still hadn't finished the book I'd started. Or that she was nearly done the Narnia books. I looked out the window at the fields covered here and there with patches of snow. "Fine, Dad," I said finally.

———

Dad's not angry. He's frightened. Water fills the footwell. It rises over my ankles and up my calves to my knees and then over the seat. We're sitting in water. I'm running out of air.

Dad shoves my shoulder through the gap in the door and out into the lake. He's forcing me out of the truck, but I grab him, first his head, then his shoulders, and hold on as hard as I can. I don't want to go without him.

———

"You know, I was never good at reading either," Dad said.

"I didn't *say* I wasn't good at reading," I said. I just took longer. I liked other things more.

"Christ. What I mean is, I had to work at it too. Reading isn't everything." He smacked the steering wheel and looked out the window. "I just wanted us to have a good time together, you know?"

"I know, Dad," I said. "It's okay." I felt sorry for him. I didn't know why, but he seemed to get angry all the time. I looked down at my jeans. They were brand new Levi's, bought with my own money. I was wearing them for the first time. I was excited when I got them, but now when I looked at them I felt sad.

Dad pulled off the highway and onto a gravel road. It was huge, Lake Wabamum. The sky was grey-white and the lake was grey-white. We were in a gigantic grey-white dome. The sun was low in the sky. Dead grass poked through the patches of snow near the road.

"Look at all those guys! What was your Aunt Helen talking about, not to go on the ice so late in the season? She doesn't know what the hell she's talking about! I sure hope she didn't talk Rick out of going. Aunt Helen, your mother, they have no idea."

"Uncle Rick always waits for us, Dad," Janie said quietly.

———

He squeezes my fingers together so hard I think they'll break, but he keeps squeezing till I let go, and then shoves me out into the water.

It's not cold. It's just like nothing. I shut my mouth tight to keep the water out.

Dad dives into the back seat and grabs the buckle on Janie's seatbelt. The inside of the truck is full of water now. Janie's hair is wet and floats around her face. Dad unclips her and pushes against the door. Her face and hands are pushed hard against the window, her hands banging at it, her lips flattened against the glass.

———

Dad followed the gravel road along the shore for a while and then turned onto the packed-down snow where the others had driven onto the ice. He turned so hard I grabbed the dash.

"Knowing my luck, Rick's probably come and gone, we took so long getting here," Dad griped. "I'll just drive around for a bit till I find him. Did you remember the hot chocolate?"

I nodded.

"Mom packed cookies too," Janie said.

"You can have those if you get bored." He stared at the lake. "I'm sorry if you get bored. People are just different, you know? We can't help who we are. It no big deal, eh?"

"Uncle Rick's there, Dad, look," Janie said.

"Where? For Christ's sake, where?" Dad said. He drove forward slowly.

I looked too. We'd passed ten or twelve men, some of them in pairs, hunched over holes. They were dark shapes in the white-grey globe. I couldn't see Uncle Rick either.

"Keep going, Dad, he's out there, I can see him," Janie said. "Past that guy with the dog."

Dad drove on. And then I heard a loud crack, like a gun going off, and the front of the truck tipped forward. It was like those dreams where everything is in slow motion and sounds are muffled and all the people have gone and only we are left. The truck tipped forward, and then the front wheels were in the water.

———

The men said they helped me out, but nobody did. I got up on my own, when I finally found the hole. After Dad pushed me

out of the truck, I floated up and hit the ice from underneath.
Over and over, I kept hitting ice. It took the longest time to
find the hole.

I wasn't in the hospital for long. Just overnight. My new
jeans had to be cut off. It seemed like the wrong thing to be
sad about, so I didn't tell anyone. My hip was bruised. And my
right shoulder and my cheek, where the buckle hit it. The
bruises were there for a long time.

The funeral was on Thursday. Janie's face had make-up all
over. She didn't look like Janie. Her lips and cheeks were red,
from the make-up. She looked like a baby, with her smooth,
soft skin, but she also looked grown up. Like she was sixteen
instead of nine. Her hair was washed and neatly combed. They
even put make-up on Dad. I looked at their chests for the
longest time, waiting for them to move up and down.

I asked Marla, when Mom wasn't near, what she meant about
the Pichowskys, and she said she didn't remember. But her face
turned bright pink, so I knew she knew.

Marla said we were living in a flower shop, with all the potted
mums that filled the living room and the kitchen, some green,
some purple, dark glum colours. There were so many we had to
put some on the floor. We were in the news, too, the radio and
the newspaper and the television even, and Mom said, over and
over, at least he was doing something he loved. I wanted her
to say the other part, what she talked to Aunt Helen about, that
she was angry with Dad for going, after she and Aunt Helen
had told Dad and Uncle Rick it was late in the season and the
ice was rotten. She never mentioned that on the news.

I wanted her to say more about Janie, too. I'd seen her in
Janie's room, holding a crumpled blue shirt of Janie's up to her

chest, then pulling it till it ripped and crying as though she was going to break open, right down the middle, like the shirt. Just once she mentioned Janie, to one of the reporters who stayed asking more questions. She told the reporter that Janie was just a little girl. An adult has a choice, she said, but a child –. Then she saw me and Marla lingering in the doorway, as we so often did in the early days after the funeral, lingered near her, and she stopped talking and told the reporter to go. I kept waiting for her to say something, to a reporter or me or Marla, anyone, about getting Janie's clothes back and finding the five-dollar bill in her jeans pocket, soaking wet. But she never did.

KRIS BERTIN

IS ALIVE AND CAN MOVE

I'd made it through a real rough patch, and so I had to do everything I could to try and get something going that would keep me together. My brother wouldn't let me stay with him, but he did put up the money so I could get an apartment. Said he'd help me more if I started going to meetings, but I said I didn't need that shit. Said all I needed was a job, and believed it, too. Eventually I'm hired to do clean up at one wing of a building at the far end of the university campus – mostly dorm rooms, but there's a cafeteria and kitchen, a daycare, and two floors of offices for the teachers. I had to clean from midnight until it was done, which was usually five in the morning, and for the first time in years, I really try to stay on top of it and do a good job because I really have nothing else.

I got hired even though for the first week I had to smoke every five minutes, take a dump every two, and was sweating so much I looked like I'd been out in the rain. But the cleaning boss, Charles, seemed to understand. He has one of those big, bloated noses and you could see he'd been through some rough patches himself. You could never know how bad someone else has had it, but even the worst alcoholics didn't have it as bad as me. I was a special case – even the doctor said so – but it was still nice to know he had an idea or two about it. One time, he even asked how I was handling it, and I said *good*, because it was mostly true. The job gave me a place to be at the exact time most everyone would be going downtown to drive drinks into them. And it was a job that, for the most part, was quiet and didn't involve other people. Sometimes I'd see a college kid or two, shuffling around in their pajamas but that was it. And the only other people I'd see were the professors, a couple of young ones who would even talk to me sometimes. They seemed to always be working late, smoking pipes and cigars and laughing a lot. I never really let myself get in too close, because something about them seemed dangerous.

It was impossible to start the shift at the dormitory end, because any day of the week the kids would be going right until three or four in the morning, and if you cleaned it too early, you'd have to pick up trash, mop up drinks or even puke, broken glass, shredded papers, then come back and do it all over again. Instead you'd start with the offices, go down each floor, sweep, mop, and buff. Change garbages. Vacuum the mats near the doors. Clean walls once a week. Wipe down doorknobs and railings and light switches with disinfectant. Do the toilets and sinks and stock everything up, too.

Charles said I had it right. That it was best never to even see the kids, to never even lay eyes on them. A guy who had my job from before, a few years ago, he got fired for fucking one of the girls.

"Whether or not he even did," Charles said, "And I fucking tell you he *did not* so keep that in mind, too, young fella."

One night I did end up seeing a girl, at maybe quarter to four, hanging over the stairwell, watching me buff the floor. Her tits were dangling down at me in her silvery shirt and I had to do everything not to take a second look at her. Problem was it was summer, it was hot, and we were both stripped down to almost nothing. I had on shorts and a muscle shirt, and she had on that party top, and as far as I could tell, her underwear. Even with the noise from the buffer and all the space between us, I swear I could almost *feel* her body against mine. Smell her. It had been so long since I'd been with a woman, I almost dropped that big hand-operated thing down the stairs a dozen times.

She kept saying stuff like *you're hot*, and *you're younger than the other guy*, and *I like your tattoos*. Shouted them right down on top of me so it bounced off every surface and into my ears. And to be honest, I was scared, scared all around. For my job and my life and to even be seen with her. But I was most scared of what she might think if I actually went for it, if she got a good look at my face and eyes and smelled the stink coming out of my pores. So I put my head down and pushed hard on the handles, as hard as I could, got out of there with the job half done, my prick sticking straight out in front of me.

And so I kept away from there until the very end of the night for both those reasons, and because the only way for things to get back to normal was for me not to lay eyes on any bottles, not to even smell the stuff or look at it. I knew I couldn't even look at someone when they're screwed up and having a time. Doctor told me I had to do whatever I had to do in order to

make it work, and the old guys who'd been able to quit altogether all said shit like *it never gets easier* and I had to believe it
because what else could I believe? Even all the pamphlets said
the same thing, and I imagine the meetings would, too.

Being alone might not have been the solution I needed,
though. For the first part, it was. When my system was changing, trying to turn itself into something that didn't run on grain
alcohol and bar food, I needed to be alone. When I would have
sudden bursts of energy and the air smelled fresh, when all I
wanted to do was tell the world how beautiful it was, when I
was so emotional the taste of Mike and Ikes nearly moved me
to tears, I knew it was good no one was around. Same as when
I'd have a real downward dip and I would be so angry at
absolutely nothing – angry at dirt and streaks and myself and
the walls – those were times it was good to be alone. And then
when I'd have a blackout, and I'd come out of it, scared and
confused and I would have a moment where I wasn't sure if it
was a new day or one that happened a long time ago. Those
were times I was glad to be alone.

And then other times it would've helped to have someone
there. Part of drinking so much that your brain is permanently
fucked means that you have trouble staying focused on tasks,
or else you can get distracted from the ones you need to be
doing by ones that don't matter. For a while I got to counting
all the bricks at eye level. I got to thinking for a while that if
the number of bricks came out odd, it was an omen that things
were going downhill again. I'd feel grim and grey and once
even thought about opening one of those big green windows
in the bathroom and stepping out headfirst. When it was even,
I'd get a burst of energy and I'd hear a whistling sound like my

life was flying down the right path. Those were things that another person could have kept from coming.

The brick count came out odd a few too many times and so I started to get the idea that the building was against me. It wasn't a thought that occurred to me – it was just that one day I realized it was what I believed, was what I had always believed about the place. Almost immediately after I realized it, I started to see it everywhere.

There was a brick missing from one of the walls, low and on a corner that I hadn't noticed. I'd walk by it, or just clean the little red crumbs where the hole met the rest of the wall. It wasn't until I realized that the dirt and bits around it on the ground were from someone's foot, climbing on it, that I paid it any attention. When I stuck my foot in it and take a step up, I realized there's another brick missing, a whole arm's reach up near the top. I felt something slimy up there and let go, and a moment later a few white things went plop onto the ground. At first I thought they were worms – maggots – and I froze, held my breath while my brain tried to work it out. With what I have, figuring things out can take longer than it should, and it was only when I smelled my hand that I finally realized what they are. It's a horrible smell. Latex and come. Somehow that was worse than maggots and I heard myself scream.

The scream started a chain reaction and then other people are screaming, too. Shouting, yelling, a bunch of men's voices coming down the hallway. I watched a group of kids bust through the atrium, carrying something over their heads. They were chanting. Saying *Edmond Burke*, the name of the building. I could feel something bad coming off them so I went up the stairs to the cafeteria and stood behind a bunch of garbage bins just to get something between me and them. Then I noticed what they were holding. A person. A girl. The girl from the dorms – no pants on, just sneakers and that silver shirt. At first I think they're going to throw her through one of the windows, but then they open the door and throw her outside. It almost looks like a prank, until they chuck her right at one of those boulders near the doors, the ones that kids sit on. She lands on her back and makes a terrible sound but I don't stay to watch the rest.

I scramble into the cafeteria. Hide. Hide for so long that I fall asleep. When I wake up, it's still dark, but I leave that whole area alone, don't even go back to it. The next day I don't get in trouble for my shitty job, and there's no blood or skin or teeth or sign of struggle and the boulder looks fine. The condom is still in my uniform pocket though, and there are more used ones in the missing brick. To me, it looked like a pattern, but when I was feeling like that, everything did.

And then, a voice in my head said, *something in this place makes you crazy.* A moment later, it added, *you probably have it too.*

The next week, one of the walls collapses. I was the last person to be told, and so I just come across a whole mess of caution tape and scaffolding and tarps and dust where I was supposed to be cleaning. When I call Charles, he apologizes and tells me to just leave that part and move on.

"Yeah, the fucking thing just let go. Been spitting rocks the size of grapefruits out the front of it for years. One kid even got hit in the '90s," Charles tells me. "The whole fucking thing just let go. Two kids died. Girls. Happened to be walking through the door at that exact moment. There's gonna be a hell of a lawsuit."

Avoiding the mess fucked with my hours, because it took a solid two and a half off of them, but I don't say anything. Instead I put my hand in a locker and slammed the door a few times. I knew at the time that it wasn't productive but it made a kind of sense. It was about my hours, but for those poor girls, too, like if I felt bad pain it could somehow straighten things out for them *and* me.

When I look back I know I'm acting this way because I refused to take the pills they said I needed after my hospital stay. I thought refusing them would make me stronger, that if I could get through on my own, it would be for the better. And so in that state, thinking about what the bricks and the kids and the wall meant kind of made me decide things I shouldn't have. Like that the building was alive. That it did stuff to people, and did stuff on its own.

It gave me something to do for the rest of my nights, on my smoke breaks, in the toilet bowls. Gave me something to look for when I was doing the floors, gave me cracks to see in the ceiling and little differences to notice. I was sure the school was moving. Maybe it was all marshland underneath or a slow sinkhole or something, but there were signs of growing and shrinking, no doubt about it. The more I thought about it, the more I remembered stuff that had been one way and was now another, like a whole door that used to be under the stairwell, and the giant mirror that was right next to the south double doors that was just gone.

"What happened to that stuff?" I would ask out loud. I wanted to ask Charles but then I wasn't really sure if he was on our side or *Edmund Burke*'s. I wanted to go look for the girl in the silver shirt from all those weeks ago, but I was both scared

I wouldn't be able to find her and that I would, that I'd lose my job up there on a hot, sticky night.

I mostly didn't think about the building during my daytime. I'd just watch TV and smoke and take walks, but more than a few times I catch the tail end of an idea of a memory I'd once had that could help with my theory. Memories are hard to hold onto without booze, and I even thought about buying some Russian Prince just so I could make my brain work right – not even to get drunk, just a few ounces to grease the wheels and get things going.

I didn't give in, though, not then. I'd get into bed and sleep when I felt like that, and eventually my missing memory came to me. Spider-Man dealt with this shit once. A living building. It was a museum and it tried to kill him. And a green guy was in it. Like a mummy or a zombie, all rotten and shit, and he controlled the museum. He made chandeliers fly around and wax cavemen chase Spider-Man around. In the end, a suit of armour cut Spider-Man's head off. Or no – Spider-Man cut the green guy's head off. But it grew back.

I tried to explain it to the guy at the comic shop and he said he wasn't sure which issues I meant. He said it sounded more like a *Twilight Zone* episode but I said no, it's definitely a comic. I read it as a kid, and then again at the library in the can back in '01. It was a pretty dull day so him and me went digging through the oldies and I realized it wasn't a zombie, it was Spider-Man's enemy, the Lizard. We found four Spider-Man comics with museums in them, but only one of them had the lizard. It wasn't the right comic, but it was close enough that I bought it. Read it at the McDonald's nearby and even though it wasn't the one I remember, it seemed so familiar that it made me feel better, even if it didn't tell me how to solve my problem.

I lost the comic book before I could read it twice, but I saw the Lizard guy the next night in a dream. He was standing in the hall at the school, upstairs near the toilets, and he had a mean hard-on sticking out of his pants and lab coat. Was hissing and laughing and playing with himself, trying to keep it going so he could give it to me. He didn't look real – looked like a guy in a costume but I got the idea that maybe the costume was alive, growing on the guy like moss.

"Don't come forward," I said, but of course he did.

As he came at me, I got a jolt of pain in my guts like I'd been knifed and I fell backwards over my mop bucket, tipped the thing over, and within seconds I was soaked in brown water.

The green guy's rubber feet squeaked after me and it was then that I realized I wasn't dreaming, I was just seeing shit. I heard the echo of my own voice spiralling down the halls and bouncing off the floors and then it was quiet. Then I saw just how dark it was outside. That it was just another night and the hall was empty. The doctor warned me I was probably gonna see shit. He said I'd feel good for a bit and then it would be like detox all over again. And it would be bad. I thought it had come and gone but there it was after all. It doesn't take long to realize I'm going to need those pills he talked about.

I barely finished my cleaning that night because I was so fucked up over the Lizard. I kept looking over my shoulder and even fell down the stairs because of it. Ended up scraping my hands and bashing my knees and it took everything, everything in me not to walk to Ron's or whatever bar would let me in at eight a.m. to drink my face off.

—

It hurt to go to the doctor. To say that I fucked up and I couldn't straighten myself out on my own, but he was nice about it. He said what he said before, that it's not an option to go without the pills. That a guy as young as me can still make it if we get on top of it. He prescribed the stuff, which is usually for old people, but said it would help me keep my head straight. He also gave me a chart of stuff to eat, vitamins to take. Said that people who have alcohol dementia need nutrition more than anything else. It's important to eat three meals, make them healthy, and never miss them.

I realized too, that I hadn't been drinking enough water, just a few cups of coffee and a can of coke to stay up. The doctor straightens all that up though, and after a while, I actually feel good. I start getting that high all the time and for a while the job gets better. With something as easy as the right food the right amount of times, the right pill at the right hour, things make more sense. Three weeks is all it takes for me to feel like a teenager again. At night, the school is quiet, like a church, and when I clean it, it's like a whole new place to me. It's like I've just come back from another planet – one that looked just like this one, except without straight lines and right angles. I stop seeing shit, hearing shit, thinking insane thoughts, and more than once I have a hard time remembering what it was even like before the pills.

It stays away from me, and I don't even think about the building growing or moving, or controlling people's minds. I just about forget all about it until I find that comic book in a bag with a bunch of porno magazines and mouldy burger wrappers. I laugh out loud, and remember how crazy I was being, like it's so far away from where I am now. But then, I look inside, look a little *too* close at one of the pages and that Lizard is smiling too hard, his mouth *too* wide. And I feel it, like it's all fresh. I close the book. Throw it out.

One night the professors get me in their office. I'm going by with the dust mop and one of them shouts, *Hey*, and I stop. I don't know why I stop. One of them has a sixty-ouncer, drinking right out of the neck with one hand like the kids would do, except it's a fancy Scotch I've never heard of. I get the sense from looking at them that maybe something had gone wrong for one of them, and maybe the other was the kind of person who'd go along with anything. Then he passes the bottle around the room a few times, and when it gets to me I watch my hand bring it to my mouth. Feel my mouth open, my throat take it and send it down to my belly, and feel everything get dull. Even though I stand there and joke with them and listen to their shit, it takes everything to keep it together. I feel like I'm falling backwards into something like a bed, but warmer. Something like water, but softer. I realize that I believe the building is moving again. I believed it with my first sip. And more, I've always believed it.

I want to say something like, *No sorry, I don't drink*, say it now and launch it back ten minutes ago, but I can't. I realize that going to meetings and all that probably would have trained me to say it. I would have said it when I met them, would have shaken their hands and told them about my disorder or disease or whatever you call it.

Then we're outside, and I'm on my hands and knees, showing them the slope in the ground made by the building as it moves forward.

"That's amazing," one of them says.

"This place is fucking haunted to shit anyway," the one with the beard says. "All I hear is people saying they wish the department was somewhere else. Jane saw a ghost here once."

"Fuck Jane," the other one says, then the bottle goes around again and we're leaving to get more and I don't even think about my mop and bucket, up on the third floor. Don't think about the unlocked maintenance room, the extension cord running down an entire hallway into a stairwell. The six dirty washrooms that need to be cleaned.

We're at a bar after that, and they got us each a pitcher and we're in a place that doesn't even care if we drink right out of the jug. Then I realize we're at Ron's, and I brought us here. Nick's behind the bar, watching me, and I get the sense that maybe I'm dreaming, maybe I've floated here in a dream and really I'm in bed, groaning and rolling around and kicking the shit out of the sheets. Maybe I'm still good, and I haven't drunk a drop and everything's okay.

"I need to put together a resume," I tell the professors. "I need to get a new job."

"Take out an ad," the younger one says. "I'm sure you can do a lot of jobs."

"I'm alive," I tell them. "Got two legs."

"Is alive and can move," the other one says, moving his hands like he's creating a headline before our eyes.

There's a long black piece in my memory like a blindfold and then I'm on a beach with my shirt off.

"Look at that," one of the girls says. There are girls.

We look out across the harbour at the city and even though it's late, the lights and the fog and the sky all around it are this deep purple, green at the edges like a bruise. There are clouds overtop of it that aren't over us, and you can see the little flashes of lightning way in the air as things get ready to open up.

"The school's moving," I tell the professors. "In the past two months, it's moved two feet. That's why the wall collapsed."

"Of course it is," one of them says. "According to my research, the whole city's on the move. It wants to get into the Atlantic."

"Really?"

"It's a living thing, the city. I know that sounds like a joke, but it grows and changes and learns. Does stuff. Just like us. Except it runs on people."

"That's bullshit," I say, but I can feel myself getting scared. "Gonna need a new job."

"He's a professor," one of the girls says in a voice I don't like. Everyone looks at me like they're serious, though. Like I'm not being fucked with.

"Your body runs on a bunch of smaller things going around and doing stuff. Your blood, your cells, antibodies, bacteria, all that stuff. A city's the same thing, except we're those little guys making it work, keeping it alive. You see?"

"Yeah," I tell them. And I do. I can actually see it in my mind, all of us climbing over scaffolding and driving our cars and walking up and down the streets like water through a pipe. I want to ask them if they know somewhere I can get a job, but then someone passes me a drink and I realize I don't know anyone's name, don't even know who or what they are.

"The city's gonna dump us all into the ocean," the bitchy girl says. "You think two feet is impressive? Try a kilometre a year. That's how fast the city is trying to kill us."

"It's true," the professor says, but this time I can hear some-thing in his voice. Then his friend speaks up and I realize they've been bullshitting me, going around in circles making shit up.

Smoke pours out of the other professor's bearded mouth as thick as taffy, and he says, "Oh yeah, the world's coming to an end. This is fucking it."

Then there was thunder, and that feeling you get inside, that rumble that wants you to run away like an animal on a nature documentary, and I could almost see it. I could see that bruise colour spreading through the sky, and then I saw it. Everything shook and I felt it right in the middle of me and the city actually *moved*, moved a whole block over. Like *ka-chunk*, and there it was, settling in, nestling into place like a cat. And the thunder got louder and louder and the sky lit up again and when it was over, when the noise from the sky got quiet, almost everyone was laughing like crazy. I could feel something coming, something coming right up from inside of me, so I make a point to try and drift off to that place where everything gets dark and I can sink into myself like a stone down to the bottom of my thoughts. Then something bad happens.

Three years later I go back to that school and eyeball from the corner of the steps to the tree, and count out the paces and put my hands flat on the earth and I swear it's taking a *goddamned* walk up the city. I'm completely dry, and I'm on my medicine, and I've been stone-cold sober since I was back on the street but I swear it's moved. It's a cold fall day and I know it doesn't make sense, but it's all there. And I can still see that same dark shit in all the kids that look at me like I'm some kind of monster dragging my belly in the dirt, but it's actually the other way around and they'll never know it.

TREVOR CORKUM

YOU WERE LOVED

"El, are you there? Elliot? *Pick up the goddamn phone.*" I slide my left cheek along the frosted window, place one of my palms against the white glass so it leaves a kind of caveman handprint, a brief, skeletal X-ray in melted relief. I don't really care to answer. Her voice on the machine is panicky, needy and messed up in its despair. It's early in December. Snowing outside. I used to sit like this for hours as a kid, tracing icy snowflakes, watching the weird light change as it poured into cold rooms, through all those intricate patterns and crazy designs.

Finally I pull away. Grab the chilly receiver. Wrap a scratchy blanket around my naked shoulders.

Hey, Mom.

Exhausted, feeling trapped already, I collapse into the dumpy armchair. It's green and fancy in a retro way, something I rescued from an alley last summer. Around me are pages of an essay I'm supposed to be working on for a course in Canadian history. *The Influence of the Trade Union Movement on*

Canada's Migrant Workers. Underneath these papers in a well-worn baggie, the flaky remains of some B.C. bud I traded for a blow job from a jacked-up skinhead at the bus terminal.

Oh El.

Instinctively my fingers begin to roll. I think I can hear something new in her voice. She's crying, of course. Which isn't so unusual. She cries like the women on TV, like the love-worn and the heartbroken, like her life is some never-ending drama etched into bright 3-D. But her sobs now sound as if someone is beating her chest with a boxing glove, so hard that the tears are being pounded, literally being pounded right out of her.

For a beat, a whisper and a half, I'm afraid.

Then I clear my throat.

Around the time of this phone call, many years ago, my mom lived a quiet life in a rundown farmhouse outside a village called Warsaw. She lived there all alone until she died. Warsaw is about half an hour or so outside the armpit of a faded industrial city I moved away to for university, about a million and a half years ago. Her house was the house I grew up in, a place we only rented, and though the land had been hacked off and sold back in the days when Sonny and Cher were still a couple, I used to pretend sometimes that it was ours. I had childish Dungeons and Dragons–type fantasies where we were the feudal landowners and the piss-faced farmers our lowly serfs. Wandering around in camouflage shorts through the sad Christ-like cornstalks, beheading stray sunflowers with a sword carved of wood, I used to imagine too that in a different kind of life we had a whole other family history, descending not from the stone-hearted Vikings, with their raping and pagan pillaging, but blending in instead with everyone else around us in that fucked-up little corner of the world, heirs to a solid line of God-fearing Irish-Catholic drunks.

Other times, horny and so bored out of my mind it seemed fun to think about killing myself, if only in the theoretical, the way you imagine winning the lottery or living forever, I'd get on my BMX and bike past the rows of corn up our long gravel road to spy on our fun-loving neighbours. Cycling past the lake and the fake European châteaus with their gingerbread-laced verandas and fancy designer solar panels, I'd wonder what it was like to be part of this ass-kissing leisure class, who seemed not necessarily rich, but full of a kind of bullshit I could never get away with. Men in ironed golf shirts practising their drive, tanned kids playing pick-up games of laser tag, women in tight sundresses drinking iced tea and peach schnapps under long covered porches, keeping one eye on the kids and joking in a sexual way about the men.

I didn't want this world. It made me feel guilty and ashamed. But maybe something like it. Maybe just a slice of it. A made-for-CBC documentary, where intimacy was a Cracker Jack prize, some hard, sweet surprise, not just a nail-spiked Molotov cocktail hidden inside a slot machine waiting to blow up in your face, on what you thought was your lucky day.

After her phone call, I must have fallen asleep. I wake up a few hours later, soaked and sweaty in my briefs. The heat in the apartment is cranked. It's dark outside and I feel disoriented, bloated by the sensation that I have fallen out of time.

Around me the walls vibrate. Hello, you little fucker, you cocktease Friday night.

When I get up I notice I have just a few cigarettes left. So I put on jeans. Outside the street is freezing. The stars are at their finest: twinkling, sleazy little ghost eyes. Ropes of Christmas lights flicker, gaudy silver garlands rustle from ornate street-lamps, the storefronts themselves are haunted with cotton snowmen and gaunt-looking plastic Santas staring out like orphans at the world. As I slip along the sidewalks, the cold nudges its fingers under the edge of my coat. I think I might walk toward the river later, past the factory where they roast the oats and where even in the middle of winter ducks huddle like nuns along the banks. I like that kind of silence beside the river, the maple smell of the oats, the shadows under the bridge where you can sit on the concrete pilings and no one will ever find you.

I tell people, in the world I live in now, that I grew up in the sticks. I say I was born in *God's Country, Ontario*; I make it into a joke, something dark and unimaginable, like we were so poor we had to shoot mutated squirrels and scrape half-flattened roadkill from the side of a secondary highway for our special Viking soup. I tell them my mother made me clothes from old curtains stained with turpentine; that I was so lonely as a kid I created imaginary friends in the faces of rotting pine trees in the forest at the edge of our property and learned to kiss by pressing my lips against the itchy bark, whispering their terrible names like a mantra. And that later, much later, I'd dream that there were lost hunters and rugged backwoods bachelors who would find me wandering around like this in the eerie back fields and want to do cruel, unimaginable things to my unloved body.

Only some of this is true.

Other stuff?

I did have a TV, though we only got two channels. My mom and I fought over the *Jeopardy* questions. I knew the names of every GI Joe and believed I was in love with Hawk Eye. I had a Commodore 64 (a gift from my long-dead grandmother) and later on a second-hand Nintendo. I could wrap the first Zelda game in a single sitting. I could kick Super Mario Bros.' ass and give the sequel an equal spanking. Offer me a new game and I'd master it in a week. I was a genius that way.

I also enjoyed masturbating. I was a genius in that way too. The first time I had an orgasm I was twelve, humping an abandoned Victorian couch in the dark comforting cave of our unfinished basement.

I wrote fan letters to Ricky Martin, when he was still a part of Menudo. I imagined the two of us on tour together, how he'd hold my hand in the bus and teach me Spanish.

For a year I collected Scratch 'n Sniff stickers in a flower-covered photo album from the bargain bin at Zellers. I traded them at recess with the girls.

All of this is true.

Inside the tavern later it's pretty dark. Amid the hollering and the smoke I can feel myself start to unwind. The place is maybe half full. It's a rough sort of place set in the refurbished bunker of an old radical union hall. I take off my scarf and let my eyes adjust to the light, finding a spot at the long bar beside an older guy I've seen before. Rick, I think his name is. Rick Mc-some-thing. He's maybe forty, and going grey. A big dude. Tall.

"Hey," Rick says, nodding and clearing a spot. His eyes are

watery, wired and alert, then softening a bit, as if he has turned down the volume. The bartender that night – a woman named Louise, hair dyed red, a rough patch of acne fucking with her chin – hauls out a bottle of Molson. I raise my beer to Rick and we clink ceremoniously, as if we are toasting a buddy's wedding. There are other people at the bar, guys like Rick who work the factories, women in leather pants, puffing cigarettes and teasing their bleached bangs. A whole sad crowd of nut-cases and half-assed pretenders.

"Who's playing," I say, although looking up at the screen I can see right away it's the Blackhawks and the Bruins.

"Bruins."

I can feel him watching me sideways.

"Nice," I say, gulping.

You can't hear much of the game. In the bar all you hear are glasses clinking and the spitfire of a dozen conversations. I look at myself in the mirror across the counter, bony cheeks, what passes for indifference in the eyes. I finish what I'm drinking. After a couple of minutes the screen switches to a commercial. Rick starts staring again. I have this kind of paranoia, from all the weed I've toked, that he can see inside my brain.

"What?" I say, swivelling around on my stool.

"Nothing."

I don't know him. Not much. We've talked about hockey, spouted some bullshit politics. He smiles, licking his lips like a drunk. I like this liquid need about him, the eager hangdog show, how he stays close to me and presses his shoulder up against me and laughs and tries to listen to what I say. He's a good listener. But I don't feel much like talking.

"How's school?" he says, eyes drilling down.

I shrug.

"At least you're getting an education."

"I better be, for how much I'm fucking in debt."

Louise comes over. Rick makes the turn of the finger to show he'll buy the round.

When Louise brings the beer we toast again.

"Here's to Mr. Smartypants!" He squeezes my shoulder, lets his hand linger for a beat. It's warm. I can see the trail of tiny veins swelling beneath his eyes, broken red rivers carved into saggy cheeks. On the screen the Bruins score.

I put down the bottle. "How about you?"

"Me? Work blows. I haven't gotten laid in awhile. What the fuck else is new?"

He laughs. His eyes fish, dig into the ponds of mine, and he smiles like we're sharing a joke, like he wants me to smile, too. So I do. And I start to feel better. A couple of girls in the corner are laughing over pinball, rocking the machine back and forth, until Louise shouts over for them to knock it the hell off. Seeing these girls, hearing their laughter, their recklessness – I think about my mother. Her voice, so desperate, only a few hours earlier. It makes me feel shitty all over again. But I stuff that shitty feeling into my pocket.

The reality of my story was like nothing I saw on TV. There were no slow-moving love scenes, no laughter in the parental bedding unit late on a weekend morning. If anything, it was a low-budget, family-values, after-school special produced for PBS in the Reagan era and sponsored by Big Tobacco. I never knew my dad. My mom raised me solo. She turned twenty-five the day they met, a line cook working the oil patch in Alberta.

She swore to her dying days that the only thing she could remember was that he was a funny guy and very blond. A mythical Swede, a jack-in-the-box Leif the Lucky. They dated for a few months. They even pretended they were in love. Then one month she missed her period.

For years I would dream of my dad pretty much all the time. I thought about what he looked like, what kind of food and cars he enjoyed, if he was married or lived alone. I wondered who he was as a kid. If we would have been friends. I wondered if he resembled me. If his body was tall and wiry, if his penis curved to one side, if he had a chest like a hairy linebacker.

I wondered if he was religious. How old he was too, the first time he had sex.

I wondered if he ever thought about me.

I went through a period early in elementary school where I'd draw pictures for him in art class, stick drawings of the forests, blotchy watery paintings of all the rocky lakes, etchings of spaceships and aliens in cheap waxy paper that would disintegrate in the rain.

I'd sign them all. Each and every one. And add a column of Xs and Os. Save them up in a special pizza box hidden under my bed, wrapped in second-hand Christmas paper, to give to him when I was big enough and could finally get out there to find him.

To Dad.
For My Best Bud in the World.
Happy Father's Day!

When I get up to say goodbye, Rick grabs me. His place is around the corner, he says. Do I want to head back? The bar is bright, people staggering around like little kids, everyone hovering expectantly over their seats, searching for their coats. It seems early.

I look up. Around us, under fluorescent, Louise is wiping the bar, getting ready to count her tips. Rick's eyes are damp. Bits of his grey hair stick up here and there in tiny spikes.

"Sure," I say. "Let's do it."

When my mom told my father the news about her unplanned pregnancy, over lukewarm sloppy screwdrivers in his tiny foreman's trailer, he looked down at her very strangely, as if he was about to smile, then he changed his mind, and punched her hard a few times in the gut. She had expected celebrations. At first she was so shocked she forgot to lift her arms to protect the invisible fetus growing and developing inside her. But when he raised his fist the third time, she finally learned to duck, to turn her stomach away from him down toward the floor, and the blow instead caught her in the side of the face.

It's cold. But I don't really feel it. Just a bite of it at the neck. There's a moon rising slowly over the James Street Baptist Church. Rick lives near this church. He lives in a big brick building with a wooden porch and a tricycle in the snowy yard and some black bags of garbage frozen to the curb. A metal sign flapping and squeaking in the wind says *Dearborn House. Apartments for Rent. 742-5656.*

"We're here," he says, pulling out keys. We stumble up some steps and a woman with a feather boa shoves past. She calls Rick a perv. Her heels click like nails on the splintered wood.

"That's Rosie," he whispers. "Our whore."

We go down a narrow hall with several doors. There's the sound of staccato gunfire, something from a DVD, and a baby mewling from somewhere, which may or may not be real. Also some weird low moaning, human or animal, leaking out from one of the apartments.

"Welcome to my kingdom," Rick says, pulling open his door.

His room, like mine, is nothing much to look at. There's a bed against the wall with a green blanket twisted over some sheets. There's an armchair and a small TV sitting on a box near what used to be a fireplace, boarded up now and painted black. At the far end there's a table, two chairs piled with dirty clothes, a kitchenette with a sink, and one of those mini fridges crowded up on top with scummy dishes. There's a calendar over the bed, stuck on the month of July 1992, with two naked Thai girls curled up like sleeping sisters in the middle of a zebra-skin rug.

He closes the door, rubs one of my shoulders in a half-massage, squeezes my elbow in a comradely way before heading to the kitchenette. "Drink?" he asks from the counter. My face is warm. There's no empty chair, so I sit like it's a first date on the edge of the dumpy bed.

"Sure."

Back turned, he pours. My eyes are ultraviolet pinpricks sucking up the light, but my legs and thighs are like stones. Soon he's right beside me, and again we're toasting our booze, this time sipping it up from cheap ceramic teacups.

"Like it?" he says, watching me gulp. "It's homemade. From a friend in Montreal."

I've had the homemade stuff before. This shit is sweet, fresh, like apple cider. Part of me notices that Rick is barely touching his. Instead he's put on some electronic house music. He's nodding his head and standing like a giant above me. He dances to the tunes, exaggerating his jives and humpy hip twists. I stagger up and try to move and groove, feeling suddenly sad and far away from my body, like an angel or Peter Pan. I end up, after a while, dropping the little mug onto the floor.

I watch it roll under the table in fascinating slow motion.

"Sorry," I mumble, trying to slide down to pick up the cup. But Rick grabs my shoulder, pressing knobby fingers into my deltoids, guiding me back to the bed, pecking me chastely on the cheek.

"Easy, sailor."

Secret video footage would show my father returning to base camp early the next morning carrying roses. My mother, weaned on a steady diet of Carole King and James Taylor in the pre-Oprah seventies, sensed an impending proposal, and pressed her nail-bitten fingers to her lips like a lovesick teen-aged girl. But the most he could offer in the form of tangible love was a promise to pay her expenses if she visited the clinic in Edmonton, where the sluts and the Indians would go.

Don't you even love me, she wanted to shout, like she was an Oscar-winning heroine in some high-stakes Hollywood block-buster, crying on cue in a close-up.

From the squeaky bed in Rick's stuffy apartment the ceiling begins to spin. I start shaking, afraid, 'cause I can't seem to keep my head on top of my neck.

"Don't worry," he says, cradling my skull. I see him start to unbutton the top of his shirt. Hair, black furry tufts, puff out over the button. He continues to undress, making it into a show, like I'm paying for it. Soon a small gut flips out. His stubby fingers cup the front of his jeans.

"Do you want more to drink?"

I manage to shake my head.

"What do you think?" he asks, palming the soft bulge inside his pants.

I try to speak. I do. But no words, no sighs or declarations come to my rescue. Just a fey sloppy *unnh* sound, like I have a motor-neural disease, something like cerebral palsy, like a gag has been shoved deep into the gut of my mouth.

All of this appears to please him.

"Do you live alone?" he says, running one hand through my hair, slipping the other over my cheek, forcing one of the meaty fingers into my mouth.

I can't answer at all. His finger's in my throat. I can't even really move.

"It's not good to live alone, you know."

He runs a greasy fingertip, damp with my own saliva, in an arc across my forehead. I can feel the cool spit hit gravity, river like invisible gravy down into my ear. I used to drool when I was a kid. My mom told me to be careful, be brave, try to be a big boy now, or she'd have to get me a chin cup, and force me to wear it to school.

She claimed she refused the abortion, I learned from her sister light years after her death, because growing up in Ontario she had dreams of what it would be like to be a mother. She had fantasies of falling asleep at night listening to a child's breathing. She wanted to feel a stream of warm milk being suckled from her breast, just like in the European movies. And she wanted to hold a little baby in her arms – a creature so tiny and helpless, so entirely dependent on her – and to know that in the flimsy black-and-white tragedy of her life, here at long last was the proof that God loved her.

The irony of this fantasy is that we were never a physical family. Not the kind of people who ever touched. We were only two. There were rarely goodnight kisses, no hugs at the end of the day. No running home breathless from school for chocolate-chip cookies and an armful of tender caresses before *Degrassi Junior High*. No baths at the start of the night.

I don't know why.

Rick strokes me gently, brushing the matted hair up and away from my sweaty face.

"That's a good boy."

It's cold. I know it's time to zip up my hoodie, all the way to my throat, and get the fuck out of there. But my arms are totally punked.

"You're cold," he says. He kneads the thin muscles of my back some more, kisses me again on the forehead. He strokes my hair too, appears to ruminate or consider some larger existential question. Then he grunts. Pig-like. Slips a calloused hand inside my pants.

"Poor Elliot. We should really warm you up now."

I try not to think. I manage to shut my eyes. In the background the music changes to a local radio call-in show, and Beth from St. Thomas High would like to hear some U2. There's a whoosh as he slides toward me on the tiny bed. He hooks his arms around me and sits me up like an old man or a doll, unzipping my stupid hoodie, pulling my numb arms out one by one, tugging each frayed sleeve until my hands and fingers are free. After that he stretches the faded Leafs T over my fuzzy head. He spends a lot of time on my chest, biting and pinching the nipples, caressing the bony shoulders, squeezing the skinny biceps, then leans down to lick me under the ear, juicy and dog-like, along the tender jugular.

"You like this," he says, nuzzling down. He whispers this, and I feel his warm beer breath tickling my stomach. While he's down there, he peels me out of my jeans. When he's got me lying back, he sighs, studying me for a minute and then stroking the inside of my thigh, playing with my shaved balls through my shorts. Here my blood betrays me, pooling into my groin, racing its biblical way from one hidden vault into another, one tight vein into the next, until I'm stiff and shamefully hard.

On the phone that afternoon, that snowy afternoon, she clears her throat, then speaks after what seems like a long time. She's calm all of a sudden. Composed now, even important sounding. Like she is being interviewed for the afternoon news or one of the famous talk shows. Like her life, finally, is beginning to make some sense, framed in this tragic new twilight.

I heard from the doctor today, El. Remember I went to Lindsay? For all those weird tests? Well I got a call today. And guess what, El? They found something.

I picture her in her *Cagney & Lacey* nightgown, hugging the rotary phone and pacing at the far end of the hallway upstairs. She'd be itching for a smoke. Jonesing. Picking at her teeth.

She tells me the gritty details, but doesn't say breast. She says she has a lump, but in a self-conscious, whispery voice, so I understand right away what she means.

Rick stands up. He watches me a couple of minutes, while clouds of tiny crickets float inside my eyes. There's a scratch at the back of my throat, sweat like a humid lake under my arms.

He finishes undressing. When he gets back into bed, I can tell by the heat on my right shoulder that he's naked. He rises, crouching over me, pressing his warm dick, the sweaty pubes, up against my cheek. Then he starts to stroke himself, moaning, tapping my lips with his penis, then more quickly, rubbing the head of his cock across my damp forehead before slipping it into my mouth, telling me it's good, it's so fucking sweet, how proud he is that I can take so much at once.

"Elliot. Oh fuck."

I try not to puke. Drool leaks out and pools into the crook of my neck. When I finally start to gag, he pulls out fast, edging, and this movement creates a loud suctioning noise. I heave a few times, pull away, curling up, a man-sized gimpy fetus. But before I can recover he grabs my shoulders and flips me onto my stomach, wrenches down my shorts and pushes me face-first onto the mattress.

"It's okay, buddy. You're okay."

But I'm not. He's fucking heavy. In the tiny padded panic room deep inside my mind I feel rational, calm – at least I'll remember it this way later, thinking *at least I survived the fall* instead of *this is what it's like to suffocate*. It's the feeling I had as a kid, crawling into the dryer while my older cousin stood outside and held the door shut with the weight of his body, cranking the machine up to full load and laughing, watching me go round and around.

I manage to twist my head an inch, maybe two, but no air. Just a puddle of pissy drool.

My body makes an unrecognizable sound, a squishy girlish whine.

There's the ricochet of TV gunfire whizzing through the apartment wall.

"I bet you like this," he says again, as if I hadn't heard him the first time.

I'm your mother, she used to say, when I'd ask her as a kid why I had to listen to her, why I had to turn down the music or get the truck back by midnight or try to improve myself out in the world by going away to university.

Just because I'm your mother.

A few seconds later, one of his fingers wiggles down, testing the air like a divining rod before digging into my ass. It pinches and aches in ways I am unprepared for. If I was a believer, I would whip up some half-baked prayer, ask God or one of his henchmen to spare my Levitical body. Instead I disappear. I close the lonely eyes inside my eyes. He slides a meaty finger farther in – no lube – then two, then he climbs all the way onboard and levers himself into me and buries himself deeper and deeper, all the while balancing his weight on my hips and slapping my goose-pimpled ass cheeks like a slightly depressed percussionist – with a reasonable amount of energy, but without any real emotion.

—

You're just like your father, she said, on more than one occasion. Mostly when I was doing something that didn't please her, being stubborn about fixing the VCR, or slamming one of my work boots into the kitchen door, because she wouldn't stop lecturing me.

Sometimes you remind me exactly of your father.

Eventually, before he's done, before he's had his fill, I black out. When I wake up later, sewer mouth, drill bit to the head, the apartment is still dark, with just the soft light from the streetlamps casting a long dirty glow across the bed. It takes a moment to make sense of where I am. I'm damp. Still shivering.

When I get up, sheet draped over me, pain winches through me, gathering like a cinch low inside my gut.

"Well, look who's wide awake now! Did you have a nice sleep?"

I want his voice to be tough, brittle and full of evil, a monster from kids' TV. But it's quiet, soft, disappointingly feminine, as if it's been punctured by a hatpin and deflated. He's there in one of the kitchen chairs, regal and fully clothed, a cavalier Gargamel, stroking a mangy Siamese cat who must have been hiding before.

"Welcome back, Elliot."

It's hard to stand. But eventually I do, pulling the sheet around me like a kimono.

"Your things are on the end of the bed. If you need to borrow anything . . ."

A couple of steps later and I locate everything, folded into a neat pile.

I find my white Jockeys and struggle, keeping my back

turned. A warm line of blood, a thin greasy trickle, blots the seat of my shorts. I just know it.

He's watching me.

I hurry to pull on my jeans.

"I had a good night," he says, breathless. "I hope you come back again. I mean it. If you're ever bored or lonely."

Let the record show that when she told me her news that snowy afternoon, when she needed me the most, at last and for real, I refused to come to her rescue. A person should always be judged, a man once said, by his actions and not his intentions. I believe this is true.

Perhaps I didn't know what to say. I thought about this after the call, rubbing my sweaty face against the window. Watching that freakish light in the apartment disappear, the sky splitting up above me into splinters of chemical orange, I could feel my body grow tense, and my lungs tighten inside me, like I was being lowered into a pool or an iron casket. I tried to stay calm. I tried to imagine the nervous joy she must have felt, and the wonder, seeing me for the first time as my head ripped through her insides and I breathed and choked in the world: whether my birth gave her any hope; whether it made her less afraid; what this might mean for her now.

After a couple of hard tokes I started to relax.

I think I was embarrassed by my silence, but I must have made some noise. Or said something else eventually.

Because after a while we hung up, and when we did I felt relieved.

As though as long as she wasn't near me, as long as I could forget it, none of what she was saying could ever touch me.

ABOUT THE CONTRIBUTORS

Kris Bertin works as a bartender and bouncer at Bearly's House of Blues and Ribs in Halifax. He has had stories published in *The Malahat Review*, *PRISM international*, *The New Quarterly*, *The Antigonish Review*, *Riddle Fence*, *Pilot*, and others. Kris recently put all of his favourite short stories into a pile and named it *Bad Things Happen*. He is currently working on a novel. He is from Lower Lincoln, New Brunswick.

Shashi Bhat is the author of the novel *The Family Took Shape* (Cormorant Books, 2012). Her short fiction has appeared in several journals, including *PRISM international*, *Event*, *The Threepenny Review*, *The Missouri Review*, and *Nimrod International*. She was a finalist for the RBC Bronwen Wallace Award for Emerging Writers in 2009, and has been nominated for the Pushcart Prize. She received her MFA in fiction from Johns Hopkins University. She currently lives in Halifax, where she is an assistant professor of creative writing at Dalhousie University.

Astrid Blodgett's short stories have been read on CBC Radio's *Alberta Anthology* and appeared in *Meltwater: 25 Years of Writing from Banff Centre*, *Alberta Views*, *Prairie Fire*, and *The Antigonish Review*. Her first collection of stories, which includes "Ice Break" and is tentatively titled *Let's Go Straight to the Lake*, will be published by The University of Alberta Press sometime in the near future. Astrid lives in Edmonton.

Trevor Corkum's fiction and non-fiction have appeared in *The Malahat Review*, *Grain*, *Event*, *The Antigonish Review*, and *Prairie Fire*. "You Were Loved" is part of a manuscript of short fiction completed under the tutelage of story magician Zsuzsi Gartner through the University of British Columbia's Optional-Residency MFA Program. He currently lives in Halifax.

Nancy Jo Cullen is the fourth recipient of the Writers' Trust of Canada's Dayne Ogilvie Grant for an Emerging Gay Writer. She is the author of three collections of poetry with Calgary's Frontenac House Press and has been shortlisted for the Gerald Lampert Award, the Writers Guild of Alberta's Stephan G. Stephansson Award, and the W.O. Mitchell Calgary Book Prize. She holds an MFA in Creative Writing from the University of Guelph-Humber. Her fiction has appeared in *The Puritan*, *Grain*, and *filling Station*. Her short story collection, *Canary*, is forthcoming from Biblioasis in the spring of 2013. She is at work on a novel.

Kevin Hardcastle is a fiction writer from Simcoe County, Ontario. His short stories have been published in *Word Riot*, *subTerrain Magazine*, and *The Malahat Review*. An excerpt from a novel-in-progress was recently published in *Noir Nation: International Journal of Crime Fiction*. He has studied writing at the University of Toronto and at Cardiff University.

Andrew Hood is the author of the short story collections *Pardon Our Monsters* (Véhicule Press, 2007) and, most recently, *The Cloaca* (Invisible Publishing, 2012). He has lived in Guelph,

Montreal, and Halifax, and may currently be living in any one of these places.

Grace O'Connell is the author of *Magnified World* (Random House Canada, 2012). She is the Contributing Editor for Open Book: Toronto and the books columnist for *This Magazine*, and her work has appeared in various publications, including *The Walrus*, *Quill & Quire*, and *EYE Weekly*. She holds an MFA in Creative Writing. "The Many Faces of Montgomery Clift" has also been nominated for a National Magazine Award. Grace lives in Toronto.

Jasmina Odor is a fiction writer and an instructor of English and Creative Writing at Concordia University College in Edmonton. Her stories have appeared in *The Fiddlehead*, *Coming Attractions: 05*, and *The New Quarterly*, which first published "Barcelona." She has recently completed a collection of short stories and is now working on a set of stories about empathy – empathy in its relationship to justice and in its potential to lessen the suffering of others.

Alex Pugsley is a writer and filmmaker from Nova Scotia. As a screenwriter, he has written for performers such as Scott Thompson, Mark McKinney, Dan Aykroyd, Seán Cullen, and Michael Cera. He is the co-author of the novel *Kay Darling*, and his fiction has appeared in *Brick*, *Descant*, *The Dalhousie Review*, *McSweeney's Internet Tendency*, *This Magazine*, *The Queen Street Quarterly*, and other periodicals. "Crisis on Earth-X" is the fifth published story in a narrative series about the McKee and Mair families, set in twentieth-century Halifax.

Eliza Robertson studied creative writing and political science at the University of Victoria. She is now pursuing her Masters in Prose Fiction at the University of East Anglia, England, where she received the 2011–12 Man Booker Scholarship. Her work has appeared in journals and anthologies in Canada, the United Kingdom, and the United States, including *The Journey Prize Stories 22* and the Willesden Herald Prize's *New Short Stories 6*. She is writing a novel and gathering stories for her first collection.

Martin West's work has published in magazines across Canada. "My Daughter of the Dead Reeds" is part of a larger collection-in-process about the Red Deer River Badlands in Alberta, some of which has appeared in *PRISM international*, *The Fiddlehead*, *Grain*, and *Front & Centre*. Another story from that collection, "Cretacea," was shortlisted for the Journey Prize in 2006.

What is the best advice you've received about writing?

Kathleen Winter: My short story editor, John Metcalf, told me I did not know how to write an ending. He told me to pretend I was sitting in a theatre, watching my story onstage, from the beginning to the penultimate scene. Then what happens? Watch and see. That's what he said, and that's what I do now. It's great. I get a lot of surprises.

Kathryn Kuitenbrouwer: I was given the advice early on that to write a story (a novel or a short story) one must have an idea captivating enough to sustain the project for the duration it might take to finish. I always ask myself before beginning whether the thrust of a story truly interests me. The idea needs to feel energetically urgent.

Michael Christie: For me, the idea that I often cling to, perhaps as one would a life raft, is this: Write what you like to read. Of course encoded within this comes the sneakier statement, which is: Like to read. It's terrifying to know that there are aspiring writers out there who don't actually love to read. This seems like a terrific waste of time to me. There are plenty of rewarding things to do out there other than write. But for me, it's the naked awe that I feel in the presence of a great book that impels me to attempt it myself.

Trevor Corkum: Best advice for any writer is to write the stories only you can tell. We're all hungry for stories that reflect the truth of what we know personally about the world, based on our own particular histories and desires and regrets. Write the story that really terrifies you or moves you or embarrasses you or obsesses you in some way. Good writing always has some element of emotional risk, something at stake.

Eliza Robertson: Talent will only get you so far – you need to work your ass off.

Kevin Hardcastle: That you have to put in work, put in hours like you would at any job, and keep producing. There are a few rare moments when you feel like you are really creating something special, when you are in a kind of zone, but in my experience that all comes from sitting in front of a computer or typewriter for an extended amount of time and churning out pages. If you can put in hours like that you not only sharpen all your tools and produce better work, but you also tend to become more objective and less precious about your writing.

Jasmina Odor: About writing in general, as a life practice: to care about the craft and the integrity of the writing first and everything else related to writing second.

Grace O'Connell: Lisa Moore, who was my mentor during my graduate work, once told me she was having trouble getting a character to the store, where she needed him to be. A friend said to her, "Why don't you just start at the store?" I think that's good advice for writing – a lot of times, the problems you encounter exist because you're stuck in thinking one particular way. When I come across sagging scenes, I ask myself, "Can I just start at the store?"

Martin West: Tell your own story and tell the truth. Anything less serves the art form poorly.

Shashi Bhat: One of my former professors said a short story can't take place on just any day; it has to be the day that everything changed forever.

Nancy Jo Cullen: As hokey as it sounds, all stories have to be about some kind of journey, they have to move forward in space or time, or else they are simply description and feel somewhat static.

Andrew Hood: Trevor Ferguson once told me that, in the current climate, it's against all odds that anyone will ever read anything you write, let alone like or understand it, so you can feel free to write your goddamn heart out. He said it with a few more flowers, though.

Astrid Blodgett: Keep writing.

What advice do you have for someone looking to publish a story in a literary magazine?

Kathryn Kuitenbrouwer: I would advise new writers to try to get to know people in the industry as well as getting to know the different approaches to writing each journal takes. The best advice is to send your best work to the magazines and journals publishing authors alongside whom you would like to be published.

Michael Christie: Some helpful rules of thumb: Don't send something off before you've had a fresh go or two at it. Pick your literary magazine carefully according to the style or subject matter of the story. Take rejection seriously, but don't take it personally. Try to write about anything other than the things you think you ought to be writing about. Look at a story that you find amazing, then look at your story – see any difference? Also, don't make fun of your characters. Also, brilliant stories get rejected all the time, but so do terrible ones. Also, don't be cryptic. Also, don't be uselessly clever. Also, don't be boring. Okay, I'll leave it there.

Kathleen Winter: Get the thing into the best possible shape. Then put it away for two to four weeks. Then take it out and fix all the things that have mysteriously come to the surface to mock you. Then send it out. Don't let a day go by when you don't have a piece out there. Always have bait in the ice-fishing hole.

Jasmina Odor: Care about every word of the writing, about the story as a living thing. If it is living, someone will recognize it. The more practical advice is to read the magazines, a bunch of them. Set a high tolerance for rejection letters, and send out regularly, diligently; don't shelve a good story because one or two magazines have rejected it.

Martin West: Find a magazine that suits your style. The Canadian literary scene is small and very conservative, so submit like an eagle; circle before you strike.

Trevor Corkum: Be persistent, and send only your best work. Rejection doesn't mean your story sucks. It may just not be right for a particular publication. Also, rejection may turn out to be a blessing in disguise, because it may also be a sign that the story still needs some tender loving care, more time to ferment. The goal should be to publish excellent work, not just to be published.

Nancy Jo Cullen: Read literary magazines. Send your stories to magazines you like. And try not to take it personally when your story is rejected. There are so many stories being read by editors, if your story is rejected it doesn't necessarily follow that it's not a good story. Send it out again. And if you're lucky enough to get advice or comments on your story, consider it carefully. If you can make your story better, then do so.

Shashi Bhat: Don't forget your SASE. Create a spreadsheet to keep track of all your stories and where you've submitted them. Read lots of stories, or don't expect other people to read yours.

Kevin Hardcastle: The best bet is to always be writing and submitting while you are waiting for responses to recent submissions. Waiting for things to happen without having some new work on the burner is a real good way to end up disappointed and disheartened. Getting interest from a publisher or an agent is never a guarantee that you will see your work in print anytime soon, so you have to keep writing and submitting whenever you find yourself in a holding pattern.

Eliza Robertson: Submit, submit, submit, submit! Simultaneously, if the magazines let you. Also, contests. The fees add up, but the turnaround time is quick. My first three publications were through contests.

Kris Bertin: Don't be a baby.

What is your favourite short story or short fiction collection, and why?

Michael Christie: I have many favourites, but one of those is *Jesus' Son* by Denis Johnson. The compression, the immoral daring, the surprising bursts of sheer lyrical beauty, the pathos, the dead-on description – this book does everything right. I've read that except for a few errant sentences, *Jesus' Son* is as close to a perfect book as a human being is ever going to get. But I don't agree. I've yet to find those bad sentences.

Kathryn Kuitenbrouwer: I don't have a favourite. I love the short stories of Chris Adrian, Ian McEwan, Flannery O'Connor, Deborah Eisenberg, Bill Gaston, Yoko Ogawa, John McGahern, Kenzeburo Oë, Grace Paley, and Annie Proulx. Lately, I've been reading stories by Selena Anderson, whom I discovered through the journal *Glimmer Train*. She's one to watch. I can't wait until she publishes her first book.

Eliza Robertson: Lorrie Moore's *Birds of America*. I've never laughed aloud so often. Every few pages I had to find someone to whom I could recite the funny dialogue or passage. But her stories also have a way of grabbing you by the throat.

Grace O'Connell: I love Alice Munro, but for a best single collection I think I would say *Open* by Lisa Moore.

Kevin Hardcastle: I covet all of Ernest Hemingway's short fiction and can't really choose one collection outright. Of his individual stories, though, "A Clean, Well-Lighted Place" is the one that had the most impact on me. It is one of the best short stories ever put to paper. Another perfect story is Alistair MacLeod's "The Boat" from *The Lost Salt Gift of Blood*. I gravitate toward fiction about working-class men and women, especially those in rural places who have trades or ways of life that are being threatened but still endure. I also need something to be at stake in a narrative I'm reading. I believe Cormac McCarthy said that he has no interest in writing that doesn't trade in issues of life and death, and I tend to agree with him.

Trevor Corkum: Too many to mention just one, but I'm a big fan of anything by George Saunders. He's a master at finding the right form for the spiritual, material, and existential messiness of our time.

Jasmina Odor: So many great ones – Raymond Carver's story "Blackbird Pie," Lisa Moore's "Meet Me in Sidi Ifni," Mavis Gallant's "The Moslem Wife." Because they are true, precise yet terrifically rich, and endlessly readable. You can read them and reread them and always feel that they are full of history, that the language hits perfect notes, and also that you can't ever quite "crack" the art of them, how they were built – you may think you understand the structure and the threads, but then there is always some place where the story goes beyond what you can imitate or reduce to its parts.

Andrew Hood: I love Amy Hemple's *Collected Stories* and Lorrie Moore's *Collected Stories*. I feel safe when I've got these books handy.

Nancy Jo Cullen: It's hard to name a favourite, but a collection I really, really liked was *Our Kind* by Kate Walbert. The entire collection is written in the plural first person, which completely wowed me. And a story I love is "Half-Past Eight" by Edna Alford. The characters of Tessie and Flora are brilliant. They're funny and a little tragic, but if you told them that they'd pop you one.

Shashi Bhat: There are so many: Lauren Groff's "Delicate Edible Birds" for its exquisitely crafted language; Stuart Dybek's "Pet Milk" for its speed and nostalgia; Aimee Bender's "The Rememberer" for its inventiveness and compression; Isabel Huggan's *The Elizabeth Stories* for how she pushes her characters so much further than I expect them to go; Tobias Wolff's "Bullet in the Brain" for the way it moves from cynicism to earnestness; Ray Bradbury's "All Summer in a Day" for how it's sci-fi and yet entirely human; Haruki Murakami's *After the Quake* for how it thwarted everything I thought I knew about narrative rules.

ABOUT THE CONTRIBUTING JOURNALS

For more information about the journals that submitted to this year's competition, The Journey Prize, and *The Journey Prize Stories*, please visit www.facebook.com/TheJourneyPrize.

The Antigonish Review is a creative literary quarterly that publishes poetry, fiction, critical articles, and reviews. We consider stories, poetry, and essays from anywhere – original or in translation – but our mandate is to encourage and publish new and emerging Canadian writers, with special consideration for writers from the Atlantic region who might otherwise go unrecognized. Submissions and correspondence: *The Antigonish Review*, P.O. Box 5000, St. Francis Xavier University, Antigonish, Nova Scotia, B2G 2W5. Website: www.AntigonishReview.com

The Dalhousie Review has been in operation since 1921 and aspires to be a forum in which seriousness of purpose and playfulness of mind can coexist in meaningful dialogue. The journal publishes new fiction and poetry in every issue and welcomes submissions from authors around the world. Editor: Anthony Stewart. Submissions and correspondence: *The Dalhousie Review*, Dalhousie University, Halifax, Nova Scotia, B3H 4R2. E-mail: dalhousie.review@dal.ca Website: www.DalhousieReview.dal.ca

The Fiddlehead, Atlantic Canada's longest-running literary journal, publishes poetry and short fiction as well as book reviews. It appears four times a year, sponsors a contest for fiction and for poetry that awards a total of $5,000 in prizes, including the $1,500 Ralph Gustafson Poetry Prize. *The Fiddlehead* welcomes all good writing in English, from anywhere, looking always for that element of freshness and surprise. Editor: Ross Leckie. Managing Editor: Kathryn Taglia. Submissions and correspondence: *The Fiddlehead*, Campus House, 11 Garland Court, University of New Brunswick, P.O. Box 4400, Fredericton, New Brunswick, E3B 5A3. E-mail (queries only): fiddlehd@unb.ca Website: www.TheFiddlehead.ca Blog, with original content: TheFiddleheadNews.blogspot.ca

Founded in 2008 by author Emily Schultz and artist Brian Joseph Davis, **Joyland** is an online and print literary magazine that curates fiction regionally across North America and internationally. Praised by *Time Out*, *The Atlantic*, and the CBC for our unique approach, *Joyland* has published acclaimed and emerging authors alike, and, in 2011, we received three Distinguished Mentions in *Best American Short Stories*. Editors: Brian Joseph Davis (New York), Kevin Chong (Vancouver), Jim Hanas (US South), Emily M. Keeler (Toronto), Kara Levy (San Francisco), Charles McLeod (Midwest), David McGimpsey (Montreal/Atlantic), Mathew Timmons (Los Angeles). Submissions: joylandsubmissions @gmail.com Correspondence: joylandfiction@gmail.com Website: www.JoylandMagazine.com

The Malahat Review is a quarterly journal of contemporary poetry, fiction, and creative non-fiction by both new and celebrated writers. Summer issues feature the winners of *Malahat*'s Novella and Long Poem prizes, held in alternate years; the fall issues feature the winners of the Far Horizons Award for emerging writers, alternating between poetry and fiction each year; the winter issues feature the winners of the Creative Non-fiction Prize; and the spring issues feature winners of the Open Season Awards in all three genres (poetry, fiction, and creative non-fiction). All issues feature covers by noted Canadian visual artists and include reviews of Canadian books. Editor: John Barton. Assistant Editor: Rhonda Batchelor. Submissions and correspondence: *The Malahat Review*, University of Victoria, P.O. Box 1700, Station CSC, Victoria, British Columbia, V8W 2Y2. E-mail: malahat@uvic.ca Website: www.MalahatReview.ca

The New Quarterly is an award-winning literary magazine publishing fiction, poetry, personal essays, interviews, and essays on writing. Now in its thirty-first year, the magazine prides itself on its independent take on the Canadian literary scene. Recent issues include The QuArc issue (a 290-page flip book on the interstices of science and literature undertaken with *Arc Poetry Magazine*) and The TNQ Extra (writers on their collections and obsessions). Editor: Pamela Mulloy. Submissions and correspondence: *The New Quarterly*, c/o St. Jerome's University, 290 Westmount Road North, Waterloo, Ontario, N2L 3G3. E-mail: editor@tnq.ca, orders@tnq.ca Website: www.tnq.ca

PRISM international, the oldest literary magazine in Western Canada, was established in 1959 by Earle Birney at the University of British Columbia. Published four times a year, *PRISM* features short fiction, poetry, creative non-fiction, and translations by both new and established writers from Canada and around the world. The only criteria are originality and quality. *PRISM* holds three exemplary competitions: the Short Fiction Contest, the Literary Non-fiction Contest, and the Earle Birney Prize for Poetry. Executive Editors: Erin Flegg and andrea bennett. Fiction Editor: Cara Woodruff. Poetry Editor: Jordan Abel. Submissions and correspondence: *PRISM international*, Creative Writing Program, The University of British Columbia, Buchanan E-462, 1866 Main Mall, Vancouver, British Columbia, V6T 1Z1. E-mail (for queries only): prism@interchange.ubc.ca Website: www.PrismMagazine.ca

Founded in 1627, **The Puritan** is an online, quarterly publication based in Toronto, committed to publishing the best in new fiction, poetry, interviews, and reviews. *The Puritan* seeks, above all, a pioneering literature. *The Puritan* embraces work wherever it lands on the conceptual spectrum, so long as it is original, intelligent, and engaging. The journal's literary content is supplemented by in-depth, probing interviews and critical reviews. *The Puritan* also sponsors the annual Thomas Morton Memorial Prize in Literary Excellence, a contest that rewards the best poem and short story submitted each year. Founding editors: Spencer Gordon and Tyler Willis. Submissions and correspondence: puritanmagazine@gmail.com Website: www.Puritan-Magazine.com

Taddle Creek restores the sanctity of the literary magazine, fusing traditional editorial and design values with non-ephemeral, modern-day urban fiction and poetry to create a product unassociated with any one literary movement. Works found in *Taddle Creek* are not easily categorized: intelligent yet stylish, sensitive yet cavalierly violent, self-absorbed yet socially aware, humourous yet disturbing. Each issue also includes a combination of illustrations, comics, essays, interviews, photographs, grammatical rants, and whatever else suits *Taddle Creek*'s fancy, resulting in a most unlikely literary journal–general interest hybrid. In short, *Taddle Creek* is the journal for those who have come to detest everything the literary magazine has become in the twenty-first century. Editor-in-Chief: Conan Tobias. Correspondence: *Taddle Creek*, P.O. Box 611, Stn. P, Toronto, Ontario, M5S 2Y4. E-mail: editor@taddlecreekmag.com Website: www.TaddleCreekMag.com

Vancouver Review is an iconoclastic, irreverent, and independent cultural quarterly that celebrated its eighth anniversary in 2011 and is currently on a publishing hiatus. This Journey Prize– and National Magazine Award–winning journal focuses on B.C. cultural, social, and political issues, and publishes commentary, essays, and narrative non-fiction, as well as fiction and poetry in every issue. In the Blueprint B.C. Fiction Series, launched in the summer of 2007, *Vancouver Review* explored the zeitgeist and geographic implications of the province through illustrated stories by first-time and established authors. Editor: Gudrun Will. Fiction Editor: Zsuzsi Gartner. For information on when submissions will be accepted again, please see our website: www.VancouverReview.com

Submissions were also received from the following publications:

Broken Pencil
(Toronto, ON)
www.BrokenPencil.com

carte blanche
(Montreal, QC)
www.carte-blanche.org

The Claremont Review
(Victoria, BC)
www.TheClaremontReview.ca

dANDelion Magazine
(Calgary, AB)
www.DandelionMag.ca

Descant
(Toronto, ON)
www.descant.ca

EVENT
(New Westminster, BC)
www.douglas.bc.ca/visitors/
event-magazine

ELQ/Exile:
The Literary Quarterly
(Holstein, ON)
www.ExileQuarterly.com

Found Press Quarterly
www.FoundPress.com

FreeFall
(Calgary, AB)
www.FreeFallMagazine.ca

Geist
(Vancouver, BC)
www.geist.com

Grain
(Saskatoon, SK)
www.GrainMagazine.ca

Matrix
(Montreal, QC)
www.MatrixMagazine.org

The New Orphic Review
(Nelson, BC)
http://www3.telus.net/new
orphicpublishers-hekkanen

On Spec
(Edmonton, AB)
www.OnSpec.ca

The Prairie Journal
(Calgary, AB)
www.PrairieJournal.org

Prairie Fire
(Winnipeg, MB)
www.PrairieFire.ca

Queen's Quarterly
(Kingston, ON)
www.queensu.ca/quarterly

Riddle Fence
(St. John's, NL)
www.RiddleFence.com

Room
(Vancouver, BC)
www.RoomMagazine.com

subTerrain Magazine
(Vancouver, BC)
www.subTerrain.ca

The Windsor Review
(Windsor, ON)
www.WindsorReview.
wordpress.com

PREVIOUS CONTRIBUTING AUTHORS

* Winners of the $10,000 Journey Prize

** Co-winners of the $10,000 Journey Prize

I

1989

SELECTED WITH ALISTAIR MacLEOD

Ven Begamudré, "Word Games"

David Bergen, "Where You're From"

Lois Braun, "The Pumpkin-Eaters"

Constance Buchanan, "Man with Flying Genitals"

Ann Copeland, "Obedience"

Marion Douglas, "Flags"

Frances Itani, "An Evening in the Café"

Diane Keating, "The Crying Out"

Thomas King, "One Good Story, That One"

Holley Rubinsky, "Rapid Transits"*

Jean Rysstad, "Winter Baby"

Kevin Van Tighem, "Whoopers"

M.G. Vassanji, "In the Quiet of a Sunday Afternoon"

Bronwen Wallace, "Chicken 'N' Ribs"

Armin Wiebe, "Mouse Lake"

Budge Wilson, "Waiting"

2

1990

SELECTED WITH LEON ROOKE; GUY VANDERHAEGHE

André Alexis, "Despair: Five Stories of Ottawa"

Glen Allen, "The Hua Guofeng Memorial Warehouse"

Marusia Bociurkiw, "Mama, Donya"

Virgil Burnett, "Billfrith the Dreamer"

Margaret Dyment, "Sacred Trust"

Cynthia Flood, "My Father Took a Cake to France"*

Douglas Glover, "Story Carved in Stone"

Terry Griggs, "Man with the Axe"

Rick Hillis, "Limbo River"

Thomas King, "The Dog I Wish I Had, I Would Call It Helen"

K.D. Miller, "Sunrise Till Dark"

Jennifer Mitton, "Let Them Say"

Lawrence O'Toole, "Goin' to Town with Katie Ann"

Kenneth Radu, "A Change of Heart"

Jenifer Sutherland, "Table Talk"

Wayne Tefs, "Red Rock and After"

3

1991

SELECTED WITH JANE URQUHART

Donald Aker, "The Invitation"

Anton Baer, "Yukon"

Allan Barr, "A Visit from Lloyd"

David Bergen, "The Fall"

Rai Berzins, "Common Sense"

Diana Hartog, "Theories of Grief"

Diane Keating, "The Salem Letters"

Yann Martel, "The Facts Behind the Helsinki Roccamatios"*

Jennifer Mitton, "Polaroid"

Sheldon Oberman, "This Business with Elijah"

Lynn Podgurny, "Till Tomorrow, Maple Leaf Mills"

James Riseborough, "She Is Not His Mother"

Patricia Stone, "Living on the Lake"

4

1992

SELECTED WITH SANDRA BIRDSELL

David Bergen, "The Bottom of the Glass"

Maria A. Billion, "No Miracles Sweet Jesus"

Judith Cowan, "By the Big River"

Steven Heighton, "A Man Away from Home Has No Neighbours"

Steven Heighton, "How Beautiful upon the Mountains"

L. Rex Kay, "Travelling"

Rozena Maart, "No Rosa, No District Six"*

Guy Malet De Carteret, "Rainy Day"

Carmelita McGrath, "Silence"

Michael Mirolla, "A Theory of Discontinuous Existence"

Diane Juttner Perreault, "Bella's Story"

Eden Robinson, "Traplines"

5

1993

SELECTED WITH GUY VANDERHAEGHE

Caroline Adderson, "Oil and Dread"

David Bergen, "La Rue Prevette"

Marina Endicott, "With the Band"

Dayv James-French, "Cervine"

Michael Kenyon, "Durable Tumblers"

K.D. Miller, "A Litany in Time of Plague"

Robert Mullen, "Flotsam"

Gayla Reid, "Sister Doyle's Men"*

Oakland Ross, "Bang-bang"

Robert Sherrin, "Technical Battle for Trial Machine"

Carol Windley, "The Etruscans"

6
1994
SELECTED WITH DOUGLAS GLOVER; JUDITH CHANT (CHAPTERS)

Anne Carson, "Water Margins: An Essay on Swimming by My Brother"

Richard Cumyn, "The Sound He Made"

Genni Gunn, "Versions"

Melissa Hardy, "Long Man the River"*

Robert Mullen, "Anomie"

Vivian Payne, "Free Falls"

Jim Reil, "Dry"

Robyn Sarah, "Accept My Story"

Joan Skogan, "Landfall"

Dorothy Speak, "Relatives in Florida"

Alison Wearing, "Notes from Under Water"

7
1995
SELECTED WITH M.G. VASSANJI;
RICHARD BACHMANN (A DIFFERENT DRUMMER BOOKS)

Michelle Alfano, "Opera"

Mary Borsky, "Maps of the Known World"

Gabriella Goliger, "Song of Ascent"

Elizabeth Hay, "Hand Games"

Shaena Lambert, "The Falling Woman"

Elise Levine, "Boy"

Roger Burford Mason, "The Rat-Catcher's Kiss"

Antanas Sileika, "Going Native"

Kathryn Woodward, "Of Marranos and Gilded Angels"*

8

1996

SELECTED WITH OLIVE SENIOR;

BEN McNALLY (NICHOLAS HOARE LTD.)

Rick Bowers, "Dental Bytes"

David Elias, "How I Crossed Over"

Elyse Gasco, "Can You Wave Bye Bye, Baby?"*

Danuta Gleed, "Bones"

Elizabeth Hay, "The Friend"

Linda Holeman, "Turning the Worm"

Elaine Littman, "The Winner's Circle"

Murray Logan, "Steam"

Rick Maddocks, "Lessons from the Sputnik Diner"

K.D. Miller, "Egypt Land"

Gregor Robinson, "Monster Gaps"

Alma Subasic, "Dust"

9

1997

SELECTED WITH NINO RICCI; NICHOLAS PASHLEY

(UNIVERSITY OF TORONTO BOOKSTORE)

Brian Bartlett, "Thomas, Naked"

Dennis Bock, "Olympia"

Kristen den Hartog, "Wave"

Gabriella Goliger, "Maladies of the Inner Ear"**

Terry Griggs, "Momma Had a Baby"

Mark Anthony Jarman, "Righteous Speedboat"

Judith Kalman, "Not for Me a Crown of Thorns"

Andrew Mullins, "The World of Science"

Sasenarine Persaud, "Canada Geese and Apple Chatney"

Anne Simpson, "Dreaming Snow"**

Sarah Withrow, "Ollie"

Terence Young, "The Berlin Wall"

10

1998

SELECTED BY PETER BUITENHUIS; HOLLEY RUBINSKY;

CELIA DUTHIE (DUTHIE BOOKS LTD.)

John Brooke, "The Finer Points of Apples"*

Ian Colford, "The Reason for the Dream"

Libby Creelman, "Cruelty"

Michael Crummey, "Serendipity"

Stephen Guppy, "Downwind"

Jane Eaton Hamilton, "Graduation"

Elise Levine, "You Are You Because Your Little Dog Loves You"

Jean McNeil, "Bethlehem"

Liz Moore, "Eight-Day Clock"

Edward O'Connor, "The Beatrice of Victoria College"

Tim Rogers, "Scars and Other Presents"

Denise Ryan, "Marginals, Vivisections, and Dreams"

Madeleine Thien, "Simple Recipes"

Cheryl Tibbetts, "Flowers of Africville"

11

1999

SELECTED BY LESLEY CHOYCE; SHELDON CURRIE;

MARY-JO ANDERSON (FROG HOLLOW BOOKS)

Mike Barnes, "In Florida"

Libby Creelman, "Sunken Island"

Mike Finigan, "Passion Sunday"

Jane Eaton Hamilton, "Territory"

Mark Anthony Jarman, "Travels into Several Remote Nations of the World"

Barbara Lambert, "Where the Bodies Are Kept"

Linda Little, "The Still"

Larry Lynch, "The Sitter"

Sandra Sabatini, "The One With the News"

Sharon Steams, "Brothers"

Mary Walters, "Show Jumping"

Alissa York, "The Back of the Bear's Mouth"*

12

2000

SELECTED BY CATHERINE BUSH; HAL NIEDZVIECKI;

MARC GLASSMAN (PAGES BOOKS AND MAGAZINES)

Andrew Gray, "The Heart of the Land"

Lee Henderson, "Sheep Dub"

Jessica Johnson, "We Move Slowly"

John Lavery, "The Premier's New Pyjamas"

J.A. McCormack, "Hearsay"

Nancy Richler, "Your Mouth Is Lovely"

Andrew Smith, "Sightseeing"

Karen Solie, "Onion Calendar"

Timothy Taylor, "Doves of Townsend"*

Timothy Taylor, "Pope's Own"

Timothy Taylor, "Silent Cruise"

R.M. Vaughan, "Swan Street"

13

2001

SELECTED BY ELYSE GASCO; MICHAEL HELM;

MICHAEL NICHOLSON (INDIGO BOOKS & MUSIC INC.)

Kevin Armstrong, "The Cane Field"*

Mike Barnes, "Karaoke Mon Amour"

Heather Birrell, "Machaya"

Heather Birrell, "The Present Perfect"

Craig Boyko, "The Gun"

Vivette J. Kady, "Anything That Wiggles"

Billie Livingston, "You're Taking All the Fun Out of It"

Annabel Lyon, "Fishes"

Lisa Moore, "The Way the Light Is"

Heather O'Neill, "Little Suitcase"

Susan Rendell, "In the Chambers of the Sea"

Tim Rogers, "Watch"

Margrith Schraner, "Dream Dig"

14

2002

SELECTED BY ANDRÉ ALEXIS;

DEREK McCORMACK; DIANE SCHOEMPERLEN

Mike Barnes, "Cogagwee"

Geoffrey Brown, "Listen"

Jocelyn Brown, "Miss Canada"*

Emma Donoghue, "What Remains"

Jonathan Goldstein, "You Are a Spaceman With Your Head Under the Bathroom Stall Door"

Robert McGill, "Confidence Men"

Robert McGill, "The Stars Are Falling"

Nick Melling, "Philemon"

Robert Mullen, "Alex the God"

Karen Munro, "The Pool"

Leah Postman, "Being Famous"

Neil Smith, "Green Fluorescent Protein"

15

2003

SELECTED BY MICHELLE BERRY;

TIMOTHY TAYLOR; MICHAEL WINTER

Rosaria Campbell, "Reaching"

Hilary Dean, "The Lemon Stories"

Dawn Rae Downton, "Hansel and Gretel"

Anne Fleming, "Gay Dwarves of America"

Elyse Friedman, "Truth"

Charlotte Gill, "Hush"

Jessica Grant, "My Husband's Jump"*

Jacqueline Honnet, "Conversion Classes"

S.K. Johannesen, "Resurrection"

Avner Mandelman, "Cuckoo"

Tim Mitchell, "Night Finds Us"

Heather O'Neill, "The Difference Between Me and Goldstein"

16

2004

SELECTED BY ELIZABETH HAY; LISA MOORE; MICHAEL REDHILL

Anar Ali, "Baby Khaki's Wings"

Kenneth Bonert, "Packers and Movers"

Jennifer Clouter, "Benny and the Jets"

Daniel Griffin, "Mercedes Buyer's Guide"

Michael Kissinger, "Invest in the North"

Devin Krukoff, "The Last Spark"*

Elaine McCluskey, "The Watermelon Social"

William Metcalfe, "Nice Big Car, Rap Music Coming Out the Window"

Lesley Millard, "The Uses of the Neckerchief"

Adam Lewis Schroeder, "Burning the Cattle at Both Ends"

Michael V. Smith, "What We Wanted"

Neil Smith, "Isolettes"

Patricia Rose Young, "Up the Clyde on a Bike"

17

2005

SELECTED BY JAMES GRAINGER AND NANCY LEE

Randy Boyagoda, "Rice and Curry Yacht Club"

Krista Bridge, "A Matter of Firsts"

Josh Byer, "Rats, Homosex, Saunas, and Simon"

Craig Davidson, "Failure to Thrive"

McKinley M. Hellenes, "Brighter Thread"

Catherine Kidd, "Green-Eyed Beans"

Pasha Malla, "The Past Composed"

Edward O'Connor, "Heard Melodies Are Sweet"

Barbara Romanik, "Seven Ways into Chandigarh"

Sandra Sabatini, "The Dolphins at Sainte Marie"

Matt Shaw, "Matchbook for a Mother's Hair"*

Richard Simas, "Anthropologies"

Neil Smith, "Scrapbook"

Emily White, "Various Metals"

18

2006

SELECTED BY STEVEN GALLOWAY;

ZSUZSI GARTNER; ANNABEL LYON

Heather Birrell, "BriannaSusannaAlana"*

Craig Boyko, "The Baby"

Craig Boyko, "The Beloved Departed"

Nadia Bozak, "Heavy Metal Housekeeping"

Lee Henderson, "Conjugation"

Melanie Little, "Wrestling"

Matthew Rader, "The Lonesome Death of Joseph Fey"

Scott Randall, "Law School"

Sarah Selecky, "Throwing Cotton"

Damian Tarnopolsky, "Sleepy"

Martin West, "Cretacea"

David Whitton, "The Eclipse"

Clea Young, "Split"

19

2007

SELECTED BY CAROLINE ADDERSON;

DAVID BEZMOZGIS; DIONNE BRAND

Andrew J. Borkowski, "Twelve Versions of Lech"

Craig Boyko, "OZY"*

Grant Buday, "The Curve of the Earth"

Nicole Dixon, "High-water Mark"

Krista Foss, "Swimming in Zanzibar"

Pasha Malla, "Respite"

Alice Petersen, "After Summer"

Patricia Robertson, "My Hungarian Sister"

Rebecca Rosenblum, "Chilly Girl"

Nicholas Ruddock, "How Eunice Got Her Baby"

Jean Van Loon, "Stardust"

20

2008

SELECTED BY LYNN COADY; HEATHER O'NEILL; NEIL SMITH

Théodora Armstrong, "Whale Stories"

Mike Christie, "Goodbye Porkpie Hat"

Anna Leventhal, "The Polar Bear at the Museum"

Naomi K. Lewis, "The Guiding Light"

Oscar Martens, "Breaking on the Wheel"

Dana Mills, "Steaming for Godthab"

Saleema Nawaz, "My Three Girls"*

Scott Randall, "The Gifted Class"

S. Kennedy Sobol, "Some Light Down"

Sarah Steinberg, "At Last at Sea"

Clea Young, "Chaperone"

21

2009

SELECTED BY CAMILLA GIBB;

LEE HENDERSON; REBECCA ROSENBLUM

Daniel Griffin, "The Last Great Works of Alvin Cale"

Jesus Hardwell, "Easy Living"

Paul Headrick, "Highlife"

Sarah Keevil, "Pyro"

Adrian Michael Kelly, "Lure"

Fran Kimmel, "Picturing God's Ocean"

Lynne Kutsukake, "Away"

Alexander MacLeod, "Miracle Mile"

Dave Margoshes, "The Wisdom of Solomon"

Shawn Syms, "On the Line"

Sarah L. Taggart, "Deaf"

Yasuko Thanh, "Floating Like the Dead"*

22

2010

SELECTED BY PASHA MALLA; JOAN THOMAS; ALISSA YORK

Carolyn Black, "Serial Love"

Andrew Boden, "Confluence of Spoors"

Laura Boudreau, "The Dead Dad Game"

Devon Code, "Uncle Oscar"*

Danielle Egan, "Publicity"

Krista Foss, "The Longitude of Okay"

Lynne Kutsukake, "Mating"

Ben Lof, "When in the Field with Her at His Back"

Andrew MacDonald, "Eat Fist!"

Eliza Robertson, "Ship's Log"

Mike Spry, "Five Pounds Short and Apologies to Nelson Algren"

Damian Tarnopolsky, "Laud We the Gods"

23

2011

SELECTED BY ALEXANDER MacLEOD;

ALISON PICK; SARAH SELECKY

Jay Brown, "The Girl from the War"

Michael Christie, "The Extra"

Seyward Goodhand, "The Fur Trader's Daughter"

Miranda Hill, "Petitions to Saint Chronic"*

Fran Kimmel, "Laundry Day"

Ross Klatte," First-Calf Heifer"

Michelle Serwatuk, "My Eyes are Dim"

Jessica Westhead, "What I Would Say"

Michelle Winters, "Toupée"

D.W. Wilson, "The Dead Roads"